A Circle of Stars

Four Crowns
Book One

Erin Lark Maples

Lodestar Literary

This title was previously published under the pen name Courtney Fenix.

Cover designed by MiblArt.

To Mariah,
Who is a goddess in her own right
For teaching others the love of story

Someone I loved once gave me a box full of darkness.
It took me years to understand that this too, was a gift.

— MARY OLIVER

ONE

I'll admit, snow down my sweater was the most action I'd had in far too long.

When I'd stumbled out of the cab dragging two awkward suitcases, I tripped on the curb, crashed into the No Parking sign, and struggled to find any footing. I grabbed the scrawny city tree trunk in its sad square of dirt. Branches brushed the nearest awning which deposited a bucket of icy powder down my front.

Tender parts frozen, I shrieked, releasing one of the suitcase handles. Unmoored, the pink behemoth on wheels toppled forward with an unceremonious thwack into a slushy puddle.

A man with a dark mop of hair and devilish smile quickstepped around the sudden boulder to avoid taking a rigid handle to the shin. He levered the bag upright and leaned its soggy side against the wall of my new address. A *Closed* sign hung in the window.

"There are far easier ways to take a stranger out," the man said with a cheeky grin.

"I'll remember that the next time I attack someone with

a suitcase," I said as I fluffed my sweater in a vain attempt to dislodge the snow. Frigid water trickled down my skin and I slapped an arm over my chest to mask the twin bullets pointing his way. I'd shrugged out of my jacket in the stuffy taxi but now lamented the loss of its warmth in the brisk air. I vowed to strip and change into pjs the moment I got inside.

He watched me fumble in my purse for my keys. The bank mailed them on a zip tie I hadn't bothered to remove, but in the bottomless pit of my purse, they were as good as buried treasure. "Let me know when you do," he said. "I'm pretty handy with a carry on."

I stopped what I was doing to look at him. He watched me with dark brown eyes alight with laughter. *Funny. And cute— maybe too funny, too cute.* I laid out my cards. "Shouldn't need them again for a while. I'm the new owner," I said, nudging my chin toward the green door with the brass handle. "Are you the welcoming committee?"

The man tipped his head to one side and smiled. *Definitely too cute.* "Depends on who's asking." He maneuvered the second suitcase to rest near the first, then squatted to shift a stack of boxes from in front of the door. "This all you have?"

In horror, I stared at the boxes. "Those *bastards.*"

The man straightened, then frowned. He looked from me to the boxes and back. His eyes narrowed and he scanned the street. Had he been a dog, his hackles would have risen. "Who?"

"Those lazy, cheap, ungrateful...ooooh!" I pressed a hand to each temple and pressed. My heartbeat quickened. "I left them strict instructions. Color-coded boxes!"

"So the boxes...are yours?" One eyebrow rose as confusion crossed his face.

I took a deep breath and released the air through my nose. My acupuncturist back home challenged me to reconnect with my breathing whenever I was stressed. Let's just say I get a lot of oxygen now.

While I ranted, the man kicked back against the street sign. Hands in the pockets of his jeans, slight shrug of the shoulder. Behind him, the town square was largely vacant, darkness seeping in.

The frustration of two delayed flights, snow freezing my personal assets, and now the disregard for my carefully packed, diligently listed belongings pushed me over the edge. "They *are* mine. *My* moving boxes. *My* idiot movers who left *my* stuff out where anyone could take it. I'm surprised anything is still here!"

"I'm not."

His cavalier attitude rubbed me the exact wrong way. One of us had our entire life turned upside-down in the last month. The other one had nothing better to do than observe the current trials of others.

I opened my mouth to snap back, when I heard my son's voice in my head. "Mom, it's not like everyone is trying to ruin your day."

That's what happens when you give everything you have into raising a decent kid. They turn out pretty awesome and surprise you with their wisdom. Cue deep breath number two.

As I exhaled, a pair of crows settled on a tree branch overhead. The streetlight flickered. Night settled in the square like a weighted blanket. Snowflakes filtered through the air to land on the man's jacket and atop the cars. He watched me, quiet and curious.

"And why are you not surprised?" I'd moved to Prescott after all, a decent-sized city, not some tiny backwater where everyone lived in each other's business.

"Who'd want—" He leaned over to read the labels on the boxes. "—Extra Cords, Grandma's Crochet Placemats, and Photo Albums?"

"Fair point." I sighed. "Any chance you'd help me move them inside?"

Bone-weary, I didn't wait for an answer. I jostled the key into the old lock and unlatched the door. Fecund, damp air walloped my senses like a freight train to the lungs. Steam billowed out from the crack as the warm air from within met the chilliness without.

Unfazed, the man hefted a load of boxes into his arms. "After you."

I wrestled the suitcases inside and groped the wall for a light switch. I flipped on the lights.

"Where should I put these?"

I couldn't reply. All I could do was stare, dumbstruck, at the wall of jungle in front of me.

Across countertops, up a bookcase, and up a staircase wrapped a cacophony of vines. The front window was over-taken by leaves. Every open surface was covered in sprawling greenery and potted plants. Giant leaves with holes in them, long fronds with frayed edges, and everything in between fought for space in the shop.

Among the tables and a makeshift desk, boxes crowded the remaining space. Many leaned in a precarious formation. One had toppled off its stack, spilling my silverware over the floor. A formerly potted plant lay nearby, roots exposed, soil clinging to their lengths. Shards of blue ceramic and a scattering of dark soil littered the area.

"How about by the stairs?" Before I could answer, he continued, "I'll get the others." The man set the boxes in front of a black, wrought iron staircase that spiraled upward toward the second floor.

I turned a tight circle, taking in the place. I couldn't make sense of my new home.

There was a thud behind me, a stack of boxes set against another. "Well, that's the last of them. I'll let you get settled."

"Excuse me—" I had so many questions, yet only one would surface. "What is...was...this shop?"

He smirked, a twisted grin. "Would have thought that was on the paperwork."

"It said 'Apothecary.' I thought it was...lotions and soap. Overpriced towels. Belgian chocolate. I had no idea...But this..." I waved my hand at the vines, the spilled soil. "This is solid green chaos."

His face grew serious. "Hollis was a good man," he said. Then with a tap of one finger to his forehead in a brief salute, he headed for the exit.

Hollis Kohl was, in fact, my uncle. One I'd known and loved through dozens of whirlwind visits but never through an invitation to his place. He'd been in his seventies—had to be— when I received the call from his lawyer at the same moment my life in Chicago fell apart.

"Wait!" My helper was halfway out the door when I called him back. He faced me again, strain in the lines at the corners of his eyes. "You didn't tell me your name."

He flashed a sincere grin. "Joaquin." He nudged his chin toward the brick wall, carpeted in leaves. "I work next door."

Before I could pepper him with more questions, he disappeared into a swirl of snowflakes.

Faced with the reality of my situation, I panicked. Then I remembered to breathe so I wouldn't pass out, an ungainly lump of woman on the sidewalk. Then I freaked out all over again. This is the way of adulthood.

In-one-two-three, out-one-two-three, in-one-two-three... My therapist back home taught me a host of breathing techniques to take with me on this new adventure. "But they sound like I'm waltzing," I'd said, feeling ridiculous when I practiced. "Breath is a dance," she'd replied. She wasn't wrong.

I allowed myself to settle for a moment, back pressed against the wall. I closed my eyes until I was certain I could remain upright, then opened them to check out my new home. Little was visible in the wan light of the single, functional bare bulb.

"Must replace those," I said to myself, eyeing two banks of lights above what appeared to be display tables. The mental list took shape in my mind. Broom, cleanser. Glass cleaner. Trash bin. Making a list and taking action was a balm to my soul. I'd spent two decades as an event manager for one of the most prestigious wedding planners in the city. I could do logistics.

I skirted a display of some large, fluffy plant with curly edges. *A fern of some kind?* Of course I'd seen plants before, but those were more in Christopher's wheelhouse.

Christopher. Suitcases righted, I fished out my phone and dialed.

"Tell me it's fabulous," the familiar voice demanded. Soft jazz filtered in through the speaker, hushed voices mingling in.

"It's...very...green..." I said, and bit my lip. I was talking to my best friend, the one I'd worked with for fifteen years, yet I wasn't ready to admit my current state of mind. "The aesthetic is definitely lush."

"Mmm. I love a spring vibe. Fresh. Like a juice bar. Kale and apple."

I could picture Christopher now. Clark Kent glasses, head-to-toe Dior. A scarf tucked just so around his neck despite the heat cranked up in his apartment. Brandy snifter in one hand, this week's man-friend perched nearby.

"Everyone over?" I asked, a lump in my throat.

Everyone meant his handful of regular friends, an odd mashup of the Chicago arts scene and the finance district, crowding into his fifth-floor walkup. I would have given anything to be there orbiting the trendy guests, snacking on fancy cheese and big city gossip.

"Just a few. There's a big gaping hole where you should be, EJ. And a whole bottle of bubbly on ice."

I groaned. "Save it for when I visit?"

"I'll do my best. You made it safe and all that?" He giggled, then cleared his throat.

The man-friend might be attempting to wrest his attention back to the party. I rolled my eyes, a knowing smile stretched from cheek to cheek. That would be Christoper. I sat on one of the lower steps of the staircase. "Just got in the door."

"How is it? Meet any new friends? Future lovers?" He said the last word like *love-ahs* and I snickered.

"One guy helped me carry in my stuff. Pretty much the epitome of tall, dark, and—"

I paused as a shadow at the back of the shop moved, a brief shift in the darkness. I'd yet to explore the depths of the place and hadn't a clue what was back there.

"What was that? You got cut off," Christopher said in my ear.

I squinted, fighting down a bubble of terror. Nothing moved. "Oh—nothing. I'm just exhausted. Three flights and a too-short layover in Dallas. I need food, then bed."

"Okay, but at least tell me he's single and you offered him special appreciation." Christopher had made me swear that if I was going to deprive him of daily access to his BFF by moving way-the-hell out here, that I would make up for this with lots of spicy stories about my romantic conquests. Sure I'd dated a handful of guys since my divorce, but Christopher dismissed each of them with a shocking immediacy I'd struggled to explain. "The man for you will keep you up at night, for the best and most frustrating of reasons. You need a guy who will get your knickers in a twist." While I was decades from my twenties, I wasn't wearing anything close to knickers—yet.- Sure enough, those flings were short-lived—if they ever got up and going to begin with. People could say what they liked about Christopher's designs and gut feelings, but he was rarely wrong about either.

"He helped me carry a few boxes. I didn't think that warranted a hand job."

"My personal philosophy is that every moment is an opportunity to be extra friendly," he said, and I laughed.

What he didn't know, and what I wouldn't volunteer, was that dating terrified me. In Chicago, I chalked up my lack of romance to a demanding career and a son I would raise right. Christopher's and my line of work meant a lot of opportunity to meet people who weren't always at their best. Jilted exes, the brother-in-law no one likes—or worse, the rich asshole of a father footing the bill who thinks he can grab my ass because he paid top dollar for the filet mignon.

Christopher mostly left me alone about it while he managed to bag the cousin of the bride, the caterer, or any other hotty in attendance, but with Patrick off to grad school in Paris and no more events to plan, my excuses had dwindled to nothing.

"At least let me unpack the good lingerie first," I joked. A soft click behind me had me on my feet. I reached for the nearest potted plant, a spiky cactus in a palm-sized pot. *Perfect.*

"Alright. Tonight, unpack. Tomorrow, get laid. Kisses!" The line went dead.

I edged toward the back of the shop, popping on my phone's flashlight and shining the way ahead. The shop was deep. The jungle-like room was the front section, open to the second story. When I faced the back of the shop, the space behind the stairs, to my left was a workroom lined with tables and shelving. To the right of the staircase was a door to a small kitchen and a bathroom, each labeled in French. Hollis, my uncle who'd left me the shop in his will, had loved all things European.

I inched my foot forward and swung my flashlight beam across the space. Near the back was what looked like a glassed-in porch. A tiny wedge of a room, the shelving inside was filled with books. This was the only area in which there wasn't a single plant. *Reading room?* I tried the door—locked. I would have to try the keys on the ring for that one. I continued my inspection.

Light filtered in through the four glass panes in the back door to the shop. Curlicues of wood decorated the frame. Through the windows was a courtyard and a massive tree, its trunk silvery-blue under the glow of a streetlamp. Suction-cupped to the window glass was a small sign. In neat script beneath the word *Open,* the sign read, *Tithes at the ready.* I pulled the small shade down over the glass and hurried back to the better-lit part of the store.

Near the slip of a desk where a calculator, notebook, lockbox, and squirt bottle fought for space, I retrieved my purse from atop a stool. "It's nothing," I said to the big, bushy plant crowding the desk. Its leaves were shiny, like green rubber, speckled with white. "I need some sleep and a decent breakfast. Then, I'll make a game plan."

My stomach growled in protest. I wouldn't get to sleep until I ate. Airplane pretzels wouldn't cut it.

With a final glance toward the shadows of the shop, I shouldered my purse and backed out the front door, locking it behind me. The mess could wait. At this hour, I would use neon lights to guide me to some food.

The earlier snowflakes sparkled from their landing spots, giving the empty square an eerie shimmer. Cold inched in at my cuffs as the still damp skin at my chest prickled with goose bumps.

From my front door, I could see a brunch place, two Christmas shops, a candlemaker, an accountant, an adorable —but closed—bistro, and other shops framing the square.

Overhead, a sign blazed *Morgan's* in neon cursive. Was this where Joaquin worked? The place was open, it was late, I was starved. The door handle was a smooth curve in my hand as I entered the pub.

A barrage of voices filled my ears as I elbowed my way toward the bar. The streets were empty because everyone was snug inside, beers in hand. At one table, a quartet of drinking buddies shared a pitcher and watched a game on a big screen. Several groups crowded around a billiards table, the clack of balls audible in the din. In the corner, a massive dog–Irish wolfhound?–slumbered in the corner, oblivious to it all.

The pub itself was beautiful. Walls of rich, reddish wood with booths to match. A long sword hung above the bar, a mirror lining its length. There were fine carvings on the hilt and small but brilliant jewels set in the metal. I squinted but the designs swam at that distance.

I made my way to the bar to claim a stool. The bartender, a woman with a high ponytail and a ring of keys jingling at her hip, prepped a drink order. I watched her reach for bottles on the shelves, filling the jigger first with one liquid and then another.

Spotting a wrinkled sheet of paper, I leaned over the wide, walnut bar to snatch the menu from a stack. Burgers, burritos, and tots—typical. My stomach groaned, interested in all of the above.

The expansive bar wrapped a half moon shape along the bulk of the wall. Above the shelving near the pitch of the vaulted ceiling was a horse head sculpture. Its silver surface gleamed in the dim lights. The horse wore a wreath of laurel leaves as though a winner in a past race.

I flicked my gaze toward the bartender. She crouched before a squat freezer tucked under the counter, a lowball glass in one hand. The woman reached in with a pair of tongs, made her selection, and plunked a translucent ball into the glass. Then, shoulders curved, she pointed a finger at the contents. There was a brief spark of blue, and I blinked, unsure what I'd seen. With the boot of one foot, the woman tapped the freezer door closed and presented the drinks to the couple at the bar.

"I love it," the man said, swirling the ball in his glass. He wore a T-shirt that said *Sexy Beast*, the sleeves rolled up. He held the glass out to his date. "Check it out," he said to her. "Do you think I could make this?" He looked back into the glass. "Of course I could. Better, too."

I can read people. Spend as much time as I have around them at their best and worst and you get to know a few things about what makes them tick. This guy was one of those wham-bam-thank-you-ma'am types. If he got it up, and that was never guaranteed, he'd paw your boobs, pump once or twice, then collapse on top of you, dead asleep. The kind of guy who'd order a domestic beer unless someone else was paying.

He saw me staring at him and showed me the contents of the glass. Inside the sphere was the shape of a three-dimensional horse head. "Very cool," I said.

"I've got to have the mold—where do I get it?"

"Sorry," the bartender said with a sly smile. With a twitch of her neck, she flipped her ponytail over her shoulder. "Proprietary mold. You can get the drink anytime I'm here, though."

"We'll go ahead and cash out," his date said, sliding her card across the counter with a simpering smile.

Bingo, I thought. He's on her tab.

The bartender nodded, then made her way to me. "You look like a ginger mop. Why were you out in this weather?"

I frowned, lifting a hand to my hair. She was right—it was wet and lank. The shop was hot, and with all those plants, it had to be humid. "I just got here and was unpacking. Or I'm about to...anyway, I got hungry."

She watched me, measuring my words. With a quick nod, she said, "So, you're Hollis's kin?"

"You knew him?"

"Nope." She shook her head. "Not much anyway. Saw him once, but that's it. I'm new, too. Got here a few weeks back." The woman flipped a towel over one shoulder and said, "I'm Iris. What will it be? Our fries are hand cut."

"Ember James," I watched her face. Had the dismissal of Hollis been a little quick or was I light-headed from the lack of food? Whatever her status, she'd known of Hollis, which might lead to more information. "But friends call me EJ. Can you make dirty fries?"

Iris couldn't force back her smile. "New girl EJ likes 'em dirty. Got it. For the uninitiated, can you define dirty in the fry world?" She cocked an eyebrow.

I blushed. "You know, where you pile them with cheese and jalapeños and any other fun stuff you have? The kind you have to eat with a fork."

She nodded. "I like how you think. I'll see what I can do. And to drink?"

I ventured a moment of bravery. "Would you have any champagne?"

Both of her eyebrows rose now, and she blinked. "Champagne? That's not exactly our...uh...specialty at Morgan's."

I shook my head. It was worth a shot. "It's fine. I'll take a water. Should keep my head clear anyway. I've got a hot date with a stack of boxes."

Iris slid a glass my way. Parched, I took a deep drink, the ice clinking against the class. While my stomach protested the reasonable wait, I watched the pub take on a new shape with its next wave of customers. More couples tucked into booths, and a large party pushed several tables together.

Joaquin entered the pub, gaze roaming over those gathered within. He stooped to scratch behind the ears of the massive hound. It's tail thumped in appreciation. Joaquin stood and brushed back his hair with one hand. With dark eyes a shade of rich cognac, his fingers long, lithe, and promising, he was exactly the kind of man Christopher would want me to notice. Sexy, well-dressed, dog lover, and by no means a man-child.

Two others followed behind Joaquin, a man and a woman in similar dark dress. They claimed a table while he stepped to the bar to order. He leaned his forearms on the shiny surface and turned his head. Spotting me, he broke into a smile. "Hey! Welcome to Morgan's."

"Thanks–your dog?"

"Falinis? Nah, belongs to the owner. He's a good sort. Don't feed him though, no matter how big those puppy eyes get. People food gives him gas. How's unpacking going?"

Is that a dimple? "So, fun, the last thing I wanted to do was cook."

Joaquin snorted. "I bet." He caught Iris's attention, held up three fingers, and returned to me. "You won't be disappointed here, it's kind of known as the five-star dive bar. Let me know if you need anything." With that killer smile and a nod, he returned to his friends.

Trouble with a capital T, but every minute would be a thrill ride. When you're older, you evaluate potential matches with a different eye, kind of like art work. You can admire the piece for what it is, but know it wouldn't be a fit for your wall.

Alone again, but still without fries, I turned on my stool until my back was against the bar.

Joaquin claimed his seat in the booth. He stretched out against the vinyl, his arms along the back. The two with him might be a couple, but I wasn't sure. They leaned forward in hot debate while Joaquin listened to their heated whispers. Iris brought them a trio of pints and slid into the booth to listen.

After the duo laid out their argument, they and Iris turned to Joaquin, who shrugged, then nudged his chin toward the back of the pub.

In the short hallway walled in photographs a stairway led to an upper story. A figure rounded the foot of the staircase and strode forward. When he appeared in the light, my breath caught. His hair was a tangle of waves and color, dirty blond and sugar brown. He wore a black shirt buttoned to the top with a small, silver horseshoe pin on the collar, the fabric straining over a landscape of muscles. Brooding, burly, and gruff, he pushed forward through the sea of customers, leaving stares in his wake.

There was a twitch under one eye as he paused to appraise the pub. It was as though he assessed each person inside, measuring their worth. His jaw shifted.

A gaggle of women jammed into a nearby booth. They chittered like songbirds at his back.

They were right to gawk. Too rough-hewn to be movie-star pretty, he was something else entirely. He had the look of a man who could throw you over one shoulder and his prize cow over the other. A mountain man lost in the modern world.

With a nod to the room, the man stepped behind the bar and made a beeline for Iris, who'd returned to make herself busy at the taps.

"And?" His question was more grunt than word.

Iris didn't spare him a glance. She continued filling a tray with glasses. "Eleven on ten. Stag and doe. Red's about to blow, I think. Maybe the sour, too? Could use another rye and that peach schnapps you love so much. And cougar juice."

She'd spoken in code, but this man followed every word. He tented an eyebrow. "Help?"

Iris shook her head. "I've got this." Iris hefted the tray onto her shoulder and was off.

The man put his hands on his hips and sucked in the side of one cheek, his lips pursed in a look of concentration. Whether because of the lack of calories or the long day, I had the sudden urge to run a finger over his lower lip. *Down, girl.*

When his eyes, the soft blue of a summer sky, met mine, I gulped. An ice cube caught in my throat. I coughed, fist to my chest, before dislodging it into my hand.

I looked up, mortified, but he was gone. A man that big should have left a wake. He'd disappeared as though a mirage of mist.

Iris broke my search when she set a huge plate, a bottle of ketchup, and a small mug in front of my seat.

"An extra pickle and homemade sauerkraut. Heard you choking, so I made the toddy. Soothes the throat. Not a drop of drink, just honey and lemon. Mom's recipe."

Disappointment fled my system as the aroma before me met my nostrils. A pile of crisp fries—skin on, my favorite— were piled high with cheese and peppers and promised other goodies under the mound of sour cream. Lemon slices and a stick of cinnamon garnished the toddy.

I stuffed a fry in my mouth and chewed, its hot, soft insides melting on my tongue. I groaned with pleasure. "You're a goddess."

She winked at me. "Not quite—but I'll take it."

Two

Belly full, I paid my tab and headed to the Apothecary —my new home. I wasn't used to the name, let alone the ownership. Fingers white at the tips, I fumbled with the key. *What is with these old locks?* A crow cawed from the nearest tree.

"Need any help?"

Before facing the stranger, I opened that app on my phone that will blast an alarm and call the police for you, hovering my thumb over the button. Sure, someone who offers help to a woman by herself at night in a downtown area might be helpful, like Joaquin, or they might be some kind of masked person who would rob me of my extra cords and crochet, leaving my dead body for the staff of Morgan's to find when they locked up.

I turned to face my greeter. He wore a grubby pea coat and fingerless gloves. He rubbed his hands together and blew on the tips. His breath came out in great, steaming puffs. Red rims circled his eyes. He smelled of sulfur, a faint sharpness in the cold air. The edges of his shape were softened, blurry, as though an artist had erased his outline. Iris promised she hadn't spiked my drink, so I wasn't seeing things. *I might need glasses. Great.*

"No, thanks," I said, as the key settled into the lock. "Have a good night," I added, before whisking myself inside and bolting the door behind me.

I shifted to the edge of the room and watched the shop window from the shadows. The man stood in front of the door, bouncing on the balls of his feet a little. He scanned the sidewalks, as though debating his next move.

My heart leapt into my throat when he tried my door. He jiggled the handle once, then twice more. I scooted behind the giant plant with the dinner platter-sized leaves, blending in with the foliage. Hand shading his eyes, the man peered in through the large picture window. Motionless, I willed myself to remain still. Clammy sweat streaked my brow. With a final pull on the door, he stormed off into the night.

Minutes passed as I bargained with my pulse to slow its relentless rhythm. *In-one-two-three, out-one-two-three...*

Standing there, I was struck again by the warmth of the shop. There was no whirring or whoosh from vents, nor was there a click of a radiator like in my apartment back home. The shop was humid, yes, and downright muggy. No wonder my hair clung to my cheeks and my pits were wet. Sexy, this was not. Maybe Mr. Morgan's left so he wouldn't have to talk to the drowned rat seated at one of his bar stools.

Ragged from the events of the day, and shaken by the most recent, I left the shop light on. Moving a stack of boxes made it possible to mount the stairs. I lugged one suitcase behind me, abandoning the other until tomorrow.

In stark contrast to the jungle below, the lofted living area was open and uncluttered. There was a low futon fronted with a half dozen pillows and draped with a thick throw blanket. A tall lamp blinked on when I pulled the chain, revealing a low coffee table, a plush rug, and a crate filled with records and topped with a player. Speakers backed up to a wall with a small door to the narrow bathroom. A long window stretched along the alley side of the building. Its sill was lined with large crystals, a few potted plants, and several candles.

The door in the wall opposite the bathroom was closed. I reached out as though to open it, then changed my mind. A bedroom, I guessed. Whatever lay behind was Hollis's. Personal. Telling. Best handled in the light of day. With coffee.

In the tiny bathroom, I stripped, dropping my travel-worn clothes to the floor. A plant with leaves that hung over the side of its plastic pot was wedged into the small, high window. I cranked on the tap, fumbled in my bag for shampoo, then stepped into the shower.

Ice-cold water sluiced down my back. I shrieked and hopped out. My flailing arm knocked into a shelf stacked with washcloths and more crystals which tumbled to the floor. I cut my foot on the shower ledge as I flung my hands out to catch myself. "Sweet Lady Nicnevin!"

In an awkward flamingo moment, I rested my foot on the ledge of the sink and cranked on the tap. Cold water drowned out my pain and washed the blood down the drain. *Did Hollis own any bandages—or just a hundred crystals?* I hopped on one foot while I fumbled with my phone.

After two rings, a familiar voice picked up. "Morgan's."

"Hi. Iris? Um, it's me. EJ. The woman from next door. Hollis's niece. I was just there and I—"

"Of course, dirty fries! Ordered some for myself. Those are killer."

"Yes, I mean, thank you. I'm hoping you can help me. I don't know who else to call." Through the speaker, the pub's volume was cranked up to late night volume. "I tried to take a shower and the water was cold. Freezing. I'm hoping you know someone I could call. Like building maintenance? Or maybe a plumber?" Icy droplets hit my shoulders and I shuddered. When she was quiet, I backpedaled. "No worries if it's a big deal. I'm wondering if the utilities forgot to flip a switch somewhere—but the heat's on. Hmm. Anyway, if it's too much trouble, I'll—"

"I'll find someone," she said. "Hang tight." The phone went dead.

Unsure what she meant, I grabbed a towel. The place was so warm I hadn't needed one, shut up in the tiny room, but if she was on her way, the least I could do was wrap up. I opened the cabinet below the sink and found a big, fluffy stack of luxurious bath sheets. I had time only to circle myself with the cushy terrycloth—why didn't Hollis sell these?—and tuck the corner between the girls when a knock at the back door reverberated through the shop.

Scurrying down the stairs, I snagged my jacket from where it lay atop some boxes. I stuffed my arms in the sleeves and zipped it up.

Backlit by the alley light, I recognized the shape of my visitor. Head close to the frame height, a frizz of hair, broad shoulders. I groaned.

I took in my bare feet, towel-wrapped legs, and finally the boxes crammed on either side of the door for any wardrobe support. *Assorted Vases. Curling Irons.* The second box was code for my personal collection of battery-powered boyfriends, but he wouldn't know that—would he?

Another pounding on the door rattled my teeth. I took a deep breath then opened the door, bare legs and all, and steadied myself for utter mortification.

Embarrassment poured over me in waves as the beast of a man regarded me. He took his time absorbing my distress, his gaze lingering from toes to hips, to the tuck of my towel, and finally his ice blue eyes met mine. His face scrunched in what was a blend of concern and rejection, then rearranged into a stoic grimace.

Humid air from inside the shop gushed out behind me. Later, I would swear that the leafless tree in the alley atrium emitted a faint glow, threads of light flowing through its branches, as though the plants within my urban jungle called to those outside its borders.

As the man stared at me, images flashed in my head. His hair on either side of my face, his warm breath on my cheeks. A horseback ride through a lightning storm. Blood trickling from my side, a dagger angling out from my gut. Skin on skin. His—

He cleared his throat. The sound startled me out of the visions, some of them delicious, others terrifying. Arms crossed, feet planted outside the threshold, he regarded me as one might watch a moth about to invade the kitchen. *Great.* He was here to help and all I could do was play romance movie scenes in my head.

"Hi—you must be from next door." When he didn't respond, I continued. "Iris must have called you? I'm sorry to interrupt your night but the shower is freezing." I gestured down at myself, as though the towel was its own explanation.

His gaze traveled down my body a second time. His eyes lingered at the gap in my jacket where I hadn't zipped it past the swell of my breasts. As if in response, the small tuck of towel threatened to give way. I crossed my own arms over my chest, and he lifted his gaze.

"Can't help you."

"What?" Exasperation edged my tone. "Why not?" Why had he come all the way over here to offer me nothing? He didn't even do the overconfident guy thing where they dink around for half an hour with the tools you have, the same exact checks you made, and pronounce the situation in need of a professional.

He tipped his chin toward the shop behind me. "Not worth it."

I frowned. "But...I just got here. Today. I know this place is a mess, but I can move these boxes—"

Without stepping foot over the doorway, he turned to leave. "Call a plumber," he said over his shoulder. He was halfway up the back steps to the pub when he added, "Or an electrician."

I leaned into the alley, my puffy purple jacket gray in the light from the streetlamp. "How do I know which?"

"Might be sediment. Might be a breaker." He opened the back door to the pub.

I called across the gap, incredulous at his dismissal. "Do you know somebody? It's late," I said, desperation in my plea.

"In the morning," he answered, then was gone.

I blinked at his absence, shaken. Why come over here to do nothing? It was as if he'd come to see my humiliation and, when satisfied at that, left.

Aware of my vulnerability, half naked in the dark and cold atrium, I backed into the shop and locked the door. "Jerk."

The clash of warm, oxygenated air from the shop beaded condensation on my exposed skin. I dragged myself back up the stairs, pulled a sleep shirt over my head, and ran a toothbrush across my teeth. I rehashed the interaction in my head, cursing the man for all but openly mocking my need.

I wrapped myself in the throw blanket and flounced onto the futon. I'd left the light on downstairs, and its faint buzz rattled me. Stuffing my head into the pile of pillows, I curled up in the fetal position and willed slumber to take me.

In the middle of the night, the rattle of the door shook me from a dream. I clutched at my phone, wide awake, thumb hovering over the emergency button. As I counted the remaining hours until dawn, I wished for a pair of ruby red slippers to take me back to the midwest.

∽

Buzzing under my cheek shook me from a deep slumber. A line of drool snaked down my chin to where it pooled on an orange, raw silk pillow. I sat up too fast and groaned, my back stiff from the night.

My phone continued its vibration. A familiar face lit the screen.

"Patrick! I'm so glad you called. Is everything alright?"

"Mom, you sound hungover." My sensible son turned into a parental unit. "What did you do last night?"

I rubbed my face. "Give me a break, I just woke up. Have to have my coffee before I'm human, you know that."

Exasperation came through loud and clear from thousands of miles away. "It's ten a.m. there."

I looked down at the phone. So it was. "I slept in. Got in late, had to eat, couldn't find half my stuff, and the shower was cold." As the words tumbled from my mouth, I heard the subtle web of omission between them.

So did my son. "Cut the crap, Mom. What happened?" His language was tough, but his tone was worried. I could picture him in the tiny apartment he'd been so excited to snag with two of his buddies. They had a river view that made the four flights of stairs worth every step. He'd have on his favorite Cubs jersey, the one my dad bought him at a championship game. His bed would be made, every item in his tiny Parisian closet facing the same direction, his shoes in a polished line beneath. He'd been a mini me in more ways than not. A tear snuck out from the corner of my eye, and I brushed it away.

When you live with someone for almost two decades, they get to know you. The real you. The you that gets zits, can't eat too much cheese, and never puts the dishes away. They know how you like your coffee, when you've had a bad day, and the fastest way to tug your heartstrings. Then, when things change —as they do—you find yourself half a world away and missing them more than ever. For some, this is a romantic tie. For me, it's my son. To say I'd poured my heart and soul into his upbringing was an understatement. Moms know this dedication.

I exhaled. "Just a hard landing, that's all. I'll be fine. Got a big list for today. Can't wait to get to it!" I pumped far more confidence into that statement than I felt.

"Well, was I right—curated wool sweaters and coffee table books? Or did you get your fancy beauty products?"

I tucked my legs underneath myself and wrapped the throw blanket around my body. Morning sun lit the loft space. Last night's towel lay in a heap near the bathroom door. I was already out of character.

"Plants," I said. "It's a nursery."

"*Oh, no.*" My son's voice betrayed every iota of appropriate reaction.

"Come on. I can do this. It's the family business."

"Mom, think of the orchids."

"I maintain that the florist delivered them under-watered. It wasn't my fault."

"And the Ficus."

I scoffed. "I thought it was fake!"

"Don't forget the poinsettia. Last Christmas."

"It was that spotted variety. They never last as long as—"

"And the Christmas before."

"It'll be *fine*. I'm sure there's a watering can—or six. I'll make a schedule. Order one of those books, watch some videos."

"*Mom.* You'll kill them."

A smile threatened the corners of my mouth. I would have given the moon to have my son there. To throw one of the beaded pillows at him. Together we'd attack the shop the way he'd help me plan a wedding. His favorite part was staging, which I think was the motivator for his chosen career path.

"Did Uncle Hollis have a dictionary?"

"Patrick."

I heard laughter at the edge of his voice. "Because if you open the book to B for *black thumb,* there will be a picture—"

"Give me half a chance. If I'm the only living thing left in a week, then you can harass me. I'll accept every sling and arrow."

"Deal. Besides, if it doesn't work out, you can always stock soaps and lotion."

I smiled. "Maybe then I can write off my flight to see you as a business expense. I'll try every hand cream in Paris."

"Got to go, Mom. Remy is here. I'll call next week, yeah?"

All too soon, the line was quiet. The hole in my heart, once filled day in and day out by my brilliant, creative boy, ached in his absence.

I closed my eyes, willed the tears away, and stood.

"Time for coffee."

A half bag of ground Arabica beans sat next to a small coffee pot. Sadness reared its head again as I contemplated the fact that I'd picked up Hollis's life, mid-stride. Two weeks ago, he'd had coffee yet to drink, plants to tend, a business to run.

I shook some grounds into a filter, checked the water reservoir, and flipped the switch. Moments later, dark liquid dripped from the spout into the carafe. As I waited for the brew, I made tentative steps toward exploring my new place.

What was a dark and looming mass the night before became walls and tables full of individual plants crowding every inch of the shop space. The wall of vines was by day racks of small pots, their greenery so overgrown, the stems and leaves had knitted together. The front window held a display of tropicals, many blooming and eye-catching to window shoppers. A table off to one side was tiled with tiny succulents in their own plastic pots. Every few feet, a showpiece claimed attention, several of which came with trellises and faded, three-digit price tags.

Above the vine-covered brick wall hung a massive face, somehow familiar in its features. *Man,* I thought, though not without a feminine, rosebud mouth. Three or four feet across, it faced the door as though in welcome to all who entered. Around the forehead, it wore a ring of leaves, giving the character a nature-born look. It was as though my uncle, the impish former owner, still watched over his place.

Patrick's warnings in mind, I was careful not to touch any of the leafy shop occupants. He was right, plant life and I had a checkered past. I needed a plan.

The coffee pot ceased its burbling and I lunged for the contents. Several mugs crowded the counter. I selected the one labeled World's Best Plant Parent and filled it. *Fake it until you make it.*

Steaming liquid at my lips, I was mid-sip when a tap at the door rattled my frayed nerves. "What now?"

A moth fluttered down from a hanging pot to land on my hand as I reached for the door. Half the width of my palm, its wings were dappled in black. Patches of red streaked its back end.

"Hello, little fella."

Growing up in a big city, I had rare occasion to see a variety of insects. Cockroaches, sure. The occasional cricket and grasshopper. An idle butterfly in the park. Ants in the pantry. This guy was something altogether more exotic.

I held the creature up to my face as I peered through the window. A woman stood on the doorstep, a paper sack in hand. She was on the shorter side with one of those blunt, shaggy haircuts that gave her the permanent rolled-out-of-bed look people paid hundreds to achieve. I opened the door. "Morning. Can I help you?"

Her wide-set, violet eyes crinkled at the corners. "Hi," she said. "I wanted to welcome you." She spotted the moth. "What have you got there?"

"Little friend," I said. For the moth had no inclination to leave my hand despite my awkward, bent wrist attempt at a transfer onto a leaf.

The woman held up the paper sack. "I brought muffins. From Second Shot on the next block down." She pointed down the street. "I'm Charlotte," she said, and extended her hand. "But friends call me Lotte."

Moth and I shook her hand with ours. I stepped back to welcome her in and closed the door. I held up my mug. "Coffee?"

"Just had some," she said, giving the bag a little shake before handing it to me. "But thanks."

"Can't function without mine," I said. Unsure of moth protocol, I held my occupied hand near another large leaf. The moth extended first one foot and then another. Instead of transferring to the plant, it took flight only to land on Lotte's head. "Oof, careful there. He isn't house-trained. We just met this morning."

Her eyes angled up, as though she could see the top of her head. She laughed. "S'alright. I don't mind a hitchhiker."

"So, uh, Lotte. Will you stop by every morning with pastries?" I unfolded the top of the bag and extracted a blue-berry muffin. The crumbles on the top promised a carb overload.

She laughed, the sound of bells ringing. "Pastry delivery doesn't sound like too tough a gig. I own the candle shop, though." She pointed at a window across the square. "On the corner."

Through the grimy window, I could make out a store-front. Bold letters that spelled Wicks & Wax contrasted in teal against the white awning and red brick. "I'll have to check it out," I said, and held up my muffin. "Thanks for this. I just got here yesterday and I've yet to set up. Organize. I don't even know what to do with the plants, yet." I waved a hand too close to pineapple's cousin and the tip poked my finger. When I withdrew, the plant appeared to shrivel and brown where I'd touched it. *Great.*

Lotte watched me, her head tilted as my flailings sent muffin crumbs to the floor. I'd sweep them up the moment I bought a broom. Put that on the list. "So, anyway. I hope to open within a week or so."

"Wonderful," she said. "Let me know if you have any questions. I don't know everything, but I did what I could."

"What you...could?"

Lotte studied the floor a moment before meeting my eyes. "When Hollis died. I've been tending the plants the best I could. Watering, really. It's a big job, but the least I could do."

"Oh." It struck me then, that this woman had been in the shop before I had. Might have sipped coffee from the mug I now held. It was an invasion, of sorts. "Uh. Thank you." I stuffed down my impulse to ask for the key she'd used, whether she moved anything, and if she saw the awful movers dump my boxes in the street. Instead, I said, "I appreciate that. How should I get in touch?"

She pressed a card to my hand. The moth fluttered down and landed on the paper, as though to read the print. "If you need anything, I'm across the square. I'll leave you to it." With a little wave, Lotte ducked out the door.

"Okay, buddy, I've got things to do." I set the card on the expanse of soil in a plant marked *Sansevieria.*

Coffee, check. Sugar rush from a heavenly muffin, check. With a beanie tugged down over my limp, sweaty hair, I squeezed myself into the ubiquitous pair of black leggings owned by every woman for when she couldn't be bothered to put on an outfit and headed out into the morning.

Crisp winter air brushed at my cheeks as I put my feet to pavement. I needed supplies and contacts if I was going to attack my to-do list.

Two blocks away, I found a hardware store and a liquor store. With a broom under one arm and bags of cleaning supplies and champagne hooked over my elbows, I carried my purchases back to the shop.

Two hours later, I had a swept floor, boxes arranged by room, and still no idea what to do with the plants.

I huffed out a breath of air that lifted my sweaty bangs. "Time to find some lunch," I said to the moth. It had crawled up one of the plants' blades and waited, stretching its wings. "The lack of calories has me talking to bugs."

I breezed past the pub on my walk. After the brush-off last night, the last person I wanted to see was the ape of a man who'd ignored my plight. Instead, I ducked into a bistro I'd spotted next to an art gallery. The cheery tablecloths and simple menu promised hearty food.

The owners, an older couple, fussed over me. They plied me with heaven-sent cheddar biscuits and a plea to return anytime. When I paid my bill, the man passed me the number of his handyman. His wife tutted at me as I left, resting a hand on my shoulder. "Now, dear, you come by anytime. And remember, it's those of us who sense that are always blessed, never cursed."

Her words stayed with me as I walked back, my brows knitting together. What did she mean by "those of us who sense"?

Ahead, a large truck was parked in a space in front of my shop. The driver waited on the doorstep, several packages at his feet. He consulted a tablet in hand before knocking.

"I'm here," I called, picking up my pace. He glanced at me, then tapped into the device. I arrived in front of him, breathless. "Used to live at six feet," I said. "Now I'm a mile high. Got to hit that treadmill."

For the record, mom jokes are just as ridiculous as dad jokes.

The guy nodded and handed me the tablet. His interaction with me would be one of many, and possibly the weirdest. "Sign here."

"What is it?"

He shrugged. "Not my business to know." He tucked the tablet under one arm and gave me a quick grin. "Have a good day—and, uh, don't worry, you've still got it." He winked at me, dropping a glance to my spandexed curves.

"Thanks," I muttered, in a dry response.

I dragged the heavy boxes into the shop. With my personal box cutter—always on my wedding tool belt—I pried open the boxes and peered inside.

More plants. Leaves all but exploded outward as though eager to join their brethren.

Just what I needed, more collateral. *What to do with these?* I shoved the boxes to the side, promising myself I'd look up their names and care—later. I had a handyman to call.

Two hours later, with a bill for three hundred dollars and a functioning shower, I was beat.

In a box marked Kitchen Tools, I'd unearthed my favorite glass flute and bottle stopper. The champagne bottle, now two-thirds full, fit in the door of the half-sized refrigerator in the kitchenette as I took my glass upstairs. Back on the futon, I tucked the blanket over my legs and settled in for a phone call that might smother what little patience I had left.

"Honey?"

"Hi, Dad."

"Gentlemen, excuse me. It's Ember James."

Six o'clock in Fort Lauderdale. Must be at the club house. When he wasn't at work, my father lived and breathed golf.

Charles Rookwood left Chicago winters behind when my mom died. He'd moved down south, managing marketing campaigns for Floridian nursing homes. "I'm back," he said. "How is the new adventure?"

"It's...different," I said, unsure of where to start. "Did you know Hollis ran a plant store? A nursery."

"No, I didn't." I heard the concern in his voice. My father had never been a fan of Hollis, my mother's older brother, but he'd tolerated him in the name of family. They were polar opposites, and it was a wonder my mom had loved them both —but that was Mom. "What's Prescott like?"

"It's cute," I said, taking a sip from my glass and savoring the bubbles that burst against my lips. "The whole town is adorable. Old west chic. I love the brick buildings. And the sunshine."

"We've got plenty of Vitamin D down here, too, you know."

"I know, Dad." When my apartment was ripped out from under me in a surprise sale of the building for condos, Dad had offered his place as a chance to figure out my new life. He'd been hurt when the call from Hollis's lawyer made my path clear. I changed the subject to deflect any further guilt lobbed my way. "The shop is great, too. Exposed brick, wooden floors in some spaces, painted concrete in others. Lots of light."

"Well if it doesn't work, you have a place with me, sweetheart."

Below the loft, there was a rattling at the back door. The sun had yet to set, but the light through the clearstory windows above the shop was lilac and growing darker. Who could that be—was it Lotte? Or Morgan's owner, here again to see if my pathetic pleas had been answered?

The door rattled again, followed by a desperate banging.

"What's that noise?"

"Nothing," I said, erasing fear from my voice. "There's a bar next door. Customers can get a little rowdy."

"Downright obnoxious if that's what happens at all hours. You should be careful."

I shoved an ottoman under the long window as a boost and peered out. In the atrium, a figure moved back from my stoop and approached the tree, a species I didn't recognize–but that wasn't saying much. I could barely name some of the plants in my shop, all of nature seemed impossible. They extended first one hand and then the other to set their palms against its trunk.

"What do you think about that?"

"Hmm?"

After a moment, the figure bowed their forehead to touch the bare tree. Bent in this way, two bumps stuck up from their jacket, like extra sharp shoulder blades. I squinted into the dim light to get a better view.

"You and Patrick. Coming for summer break. We've got a killer pool."

I kept my eyes on the person. Defeat hung from their neck, an unseen shroud. "Sure, Dad. Sounds good." As though sensing my watch, they looked up at me staring down at them. I gasped.

"Honey?"

Without warning, a second figure was behind the first. Dark clothing, quick movements. The second person wrapped something around the neck of the first and yanked them backward off the tree. The first person struggled, grabbing at their neck while dragged backward. "Oh my god!"

"What is it? Ember James?"

"I...uh. I don't know. I've got to go, Dad. Someone's at the door."

"But it's six o'clock. Aren't you closed?"

The figures were now out of sight. I started for the stairs.

"Yes, but it's another shop owner. She sells candles. We're getting drinks."

"Glad you've made a friend," my father said, hesitation in his voice. "Call me soon?"

I faced the screen of my phone to my chest so it wouldn't glow against the night. I approached the back door, tip-toeing to the edge of the window to peek outside. In the moonlight, nothing stirred. Two crows roosted, silent among the tree branches.

Every shadow was a reason not to sleep.

Saturday morning, a resounding thwack signaled the collision of a pigeon with the arched, second story windows of the shop.

I peered over the ledge of the loft, groggy. A smudge on the glass indicated where the poor creature had crashed. I slipped into my robe and padded downstairs.

"Better make sure it isn't suffering," I said to a vine snaking out from a trellis to catch hold of the stair railing. In my new space, talking to the only other occupants around became a fast habit.

I flipped the switch on the coffee pot, donned my jacket, and stepped into a pair of slip-ons before venturing outside.

On the sidewalk, a stunned pigeon flapped, one wing immobile. Two crows watched from the roof of a parked car. They eyed the injured bird, cocking their heads as it struggled.

"Shoo," I said, flapping my arms at the black birds. "Shoo. You won't harass him on my watch." The birds hopped a dozen feet away. One flew onto the awning of the pub. Both continued to watch the scene.

The pigeon stilled for a moment, blinking up at me. Early dawn's rays set its iridescent features aflame. "You're much prettier than people give you credit for," I said to the bird.

"That they are. Here, I'll take care of the poor bastard."

Joaquin's voice coming from behind me caused my back to stiffen. There was something familiar about him I couldn't place in my pre-coffee state. I believe in trusting one's gut, and mine twisted at the early hour. I turned to face him and was startled to find Morgan's owner glowering over Joaquin's shoulder.

Few others were out that morning. A lone jogger wove through the trees near the courthouse. A woman walked a pack of little dogs in front of the candle shop. But across the square, the street was empty, its late-night businesses recently shuttered with the daytime shops yet to open.

I squinted at Joaquin. "I didn't realize you were a bird lover."

The pub owner snorted. Joaquin replied, "It's not the pigeon's fault they've evolved into a relatively useless flying rat. Humans did this to them. The least I can do is ease their suffering."

"That's what people say when they plan for the opposite."

Joaquin moved toward the bird, bending in a slow crouch. He dropped his voice to a whisper and inched a hand toward the animal. "It's okay, friend. It won't be long." The bird jerked its head, fixing an eye on the approach.

"What do you mean? You aren't going to—"

My outburst startled the bird who restarted the one-winged panic. Joaquin sent me a murderous look, his irises black in the daylight. "Put it out of its misery? Yes, that *was* the plan. And a kind one at that. You'd prefer it self-induce a heart attack instead? That it be snatched up by the first dog that walks by? Or better yet"—he gestured to the looming corvids—"let those two peck it to death?"

As if in assent or protest, the crows cawed a raucous

acknowledgement. The pub owner snorted, a smile toying at the edge of his expression.

"I just—" I began, uncertain how my intentions had been so deftly twisted by this man. He wasn't wrong, but neither was I. My hands shook as I struggled to contain my emotion. "You should see if an animal can be saved, first, before condemning it to death."

Something flashed in Joaquin's eyes, and they lightened from a rich cognac to acorn brown. "You're right." Without waiting for my response, he scooped up the bird and deposited it into his friend's sizable hands. "What do you say, boss?"

The man looked down at the bird as though it were the last thing he planned to hold, then at me. He closed his eyes and the bird stilled in his grip. A breeze whipped around us, tousling our hair and lifting the bird's feathers.

After a moment, the animal closed its eyes. Had he squeezed it to death? Before I could ask, the man opened his palms, and the bird flew off.

Joaquin spotted my finger, still raised in protest. "Perhaps I am not the only one who should be wary of poor judgment." The two men stepped back into the pub, leaving me, dumbstruck, on the pavement.

Lotte jogged by, headphones in, her all-black running gear a stark contrast to the tan and cream she'd worn when we met. Her hair was up in a knot at the top of her head. When she saw me, she paused to fold forward, her breath puffing tiny clouds in the cold morning air. "Ever think about how cool lungs are?" Her chest heaved. "You just keep going about your day and they fill, empty, and refill with no work on your part. The heart, too. Hands down my favorite muscle."

"Yeah," I said, staring at the door of the pub. "Neat."

"Farmer's market today," she said, checking her watch. "Are you going?"

I beheld my closest version of a friend in this town.

Jogging, gorgeous skin, fan of fresh fruit and vegetables. Then I consulted my own morning: jacket-robe combo, stiff from futon sleep, and larder empty except for subpar coffee. "Yes."

An hour later, I stepped off the bus, an oversized tote over my shoulder. I would play the part of someone with her shit together enough to shop for organic beets, fill a flower vase every week, and eat eggs from chickens hand-massaged and treated to endless grubs. I'd been in that role before, I could get there again.

The turnout was plentiful, both in products and customers. My first stop was to purchase a pastry from a woman with a French accent and a wide sun hat. The creation flaked over my sweater but was an envelope of the gods. Almondy-soft center, golden brown casing. Heaven from a paper sleeve.

A few booths later and I took on the identity of a local. I found granola, winter kale, and frozen empanadas. I'd patted a golden retriever, two cockapoos, and a Great Dane. In the center of the market, a folk band held court on a stage, entertaining those who'd stopped to eat and drink.

At one end of the booths was a special tent full of work benches and bicycles in various states of repair. There was a rack that sided the booth, filled with a dozen bicycles, each hung with a price tag. Several staff worked at the tables.

It had been a long time since I'd owned a bike but even longer since I'd had a car. I considered what I could do with two wheels and approached the rack. One of the workers looked up, then, intercepting my approach. She glared at me over a bike she'd lifted onto a stand, its wheels spinning free in the air. I turned my head to check behind me but there was no one. I backed away from the booth. I'd reconsider transportation another day.

I wandered down one length of the market and up the other. At a booth strung with a raffia garland, I spotted a heavenly creature holding court over a register while several other staff wove around him, filling bags with customer purchases. The man wore a newsboy hat that did little to contain golden curls escaping from underneath. The sleeves of an ASU sweatshirt, neck cut out, were pushed up to the elbows of muscled forearms. Sea green eyes appraised the customers, a wide smile greeting every question. His line was ten deep and full of other admirers, whether of the honey or the man, it didn't matter. The shelves in his booth were all but empty, his helpers scrambling to restock.

Across the booth, the man caught my eye. I froze. His wink brought a flush to my cheeks. I pretended to fiddle with something in my bag as though I'd just remembered something. When I looked up, he was talking to an ancient, white-haired woman hefting a beeswax candle.

I approached the booth, sneaking a longer look at the man. His very being was honey colored, from his hair to his sun-kissed skin. He exuded sweetness, from the bow of his lips to the laughter in his eyes. The others were a whirlwind around him, and he was the center.

The booth, Beckett Honey, was constructed from palettes painted in soft gold and navy. The banner behind the man featured a honeycomb logo at its center. Shelving contained a scant selection of candles, creams, honeycombs, and of course the showpiece, jars of the viscous liquid itself. A rainbow of labels on the shelving identified the source of the jars. Some were lavender, others clover or buckwheat. I perused what was left, selected a jar labeled Wildflowers, and took my place in line.

While I waited, I watched the other staff buzz around the

booth. There were three of them, each in an all-white outfit. None wore long sleeves despite the chill. One brushed past me, his shock of dark hair a swoop over one eye. When my bag bumped his hip, he turned to look at me, pupils dilating. His eyes were red-rimmed, his cheeks hollow.

"So sorry," I said. He said nothing and turned back to his task.

In his wake, a feather floated down to the ground. White fletching with gray streaks. I stooped to collect the treasure. I twirled it between two fingertips, admiring the iridescent, black shaft. I tucked the find into my bag and shifted the bag to my other shoulder.

With two more people ahead of me, I let my gaze wander to the crowd. Despite the chill in the morning air, the market flowed with people, the hum of hundreds checking off lists, exclaiming over tasty finds, and catching up with their neighbors.

"Hello," came a voice, fluid and smooth. "You must be new to the market. I don't believe we've met."

When I dared to lift my gaze to his, I bit back a sigh of contentment. He was all the more gorgeous up close. Rich brown skin dusted with fine golden hair, a single gold hoop in each ear—and those lips. He caught the lower one in his teeth, watching me ogle him, and I'd be damned if the man didn't smell like honey.

I gave my head a brief shake. "Hi. Er, hello. Sorry, spaced out for a second there." Cue his perfect grin. "Uh. I...was wondering if you had any more of the lavender honey," I said. "If it's not any trouble."

"We may have another jar or two tucked away back here," he said, assuring me with the ever-present smile. He turned to one of the helpers. "Have we got another lavender?"

His helper rummaged in a crate before extracting a couple of jars.

"Thanks for looking," I said. "I'm a fan of honey in my champagne, like a grown-up French 75."

"What's that?"

"A cocktail," I said. "One of my favorites."

The honeyed god handed me one of the fresh jars. "Is this what you were looking for?"

His hand overlapped mine. His skin was warm, electric. A pulse zinged from my fingers straight to a spot deep in my belly.

"It is," I said, not trusting my mouth with anything else.

He smiled at me. "Are you visiting our fair city or are you here to stay?"

This level of questioning I could manage without becoming a puddle of lust, melted by the waves of sticky, sweet heat radiating from this perfect being. "I own the Apothecary. My uncle owned it before, and I took over when he...died."

A flicker of darkness shaded his eyes for the briefest moment at my mention of Hollis. He recovered quickly, wrapping the jar in brown paper. "I'm sorry for your loss."

I frowned a little, curious what was meant by his comment. "I'm afraid I'm not half the horticulturist he was, but I'm doing my best to learn."

He handed me his card, a beehive shape. "It was lovely to meet you...?"

I plucked the beehive-shaped card from between his fingers, avoiding direct touch. "EJ," I said. "Rookwood. And you are...?"

"Rowdy Beckett," he said as I flipped over the card. "Owner of a little farm outside the city limits. I need to come by the Apothecary. I could use a plant or two in the farmhouse. Cheer the place up a bit."

"Then I hope to see you soon," I said with a smile. The woman who'd been behind me in line shot me a murderous glance at my extended delay as she stepped to his register.

I all but floated toward the market exit, my insides aflutter from the interaction with Rowdy. His touch lingered on my hand, as though he'd left an indelible mark. *It's been too long, EJ.*

It was true. The last time I remembered a man laying his hands on me was at the Davidson wedding last year. One of the groomsmen got plastered and backed me into a corner, saying I reminded him of his high school girlfriend, and wouldn't it be nice if we could relive old times. Christopher, in a rare display of aggression, yanked the guy off me and heaved him into the nearest bush where the man promptly lost his slice of wedding cake into the roses. While our boss had been livid Christopher had assaulted a guest, she'd simmered when the bride's father called to apologize for his son's behavior. Sad, but that awkward mashing of my breast was the hottest thing to happen to me in months.

The screech of rubber on brake pads interrupted my thoughts. In front of me, blocking the exit, was the woman from the bike booth, her hands tight on the handlebars.

"Careful," I said, my words carrying more bark than bite.

"Funny thing to hear from the likes of you," she said, locking her gaze on mine. Her nostrils flared as she considered me, like a specimen pinned on a table. She eyed the jar in my hands, the sprig of dried lavender tucked underneath the raffia bow. "Fool. Stay away from him."

"Who?" I said, owl-like.

"Him. *Them,*" she spat. "Edge riding isn't for the weak of heart or spirit. From the looks of it, you have neither."

"I don't know what you're talking about."

She angled the tire closer, pinning me against a trash can. "Stay out of our way, and for the sake of the Goddess, keep your distance from the Order."

"But I didn't—"

"*All* of them." With her proclamation spoken, she nosed the bike back onto the street and rode off.

Foul mood overshadowing my successful outing, I opted to walk back to the shop. My thoughts circled like storm clouds, darkening in my mind each time I recalled the vitriol in the woman's voice. The ramblings of a mad woman.

Back at the Apothecary, I dropped my bag on the stool but didn't bother to flip the open sign. There were too many barriers to business at the moment, the crabby equivalent of the Wicked Witch of the West one of the most recent.

Hands on hips, I appraised the shop. If I was to breathe life back into the place, I needed to get organized. A plan for each of my items, a possible shuffling of what Hollis left, and a strategy for moving forward.

I unpacked my purchases, setting my new honey near the coffee pot. The dregs of the morning's pot went into a mug I carried around with me as I puttered around the place. Scissors went in a drawer, the ledger stuffed with receipts went next to my purse for later reading, and I washed the inside of the shop windows. Space tidied, I addressed the plants.

For a woman who knew how to run a dual-faith ceremony and garden reception for five hundred without batting an eye, to admit my lack was painful. That I was terrible with the green and leafy organisms was a well-known fact. In second grade, we'd painted pots in which we'd planted a single, heart-shaped leaf for Mother's Day. On the walk home, I'd somehow managed to kill the plant, its brown leaf a shriveled representation of the love I had for my mom. She'd dried my tears, assuring me that kind wouldn't grow much anyway. But at senior prom, my date ignored my pleas and presented me with a gorgeous corsage. He insisted I sniff the creation and all but shoved it into my nose. Not only did I sneeze, but the flowers twisted and darkened from beneath the ribbons, the whole thing unceremoniously dumped in the trash.

Then there was the plant Patrick gave me before he left for grad school. "Don't worry," he'd said. "You can't kill this one." I did, though, its dried tentacle-leaves a testament on my windowsill. I couldn't bear to throw it out. Guilt forced me to pack the thing. Perhaps I would hide it among the greenery, tricking myself into thinking I hadn't ruined yet another thing of beauty.

"Hate to disappoint you, my friends," I said to the plants around me, "but you've been traded to the wrong team." I twisted my mouth into a grimace.

Living things were never in my wheelhouse. I left that to Christopher. He comforted the grandmothers, kept track of the ring bearers, and hung hundreds if not thousands of floral garlands from gazebos, chair backs, and all other event locations. I handled the dry details: accounts, travel, schematics, and all the legalities. I built each bride—and groom—a detailed binder of their special day, down to the bird seed thrown on their exit. We made a good team, balancing each other's strengths. Had hoped to start our own business one day. Christopher liked to say, "I find joy in the twist of the bride's neck as she tosses her bouquet. EJ finds it in the books."

Books. In the small, glassed-in room, I'd seen shelf after shelf of books. Hollis might have something for me to read on the plants. A care guide. It was worth a look.

Near the back of the shop, I tried the door to the closed room. It wouldn't budge. I fetched the ring of keys from my purse. None worked. I might need a locksmith. "Guess who I won't be asking for a recommendation?" I said to the plant nearest to me and rolled my eyes. It was one of several with the Swiss cheese leaves, this one bigger and bushier than the others.

Frowning, I reached for the ledger I'd set aside. Hollis may have tracked a watering schedule if nothing else, or maybe notes on fertilizer and ordering. I flipped through the pages, extracting receipts into one pile, scraps of notes into another. In the pages, I learned my uncle was part of a botanical group that met once a month and some kind of book club. On the pages for his last trip to Chicago, he'd penciled, "Ask Lotte to look in on the shop."

The last page of his writing was the day he died. An emotional weight plummeted in my gut. Here were the everyday notes of a man here one moment, gone the next, unaware he wouldn't live to see them through. Below a grocery list and a few measurements in inches, he'd sketched a constellation. Five-pointed stars in a neat loop, lines connecting each to the next. A note off to the side reminded him to "give the coordinates to EJ." Hollis had always been a fan of the heavens, going so far as hauling us to an observatory to witness Saturn's rings as fact outside a textbook picture. I could see him then, in a fisherman's sweater, pleased at our exclamations over the device. How sweet that he'd wanted me to see this set of stars. Perhaps I could locate them, somehow. See what he'd wanted me to find.

Holding Hollis's thoughts, his reminders, was holding a piece of him. I clutched the book to my heart, a hot tear running down my cheek to splatter on the spine.

I stood up from the staircase where I'd perched and a single, silver key fell from between the pages, pinging when it hit the steps.

THREE

I flipped the sign to open, both terrified someone would want to buy something and heartbroken when no one did within the first five minutes. Anxiety played tug-of-war with depression. This was different than when I lost my job, my apartment, and my son all in the same month but the same in the bone-crushing feeling you're pushing a boulder up a steep hill of adulthood.

Anxiety and depression are two sides of the same coin. You learn to co-exist, in a way. Like a roommate you can't evict. You land a real date after way too many years with an electric boyfriend and late-night websites full of plastic bodies. You put on the good undies and shave an extra body part or two, squeeze into the dress you hate the least, then—boom—in walks Anxiety. What if your breath smells? What if they hate pink? And purple. What if they turn out to be an ax murderer and you become a sad, cautionary tale on the news so some family adopts your beloved cat and neglects to feed it the correct food and now your cat hates you. Or rather, hates your soul, because you are now dead and can't explain any of it to your cat, not that they would listen anyway because—cat, but you would feel better about the whole mess if only you could. But you can't, so you won't, and this is why. Then Depression gets up from its all-night bender to let you know you won't get a second date so none of it matters as you'll be alone forever and the cat doesn't like you anyway.

See?

With no customers in sight, I had to shut my brain up. So, I got my hands dirty.

First, I rearranged the bigger potted plants that were shoved into the curve of the spiral staircase. I wrestled a particularly big and bushy one into place. "There you are," I said, as though it were a sentient being, and I was its caretaker. I'd read somewhere talking to your plants helps them grow. "I'll call you Mariette," I said to the monstrosity of greenery. "Mom's favorite actress. You seem fabulous." I straightened the pot and a leaf brushed at my cheek as though in thanks.

Next, I played chemist—kind of. Atop an empty rack, wedged between a pair of plant stands, was a small bowl filled with soil, an antique spoon dipped in like soup. Next to the bowl was a handwritten placard that read, *Homemade Potting Soil, $5 a bag*. In the ledger, I'd found Hollis's recipe for potting mix. This explained the box of bags and an unraveling roll of labels I'd found in the workroom. Narrow and fluorescent-lit, the workroom held shelving and grow lights, with tools discarded on every surface. Purpose set, I cleared off the counter space. Next, I hunted down a bucket and seized a giant scoop.

Sand and compost were the only two ingredients I recognized. Bags of each sat on the floor, their tops rolled down. With a grunt, I hefted them onto the counter. Next came perlite, vermiculite, coconut coir—all a mystery to me. I consulted the various containers, hunting for labels.

"Hello?"

The call of a potential customer caused me to stand up far

too fast. I bonked my head on the corner of a rack. "Sweet Lady Necneven!"

"You okay?" In the doorway stood a man with a stack of hot pink fliers under one arm. He wore a Gone Fishin' trucker hat and a pair of ripped jeans. Music boomed from the oversized headphones he'd pushed half-off his ears. The center of his forehead wrinkled in concern and I remembered to respond.

"I didn't hear you come in," I said, rubbing my head. "I'll be fine, thanks for checking. How can I help you?"

The man held out his hand. I brushed my hand off on my pants before taking his. Static zapped our fingers. I released his hand and shook my own at the wrist.

"I'm Bryce," he said. "I own Plush—down the street?" He hooked a thumb over his shoulder as though I would follow in my head.

I nodded as though I knew the place. "I've been meaning to go," I lied, wanting him to think I was the kind of fellow business owner who supported the others. Anxiety—see? "It's on my list as soon as I get this place up and running."

"Haven't been here too long, myself. Bought the place. Glad I did. You'll like it here. Folks...look out for each other." He winked at me, as though letting me in on a local secret.

He was cute, but not my type. Dimple, cleft chin, manicured nails. One of those men who claimed college was the time of their lives then mentally never left.

He whipped a paper off the stack under his arm and presented it to me. "Anyway, I'm hoping you'll hang one of these in your shop. Got some good shows coming up. Everything from jazz to funk and rock. Dance every weekend. You should come. We've got food. Beer. All the good stuff."

Something told me Plush didn't carry champagne. I moved toward him to accept the flier. There was a small bulletin board near the kitchenette with a hodgepodge of dating postings. I pinned the show list over the other layers and made a mental note to toss the old ones later.

"So you'll come?"

"Sure," I said, seeking to extract myself from the awkward circular conversation. I reached for an abandoned trowel, stuffed into the dirt in a nearby pot. Trowel in hand, I beamed an apologetic dismissal. "Well, better get back to it."

I watched as he made his way to the door. Before he left, he stopped to turn on his heel and regarded the shop, floor to ceiling, as though to case the place. Satisfied, he nodded to himself and left.

With a glance at the fluorescent advertisement, I considered my own situation. Should I be passing out fliers? "I have time," I said to myself. First there was soil to make.

Recommitted to my task, I whirled around and nearly leapt out of my skin.

Five feet from me stood a tall, lanky teen. Big blue eyes and shaggy, black hair framed his face. He backed up to the wall, as though as shocked to see me as I was to find him.

"I am...your pardon, please. I didn't mean to...I was looking for—" He held his hands up in supplication, scanning the shop as though assessing an escape route.

"Sorry—must have missed you coming in," I said, second guessing the words the moment they left my lips. Until Bryce arrived, I was certain the shop, save me, the moth, Mariette, and her plant friends, was empty. How could I have failed to notice another human? A tingle shot up my scalp. What if he'd been in here before Bryce? "I need to get a shop bell, I think."

He gave a nervous chuckle and ran his hands through the back of his hair and linked fingers at the back of his neck. His hands, long and slender, were a match for his frame. When his fingers parted his hair, it was as though they glowed a soft blue. The light trailed up his wrist and disappeared under the cuff of his long-sleeved Henley. "Look, I can come back another time. I was looking for Hollis. Please excuse me. Good day." He hunched his shoulders and shuffled for the back door, seemed struck by a thought, and then headed for the front.

I was curious about this boy-almost-man and his possible knowledge of Hollis.

"You are—were—a friend of my uncle?"

He nodded. "I come by. Whenever I'm...in town. I do odd jobs for him. For Ansel, too."

"Ansel?"

"At Morgan's. I'm a dishwasher."

Ansel must be the name of my grumpy neighbor. "Well a friend of Hollis's is a friend of mine." Guilt riddled my speech. When was his last visit? I had to tell him. "I'm—"

"No," he said, a sharp rebuke. It was all but a command. His voice lowered again, softened. "You mustn't. I...uh...am not good with names."

I lifted an eyebrow. I'd lived through the teenage stage with my own son. Many who parent girls think they have the lock on random drama, but let this mother assure you that is far from the case. "Okay. Do you have a name you'd like me to call you?"

He wrapped his arms around himself, looking everywhere but at me. "Call me Gaven. Pleased to know you."

I took a step toward him and he inched away. Odd, he'd come to my shop. "Okay...Gaven. I'm sorry to be the one to tell you this, but Hollis...died. It was very recent."

He lifted his head, blue eyes pleaded with me, wild. "Dead? But I've only been gone...oh." Pain crossed his face as he closed his eyes and pressed his lips together. "This is bad. Really bad. Who will watch...Does Ansel know?"

My surprise guest had shifted from evasive to confrontational in a snap. Questions stacked up in my mind like building blocks. "Yes, he knows."

Gaven paced the room, his agitation palpable. He fired off his own questions. "How did he die? When did it happen?"

"I was told there was an accident," I said. "The week before last. It was quick." This was the gist of what I'd been told over the phone by the lawyer's secretary.

"I must speak with Ansel," Gaven muttered, as though alone in the shop. "He'll have told Sharon. A new watcher must be named."

He was agitated, jumpy where he stood. Wary, I reached out a hand to brush his sleeve. "In lieu of services, he requested donations to go to Vester. I'm guessing it's a charity? I can find out, but I'm new and–"

"He can't have done," Gaven said, his eyes accusatory as though I'd committed a grievous error.

"It was in his will," I said with a shrug. "Of course, you don't have to—"

"I've got to talk to Ansel." Gaven approached the door.

I wanted my space back, but the mom in me worried. "Are you sure you'll be alright?"

He stopped, as though seeing me for the first time. Under a sunbeam, he shimmered at the edges, a trick of the light. "With due respect, it is your safety we must consider."

I opened my mouth to protest—with which of my questions, I didn't know—when he cut me off.

Gaven's irises went black. "Whatever you do, do not let them out of your sight," he said, his voice a harsh whisper. Before I could ask who or what or why, he slipped into the workroom and closed the door.

Blinking into the empty space, I gave my head a shake. Do I call the police? *Oh excuse me, this boy came out of nowhere— he may have known my uncle but he's on one or more drugs, so please collect him from my premises.* Or wait and see what nonsense would come out of the workroom?

The front door opened with a bang. A breeze blew in

behind the figure in the doorway, rattling a set of wind chimes near the door. This would be the last time I complained about a day starting at a turtle's pace, for the rabbit is quick to overtake him.

"Can I help you?" For the third time that morning, I greeted a newcomer. Unlike the first two, this one failed to address me.

They moved around the front room, lifting leaves and peering behind pots. Under their breath, they whispered, "Where is it? Must be here. Have the tithe, give to the watcher. Be convincing." This became a soft chant as they flitted between the plants.

When they faced me, I beheld a man with feminine features and a pixie cut, hair the color of flames. Red-rimmed eyes stared, blank and unseeing. He tilted his head, as though allowing his brain to register and explain my presence.

"Do you need assistance?" I kept my phone in hand, the back door in my sights. My pinky twitched. The shoe of my sneaker squeaked against the painted concrete floor as I stepped back from the advancing guest. "Can I call someone for you? Have them take you home?"

"Home," he said, as though the idea dislodged a barrier. He lifted his palms to me. Across them slung several strands of the palest pink pearls I'd seen. Each pearl glowed as if lit from within. "Please," he said, holding them higher and dipping his head as though in subjugation. "Take these as my tithe, mistress, but show me the way and I'll be off."

I shook my head. This was too weird, and I'd known weird. There was the wedding in which the bride's ex crashed the wedding in a lobster costume, high off shrooms. The corporate party in the Palmer House at which we'd chased prostitutes out of the bathroom. And I'd never let Christopher forget the time we hosted an executive suite at Wrigley Field. Someone streaked through the private parties, covered in ketchup, protesting the pollution of Lake Michigan.

In a pinch, I could handle the unexpected. I dialed back into my assertive reserves.

"You need to leave. Whatever this is," I said, pointing at the pearls, "is not what I do here. I'm not sure what Hollis was into, but it's not for me."

"Hollis," he hissed, and nodded with ferocity. He walked between the plants, running his hand along the leaves. "Must find Hollis."

"He's dead," I insisted for the second time today. "He's not here. He won't be here. Now. Get. Out." I stepped toward the figure, phone raised in my hand.

But he didn't leave. Instead, his eyes narrowed and he took a step toward me. "Where is it? What has thou done? You have taken it for yourself, I think. Redheads lie with a forked tongue."

For what it's worth, my hair has never been that red. Auburn highlights, sure. Bleached to a lighter marigold in the summers—yep. Red, though? No. Further, I had no clue what he meant about taking anything.

"You will take this," he said, thrusting the necklace at me. His eyes shifted in all directions, as though he were a robot on the verge of a short circuit.

I picked up the nearest object with vague weapon capabilities—the trowel. I wielded it as an officer holds a flashlight: tight to the side of my head with the business end aimed at my target. My chest heaved, but I willed my voice to remain steady. "I'm calling the police."

He stepped to me then and pressed his forehead to the tip of the trowel. A bead of blood, viscous and so purple it was black, oozed from the wound. "My dedication to freedom is unwavering. Test me as thou must."

From behind me came a shout. "Get out, reject!"

We both turned to look.

From the depths of the workroom came Gaven. He wore a pair of purple gardening gloves and wielded a rusty iron plant stand. "You dare insult this lady in her home and expect entry. Leave, foul abomination, before I run you through!"

He lunged at the person, who dropped the necklaces. Strings broke when they hit the floor, sending pearls rattling across the floor in all directions. In his haste toward the door, he crunched several underfoot. He flung the door open and was gone.

From the front door, we watched him sprint down the sidewalk. Too-big shoes slapped the pavement as his oversized sweatshirt billowed out behind. A couple blocks away, he turned down a side street and was gone.

Gaven's hair was mussed, his face sweaty. I had both newfound respect for and a healthy dose of fear of him.

"Is it just me, or is it hot in there?"

"Who was that?"

"One of the Fallen," Gaven said with a sigh. "And there will be more."

Four

"The Fallen?"

Gaven nodded as he replaced the gloves and righted the plant he'd tipped over to grab the stand. He skirted the edges of the space as though I'd forget he was there. I watched him, then, this boy of sixteen, maybe eighteen, a scarecrow in corduroy pants. A strip of leather wrapped around his wrist, a silver ring tied within.

What does one say to a teenager who snuck into their shop, might have been snooping, and then chased someone high on drugs away as though in the line of duty?

"Thank you," I said, surprising both of us. "That got terrifying."

"Oh no," he said, back to his cowering self. "It was nothing." He moved toward the door. He nodded at me, mouth in a straight line, and slunk out the door without another word. Through the front window, I saw him duck into Morgan's.

Great, I thought. Now Ansel—for this must be the owner who refused to help me—would know my shop was overrun with people seeking their next high. For all I knew, the bar owner was acquainted with Hollis's activities.

I reached for the broom. Pearls crunched under every step, digging into my nerves. I would sweep the shop of their tiny, pink presence alongside the memory of their owner.

Weary and defeated, I turned my sign to *Closed* and crawled my way upstairs to flop face down on the futon.

~

Bleary-eyed, I roused myself. My mouth was dry. I'd dreamed I was lost in a jungle, brushing back one vine only to find another. A giant snake watched me from a branch, its middle hanging down in a half loop, its tongue flicking out to taste the air.

My phone had toppled off the coffee table to buzz against the floorboards. I added *a proper rug* to my mental shopping list.

I mashed my thumbs on the screen in an attempt to catch the call. Didn't work.

Instead, *Missed Call* flashed across my screen.

"Damn." The number was local. I sighed and dialed them back.

"Waterhouse, Ingalls, and Parker." A law office, then. *Great.* The crisp voice betrayed someone with far more caffeine in their system than I.

"I missed a call from here. Just now. Ember James Rookwood."

"One moment."

I collapsed back onto the squat couch, clutching a pillow to my chest.

"Ms. Rookwood? Dan Ingalls. I'm the attorney who—"

"Hollis's lawyer." I smacked my hand to my forehead, an unseen gesture to the man on the other end of the line. "I remember now. From the documents."

Through the speaker, I heard the shuffling of papers, the

tap of computer keys. "Thank you for taking my call. I was able to transfer most of your uncle's assets fairly easily given that he'd added you to his accounts. My secretary will email you the new documents to sign."

My pinky twitched. *Breathe, EJ.* As though it wasn't hard enough to lose a loved one, a mountain of paperwork trailed behind Death. "Thank you."

"I'm afraid to say there isn't much, besides the shop. Accounts are all but drained."

I closed my eyes and winced. There'd been the smallest glimmer of hope. "I understand," I said. My tone stated otherwise.

"So, I can tell Becca you'll be by?"

"By?"

"For his effects. Safety deposit box and a few other items."

My brain was stuck calculating how I could run a business with no funding, let alone any idea how to care for the products. "Hmm? Oh. Yes. Of course. I'll be by."

With a sigh, I pushed myself up from the couch and made my way to the staircase. My feet were dead weights as I descended, the burden of reality heavier with each step.

At the bottom of the stairs, I stopped to stare at the sight before me.

Surrounding me on all sides was a wash of decay.

Long leaves on my new favorite fern curled inward, browning at the edges. Half the pots had yellowed leaves, a sickly color. Flowers drooped, petals littering the ground. A wet, musty smell permeated the room. Even my tiny table of hearty succulents shriveled as though scorched on a dry summer's day.

A shuffling sound at the door drew my attention. I watched the shadow as it fumbled with something in its belongings. I passed Marietta, her leaves drooped to kiss the ground.

Through the small metal slot cascaded a handful of envelopes. I stooped to collect them. Mail, nothing more. One mustard yellow envelope from the state department of revenue called my attention to an overdue notice. My stomach churned.

I needed some air.

~

"And I just dumped my life story into your lap and we barely know each other."

Lotte shrugged. "Listening to folks tell me about their lives is kind of my thing."

"Candles by day, therapist by night—er, afternoon?"

"Something like that," she said, running a fingertip around the rim of her mug.

I'd called Lotte to suggest a drink. The news of Hollis's estate, or rather, lack of estate, wasn't something I planned to share with my *I-told-you-so* father. I knew if I called Patrick, he'd withdraw from school and send me the money I'd scraped together for tuition. Christopher was at a bar mitzvah, and I needed advice.

"Do I sell now? Or pretend I can make it work for a few months, go bankrupt, and then give it all to the bank?"

Lotte reached out a hand to squeeze my forearm. Her touch was soft and cool, as though she was carved from marble, a goddess for the ages. "I'm sorry, this is a lot for anyone, and all at once."

"Thank you," I said. I hung my head, the hopeless situation a yoke around my neck. "I don't understand how Hollis financed the place."

"Loans?"

I shook my head. "No debt on the books. Just empty accounts. It's not as though sales were booming."

Lotte nodded, thoughtful. "Maybe he was dipping into savings. Or he could have had a benefactor..." She frowned, considering.

"If he did, perhaps they'll consider me their new charity case."

Snow spotted my jacket on the walk back to the shop. Lotte's comment had me digging through a mental family album. I wracked my addled brain for any memory of my uncle mentioning a friend, business partner, or heck, a lover with knowledge of how he kept things afloat. Someone who would have known how he stayed in business.

Two crows flapped between the trees as I walked, trading places among the branches. I stopped to peer up at them. Their black feathers shimmered in the fading afternoon light. One bird cocked its head as though considering me, too.

"Pretty birds," I said. "Are you following me?" As if in acknowledgement, the bird flapped its wings.

Music pumped out from the doorway of the next shop. Plush—Bryce's venue. Inside the big bay window, a trio held court on a small stage. The singer wailed into the microphone. His mouth was so big I could reach in and yank on his tonsils. The drummer hammered out a beat while the guitar player picked at a melody. His fret hand had LOVE tattooed over his knuckles and PAIN crossed the other hand.

The door swung open and a wave of sound washed out. A person pushed past me, brushing my shoulder. When we touched, I shivered. A carousel of images flashed in my mind of booze, the backside of a woman in front of me, my hand on the small of her back as she rocked her hips against mine, flames, and then blackness.

I reeled and braced myself against the brick wall. *What the hell? You win, Monday.*

I scurried down the street, clutching my coat tighter around my body. The crows continued to follow, alighting in each tree until I passed, then resettling farther on. Was I their prey? Soon to be roadkill in the fate of my business.

They're crows, EJ.

When I looked toward the shop, I halted my frantic pace. Someone waited between the cars. They checked a watch, then the sidewalk. Hood of their sweatshirt up, I couldn't see a face from this distance.

Movement on the roof caught my eye. Joaquin, his face peering over the ledge. Then he was gone.

I looked back at the person on the ground. Arms wrapped around themselves like a hug, they strode toward Morgan's. Just before the doors, they froze. They shook their head several times as though wrestling with a decision and paced back toward the Apothecary.

Joaquin slipped out from behind parked cars and scooted along the backside of a Sprinter van. He watched them, moving when they turned away. What was he doing?

One of the crows cawed and I jumped. The person looked toward the crow, me, us. Their eyes met mine. A woman. She brushed their hands up and down over her forearms, warming herself in the frigid air. Joaquin took that moment to step closer, a fire poker in his hands, raised to strike.

"Hey," I called. "I'll be right there!"

FIVE

The stranger's eyes were saucers, round and wary. "I'm almost there, happy to open up for you."

From between the cars, Joaquin's mouth fell open, and he stared at me. Let him stare. I remembered the almost fate of the pigeon, a rag doll in his hands. The attack in the atrium. While I wasn't sure that was Joaquin, I had a solid suspicion it was. Whatever business he had with this woman was on hold while I gave her refuge.

Joaquin whipped out his phone, his lips moving, frantic. He looked at me like I'd lost all my senses and then some before he faded back between the cars.

Maybe I had. But watching him stalk this person was all too familiar. Whoever this was, Joaquin wouldn't have the upper hand.

"Come on in," I said, fitting the key into the aging lock. "Sorry I was out. Had to get coffee." I pushed open the door and held it open. Moist, warm air wafted outward.

Without a word, the woman pushed inside. From the street, Joaquin gave his head a quick shake, his expression one of warning.

Let him be mad. He and his boss wanted compliance. They wouldn't find that from me. I wasn't sure what arrangement they'd had with Hollis, but it didn't extend to me. I let the door fall closed behind us, leaving Joaquin outside.

Once inside, the woman removed her hood and out tumbled a cascade of black hair, wavy and lush. She scanned the shop, her gaze traveling upward along the vines. The growing sunset cast a faint pink light through the clearstory windows. The complementary hue settled on the woman's cheeks.

"Freezing out there," I said, shrugging out of my jacket. "Was there something I can help you find?"

The woman eyed me as though translating my question. Ballet slippers on tiny feet rotated in place as she pored over every inch of the place, each table a world to be examined. She peered between a few plants, lifting a leaf here, a frond there. Where she touched a plant, it sprang back, invigorated.

I frowned, confused by the response. "You're welcome to take your time," I said. "I'm afraid I'm not much in the way of help with the names. Or their care." I hurried on, "But I'm learning some of them. This one is a peace lily. Aren't they beautiful? Found them in a book. Good for the air and they look a bit exotic, yes?"

The woman reached for the long, waxy stem of leaves, running a finger up its spine. As though aching for her touch, each leaf twisted at her caress.

"Or...uh," I stammered as she returned her attention to me. I backed toward the rear of the shop where the palms stretched overhead. "We have other sizes, too. Go big, they say. Make a statement. Would you...er...have a specific plant in mind?"

My nerves frayed from the day, unraveling further in the strain of hustling a response from this beautiful woman.

When she'd entered, the air stilled, as though every organism halted its existence, lying in wait for her acknowledgement.

She approached me, then, brushing her fingertips over a giant bird of paradise. Its expansive leaves uncurled, their surfaces glossy. A faint smile crossed her lips, slicked in cranberry. Almond eyes held flicks of green near the pupils. Perfume of jasmine scented the air. She was polished, striking.

Until the iron of the staircase was at my back, I hadn't noticed how far I'd retreated. I reached behind myself for the bars. "Actually, I think I might close early," I said, like a cornered rabbit to a coyote. "I've got a...date. He's...coming. Soon."

Inches shorter than me, the woman stopped just before her toes would have touched mine. Closer now, I saw the impossible symmetry of her face, a heart-shaped arrangement of features, doll-like in their perfection. Long, dark lashes framed round eyes, two dimples at her cheeks. High smooth forehead, brows that would make my aesthetician weep. Couldn't have been less than a decade younger than me yet there was a world of understanding in her gaze.

A wall of pressure held me, then, like a burst of subway air. I was pinned, breathless, against the stairs.

Without warning, her lips spread in a Cheshire grin. "Where's the weirman?"

My forehead puckered and I blinked. "The...what?

She leaned toward me and my knees buckled. Her breath was scented with cherries and a spice I didn't recognize. "The weirman. Get him. *Now.*"

Adrenaline coursed through my veins, spinning energy up from the depths. I'd dealt with bridezillas, the overbearing in-laws, and every corporate creep who'd fancied the event staff their personal property when they downed one too many martinis. I'd be damned if I'd let this woman, or anyone else, push me around in my own shop.

Through gritted teeth, I made my stance clear. "I believe there must be some confusion. I do not know who your friend is. This is my shop. If you want to purchase a plant, fantastic. If not, it is time for you to leave." My hand crackled with static when I pushed off from the staircase. I made for the desk, as though to return to business. In truth, my phone was in the pocket of my jacket. I wanted its security.

"Here," she said, dropping something on the countertop behind me.

When I turned, my eyes landed on the biggest ruby I'd ever seen. It was surrounded by a ring of tiny diamonds. A gold chain snaked out from underneath.

"What is that?" My mouth hung open. The jewel caught each beam of light and sent it outward, multiplied.

The woman pressed both hands to the countertop and glowered at me. "Proof. Now command him to attend to me immediately before I burn this place to the ground."

They say everybody has a breaking point. A mark in time in which they have breached every threshold on the way to losing their shit and there is only one level left to reach. I was there.

"Lady. There are three truths I need to make clear." At the casual address, her eyes flashed in blackness, the pupils all but disappearing. I ignored her silent protest. My lungs were on fire, and before I collapsed in a pile of panic, I would ensure the privacy to let the drama of this ridiculous day consume me. "One: I don't know who the weirman is, so you can get this cheap, costume jewelry off my counter. Two: this is my shop. I own it. Three: you will remove yourself from the premises before I call the police and have you removed." A nagging sensation worked at the edges of my mind, but I ignored it. I needed this person out of my space. I'd unpack what she said later. With wine.

In emphasis of my threat, I held my phone aloft.

Her lip curled in a snarl. "How dare you address me in such a way? I ought to send you to Nether. See how long you hold up as Sharon's plaything."

She could have been speaking a foreign language for all I knew. Whatever she meant, it wasn't happening. "Fuck Sharon. Get out." I unlocked my phone.

"Ending your pathetic life will be a gift to the Goddess!" She lunged for me, talons out. I ran from her, then turned my back against the wall, kicking my stool into her path. She jumped over it, landing on the counter with incredible strength. Who was this human grasshopper?

"Now, now, Ophelia. I wouldn't, if I were you. Come down from there and let's talk like civilized people."

Ophelia, if that was her name, crouched on top of my short counter, a predator, mid-pounce. Her eyes never left my face.

A humming filled the room as a low vibration carried all sound and motion on its wavelength. It was as though everything within the shop was more alive than it had ever been, on the brink of death or vitality. "Ballsy, even for you, Joaquin." She said his name as though it left a metal taste in her mouth.

"Now why don't you climb down from up there and we can all hash this out like friends."

Joaquin came into view. He'd stepped in from the back shadows of the shop, a loaded crossbow in his hands. The pointed tip of the arrow was trained on Ophelia.

"She insulted me," the woman pouted.

"I tried to help you pick out a plant!" My voice squeaked in defense.

The woman faced Joaquin, ignoring the weapon. "She called the Ring of Eluned costumery."

The corner of Joaquin's mouth twitched. "Could be a fake," I said. The woman scoffed.

Joaquin stood straighter. "Come now, Feelie. You know the rules. You've been denied."

"I gave proof!"

"And she didn't accept."

Ophelia's nostrils flared. Still crouched, she spun on the balls of her feet to face me. "This isn't over, hedgerider." In a graceful leap, she landed on both feet. "I will have your name." With a wicked grin, she left with Joaquin at her back, bow drawn and aimed.

Six

Absence is a funny thing. You fill a void with space, time, thoughts, yet it remains.

In the wake of Joaquin's exit, Ophelia under his watch, the shop pressed in around me. It was as if the plants stretched their branches toward their wake, seeking to follow.

Who was Ophelia and what was a weirman? I wished her back if only long enough to ask about Hollis. Gaven, too. I had far too many questions and no answers. I'd start with Joaquin.

Iris manned the bar, a ring of customers enthralled by her storytelling. I came in at the tail end.

"And that was the last time I looked under a tentacle." Patrons burst into laughter at her punchline. Several tossed hefty tips onto the bar top before moving off.

"Busy day? You look a little—parched." She slid a glass of water my way.

"Yes. I mean, no. I'm busy but the shop isn't. Yet. Actually, I'm here to talk to Joaquin. He was just there." I turned to scan the pub. "Did you see where he went?"

Iris flicked her eyes to the upstairs area, then back to me. I didn't miss the minute gesture. She met my gaze, steady and unwavering. "Haven't seen him."

"But I—"

She began collecting glasses. "Happy to leave a message, if you want."

I watched her—or rather the slope of her shoulders. "He took something from my shop, and I want to talk to him about it." Her shoulders tensed. I continued. "He knows where to find me." I flashed her the biggest smile I could muster and left.

"It's not about you," she called.

Her words locked my step in place. I turned, thrown by her comment, but she was busy with a customer. She leaned on the bar, her back to me, ponytail swishing as she chatted.

Fine. I'd asked. She would tell Joaquin I'd been there. I believed this much.

Outside, I almost plowed into a group of rowdy men. One checked my shoulder with his own. On impact, I experienced a searing heat. He turned to look at me, his eyes red-rimmed, and flashed me a lopsided grin. "Hey there," he said, grabbing my arm. "What's your hurry?"

Like a movie screen, I had a vision of my hands on a woman's hips as we ground together under flashing lights, a giant dog chasing me, its eyes aflame, a burst of light, then blackness.

I shook him off and braced myself against the wall. "Whatever," he said, and rejoined his buddies.

This wasn't hot flashes or some kind of hormonal attack—was it? I would need to find a new doctor in a new town—loads of fun—but what would I tell them? *When I touch people, I see movies of their life, like that Prodigy video.* They'd send me straight to an analyst which I may need but didn't have time for. The life of a modern woman.

My phone buzzed in my pocket. The lawyer.

"Tell me it's good news. You found Hollis's stash of gold bars."

"Good afternoon, Ms. Rookwood. I'm calling from Waterhouse, Ingalls, and Parker and—"

"Yes?" I cut her off. In front of me, at the door of the Apothecary, a crowd stood outside the door. *That's odd.* I pushed my way between the bodies.

Droplets spattered against the windows as though it were raining inside.

"Ingalls would like to make the appointment for you to collect your uncle's effects. I'm calling to schedule…"

A firefighter held a crowbar wedged into the door frame of the shop. He braced to heave when I yelled. "Stop! That's my shop!" I pushed between the last few people, breathless. I held up the key, frantic, then dropped it. "Sweet Lady Necneven!" With one hand that shook, I swiped the key from the sidewalk and fitted it into the lock.

"Do you know what happened here? When was the last time this place was inspected?" The firefighter breathed down my neck, peppering me with questions as I pushed open the door for him. He didn't stay for the answers. Once inside, he pressed his way through the shop.

I stared after him, unsure of what to do. Standing there, dumbstruck by circumstance, it occurred to me my shirt clung to my skin, soaked through. The few people still outside gawked.

Moments later, the water stopped.

"No sign of a fire," the fireman said, returning from the back. "It was only one sprinkler. Bad news is that means your system is faulty." Gray sideburns inched out from underneath this helmet. Water dripped onto his jacket. "Shouldn't be too much though. A couple thousand, unless it gets complicated."

A couple thousand. I stared at the phone in my palm

where the number for the lawyer again flashed across the screen. I clutched the phone to my head, pressing the vibration against my thudding skull. *It's okay. You'll be okay. This will be okay. Just breathe.*

"Ma'am? Did you hear me?" The firefighter peered at me.

I could only nod, willing tears not to fall.

"Building super just said they've had issues in the past." A second firefighter entered from the back of the shop. "Old pipes and whatnot."

My mouth fell open at the latest intrusion. "How did you get in here?" The tone of my voice lifted at the end, hysterics edging in.

"Owner let me in, ma'am. We are emergency personnel and—"

I jabbed myself in the chest with my thumb and cut him off. "I'm the owner!" A single tear snuck past my barrier, then another followed. *Traitors.*

The second firefighter, dry except for the drops flung in my protest, held his hands out to me. "Let's have a seat. Is there someone you could call to come help?"

I wasn't interested in placation. "How did you get in?"

Whether it was because of the glare or the rising anger in my voice, he answered my somewhat obvious question. "We knocked at the pub and he came right over. Had a dozen keys on a ring."

I fumed. The man who'd refused to help me, refused to step one foot inside my shop, had keys to the whole place. My home. "Thank you," I said, my voice a dangerous whisper.

"Could have been a lot worse," the first firefighter said, committing the mortal sin of dismissing a woman's emotions in a bid to control them.

Pressure exploded from my temples and my fingers were numb. "How soon until you're gone?"

The fireman opened his mouth to protest. My glare

stopped his next prompt. "We have some paperwork to finish up. No one was hurt but we've got to document."

"We'll be quick. You'll receive the official fine in the mail," the other firefighter added.

"Great," I said, adding this to the mental tally burying me in bills.

"Fixing it shouldn't be too bad, but make sure to get those inspections done."

I nodded, my mouth zipped shut so as not to accost an emergency professional with the barrage of thoughts I longed to shout. I wanted to be alone so I could fall apart on the much too damp floor.

Lotte stepped in through the door, then. "Gentlemen," she said with a nod. The firemen ogled the dark-haired beauty. "I've got this, you can go." As though obeying a command, they left with appreciative backward glances toward Lotte. She ignored them and crouched in front of me. She held out a thermos. "I brought soup, and I'm here to help."

Cue tears.

"How could I have missed so much?"

The firemen were gone and my sidewalk crowd had disbursed. Lotte wrapped a fresh towel around my shoulders. I sobbed over the thermos, cup of soup in hand. Lotte listened, somber.

"I am driving a train without any engineering skills while pieces fly off along the tracks."

"You are doing the best damn job you can. It's a lot." Lotte leaned a shoulder against the wall, arms crossed. She wore a delicate silver bracelet around her wrist. Numbers were stamped into the metal. Her other hand was on my forearm, an incredible comfort.

"Why didn't Hollis tell us anything? I didn't even know he had this shop—let alone that sprinklers need inspection." I looked around the soaked space. "This is hopeless!" I wailed into my soup.

"When did you last see him?" Lotte stood to grab a rag from the sink. Water puddled in ponds on the surfaces near the front windows. She mopped up water pooled between the tiny succulents. Rag soaked, she wrung out the fabric in the sink, then repeated the process.

"A few weeks ago. Said he was doing research in the High-lands and had a stopover." I smiled, remembering the visit. "Sent me a picture of rainbow-striped sheep. Was craving a slice of deep dish. Wanted an update on Patrick."

"Patrick?"

"My son. He adored my uncle. Hollis would bring him all kinds of treasures. Preserved butterflies. Exotic dried flowers. Treats from around the world—Patrick loves Turkish delight. Hollis wanted to know his favorite grandnephew was happy and safe in Paris. What I wouldn't give to go back in time and ask about his life." I paused my pity party to look at Lotte. Her back was to me. She'd stopped mopping, her hand still. I remembered the note in Hollis's ledger. "Did you know him?"

Lotte's shoulders stiffened and she shook her head. "Not well. We'd met...a couple of times. Sounds as though you two were close, though."

I stood, shrugging out of the towel. Her response seemed to discount her support of Hollis's shop, if not knowledge of him as a person. I reached for the cooled carafe of coffee, pouring that morning's dregs into a mug and downing the thick, brown swill. "I thought we were," I said. "But now...I'm not sure we knew him at all. He had a whole life here."

Lotte again twisted the rag into a knot over the sink and squeezed. Water dripped out over her hands. My body drooped with exhaustion. I was that rag, wrung out of tears, worn from the trials of the afternoon. "I have a bottle of champagne I was saving for a celebration," I said. "Care to share it with me?"

She tented an eyebrow. "A...celebration?"

I pushed back from the counter. "It is now. It needs to be."

"To new beginnings," I said, lifting my coffee cup. I'd refilled the mugs.

"To your success," Lotte said, and clinked her mug against mine. She took a sip, then licked at her upper lip. "I like this. It tickles my throat."

"Haven't had champagne before?"

She shook her head and took another sip. "No. But I'm a new fan."

"You would probably like Prosecco. Cava, too. Different versions, but all are bubbly. One day I'll go wine tasting in France. To the Champagne region. Patrick promises he'll take me when he lands his first big client. Have you been?"

Lotte lowered her cup to look at me. Her eyes were wide, like a startled rabbit. She rearranged her features into a careful smile before replying. "Sounds like a good son. Why is he in France?"

Again, she'd batted my questions back with her own. Suspicion grew alongside the headache blooming at the base of my skull. "Grad school–architecture. In Paris. He's always wanted to go. Me, too, actually. My mom loved it. Guess her adoration rubbed off. She said it was her favorite place and she'd planned to take me to see it all. Spend a month exploring the cities, then the countryside. See the museums, the catacombs—"

"That's a darker tourist spot," Lotte interjected.

I rubbed my thumb against the inside of my palm. "My mom believed in death as much as she believed in life. 'You cannot know light until you learn to breathe in darkness,' as she would say." I looked down at my hands, the slow circles soothing the flutter in my chest. It hurt to talk about Mom. Still.

"Smart woman," Lotte said, draining her cup. She plucked off a few dead leaves from a plant near her shoulder. Its vines made a small curtain of two-sided leaves: silver and emerald stripes on one side, eggplant on the back. "Your uncle's sister?"

I nodded. I followed her lead with a second strand of the same vine, gathering the spent crackling leaves in my hand. "They were very close. Every visit, he'd breeze in with his old satchel and some new, massive houseplant. He'd complain about traveling across half the country to see us before they'd stay up late into the night, talking for hours."

"He traveled a lot?"

I frowned. "Long after I went to bed, I heard him detailing his adventures. As a little girl, I reveled in his storytelling. He was a man who'd traveled around the world—or so it seemed when I was small."

Lotte made a small pile of her trimmings. "*Tradescantia zebrina*," she said, holding a leaf out to me.

"You know plants?"

"Just Latin." She brushed the dried leaves into an empty bucket. "Where is she now?"

"Who?"

"Your mother."

"She died," I said. I reached for my mug and tipped the rest of the champagne down my throat. The simple sentence was truth and pain.

"Oh EJ," she said, and set a hand on my arm. "I'm so sorry. And with what happened to your uncle..."

I stared at her hand, then into her face. "What do you mean what happened to Hollis?"

Lotte crossed her arms and stuffed her hands into her armpits. She stammered. "I...I...meant that having lost two loved ones this early in your life is...more than most have to bear."

What did she know that she wasn't saying? "It is a lot. I'm not alone, though. I have my son. And my father." I crossed my arms and regarded her. Who was this woman who wanted all of my past yet offered none of hers? "How about you?"

"Mmm?" She'd busied herself with shifting plants to check for puddles.

"Do you have any family nearby?" A pair of trimmers lay in a puddle. I snatched them out of the water and dried them on a towel.

"Joaquin," Lotte said, her eyes over my shoulder. She crossed to the door. I whirled to confront the new arrival, clippers in hand. "I'm afraid we're closed," she said, her voice heavy. She looked up at him through thick lashes.

"Especially to weapon-wielding creeps who bust into my shop."

He held up his hands. "I come in peace. Feel free to frisk me."

"Not interested," I said. The lopsided grin on Joaquin's face fell. "You owe me about a hundred explanations."

"I came in through the *front* door—" he started. When I didn't laugh, he went on, "—to give you an apology. From Ansel."

I raised an eyebrow at his statement. "For not telling me that he had a key to my shop this whole time?"

Joaquin blanched. "When the fire marshal came through a few months ago, Hollis wouldn't let the man in. Said he'd have to reschedule. Ansel never followed up. He should have."

"He's not the landlord. That's not his job—"

"But he could have reminded him," Joaquin said, cutting me off before I could press further. "We knew Hollis was—busy."

I fumed. "And why are you here, then, if he is the one who is sorry?"

Joaquin looked at Lotte. She bit her lip and looked away. *I see you both,* I thought.

"To offer my assistance," he said, arms spread wide to us. "How can I help?"

I pressed my lips together. I was torn between demanding he clean the whole place and not wanting him anywhere near me. There was this new mystery of what he was to Lotte, too.

"Who is Ophelia? And why was she about to give me the ring of Elmo?"

Lotte's eyes went wide. "Feelie was here?"

"Not someone you ever want to let in again," Joaquin said. "She was trying to show you her worth. I let her know the shop is no longer an option. She's...pushy."

"Why was she here to begin with—and who is she? What would she want from Hollis?"

Lotte disrupted my questions. "EJ was going to come pick out a candle for the shop. In trade for...this plant." She picked up a small pot, one of the ferns with frilly edges. Facing me, she raised both eyebrows. "Right?"

"Uh...yes. That's absolutely what we're doing." Why the sudden need to leave?

"How about you tell Ansel she'll be in touch when she knows what she needs. As you suggest, he *owes* her." Lotte gave Joaquin a knowing look, then pushed him toward the door. At the threshold, she kept her hand on his chest, a moment longer than necessary. They both looked down at her hand. A muscle in Joaquin's jaw twitched, as though he fought every reflex to pull her close. She eyed him with a cool gaze. Then, with a final, playful shove, Joaquin was on the sidewalk.

"Tell your boss I want that key!" I yelled as she gave him a little wave and closed the door.

SEVEN

A week later, progress was slow and loneliness threatened to swallow me whole. I was overwhelmed by the plants, both in number and the complexity of their care. Lotte made me a stack of notes, but her style of silver ink on pink sticky notes read more like a poem than technical directions. "Feel for vitality, water at full moon, trim when prickly." After hours of attempting to sort through the living items in the Apothecary, the last thing I had energy for was unpacking. Instead of finding a groove, I spiraled into a helpless, vegetative state, futon-bound. Hormones, circumstance, or a combination made for a rough start.

Sounds of revelry leaked through the brick wall. *Friday night.* I was tempted to head over, claim a stool, and dig into some fries. But then I'd have to face people, *specific* people, and I wasn't ready for that. Still my near-empty fridge pointed to an obvious need. I could get an order to go, bring it back, and watch a movie. Limited exposure and a natural end to any awkward moments. I panicked over the indecision, my stomach no longer settled enough for food.

I removed my new, pale-lavender candle from its tissue

wrappings and held it to my nose. Lotte dubbed the scent French Countryside. "For your mother," she said.

Whomever this woman was, whatever she was hiding, I felt the thread of friendship stitch tighter between us.

Candle pressed to my cheek, I wished for a way back. A return of those I'd lost. Time in their company, time for questions. Time for heart-numbing selfishness.

But that is the twist of adulthood. A woman must become the foundation, not crumble at its loss.

I set the candle on a set of shelves and tiny drawers I'd cleared and cleaned that morning. A beautiful furniture piece, the top was curved, the bottom resting on four hand-carved lion's feet. It contained a collection of crevices, nooks, and crannies of all sizes. The shelves had been crammed with half-full bottles of fertilizer, pottery shards, and a rusty pair of ancient scissors. I'd found a solid black stone on the uppermost shelf. Its glossy surface reflected the moon of my face. In the drawers, I found a collection of trinkets ranging from chipped chess pieces to bejeweled rings. They reminded me of the gifts my uncle brought from his travels. I left these in the drawers and dusted every inch. The furniture gleamed a rich ochre, Lotte's candle its showpiece.

I sank onto the stool to admire my single success. This shop was both my gift and my yoke, and I was its beast of burden. But damn it, I could make it look good, one pocket at a time.

At my elbow was the ledger. I lifted the book to reveal the key. I'd tucked it back in place, unsure of its purpose. Small, rounded, and old fashioned, a thread of ribbon still clung to the loop. I picked it up, twisting it between my fingers, curious. A sudden thought brought me to my feet. The stool grated against the floor when I stood. I rushed to the tiny, windowed room and fitted the key to the lock. With a twist, the lock clicked, and the door opened.

I shoved a stack of boxes out of the way and swung the door open. It creaked on tiny hinges, the slim, green door giving way.

The room was full of books. Every inch of the tiny room was crammed with leather-bound tomes. I reached for the first. *Mushrooms of the Forest.* The text fell open in my hands. Between the aging, leather covers were thin pages depicting a rainbow of fungus. Beautiful drawings labeled in Latin and descriptive narrative filled the rest of the pages.

I replaced the book and selected another. *Medicinal Plants of the Islands.* Canvas cover, stamped with title and author. *War and Peace. The Canterbury Tales.* The farther I reached into the room, the mustier their scent, as if I'd retrieved them straight from the studies of their bygone authors.

"More to clean," I said, replacing *Ancient Lizards.* "Tomorrow." I selected *Care of Plants in the Home* and *Drawings of Flora* and relocked the room, setting the key above the door ledge. Nothing suspicious, only a tiny library with interesting—if aged—titles.

Weary from the day, I committed to relaxation and put on my favorite slouch-fit. Oversized sweatshirt with cuffs that hung past my wrists. Loose joggers fit for Thanksgiving dinner. Thick socks, hair in a messy bun. Laptop open, I loaded a Matthew Goode romcom. I'd carried a container of almonds upstairs and dug into its contents, crunching through the opening scenes of the movie.

When one is a grown-ass adult, you have responsibilities. You also have the ability to straight up ignore those for a night. Especially when you've had a day like mine. In fact, that's one of the few benefits to being grown.

I'd come to the scene where Matthew and his leading lady are stuck walking a dirt road in the middle of nowhere and all you want them to do is kiss each other and get over their personal issues when a loud cheer sounded from next door.

I looked at the brick wall between myself and the pub. A second roar permeated my sanctuary. I sighed and clutched a pillow to my chest. Back to Goode.

Shouts again boomed through the wall. I exhaled through my nose. *Breathe-one-two-three, breathe-one-two—*

Raucous cheering, louder than before.

"Ugh," I groaned, and stood. Moonlight shone through the windowpanes. I paced the small living space, irritation building in my gut. Every few moments came another cheer. I cringed at each eruption.

At the window, I looked down to the empty atrium. Silvery-blue branches twisted toward me from the tree, a statue of time gone by. The crows—for I'd no choice but to assume they were one and the same as those who'd followed me—roosted among the branches. The roofline's shadow striped the walls. An outline of a person ran its length, then was gone.

I stepped closer to the window. A board beneath my feet creaked, the edge bending upward and out of place. Great, another repair.

On my knees, I wrenched at the board. A nail fell from a hole in the wood, a likely consequence of time and my angry footsteps.

Below where the board had lain, was an empty space. Or rather, a not-so-empty space. For there beneath the floor was another book. Cracked black leather cover, ridges along the spine, a leather cord wrapped around its girth several times. Thick with parchment, both sewn pages and loose additions, the book strained against its wrapping.

"Hollis," I whispered. "What's this?"

A tug on a loose end unlaced the ties. The book opened to a page of handwriting scrawled from edge to edge. Papers fluttered to the floor, but I couldn't take my eyes from what I held.

It was a journal of sorts, each page dated. There was a drawing of a long sword in the middle of one page, its hilt detailed on the next. Underneath was the note *Clock Maker?* Somehow the image was familiar to me and I traced its length with a finger. The pages after contained recipes between the narratives. A map of some sort, a list of poisons. His handwriting was so bold it leapt off the page like a live accounting of his thoughts. Dark ink, a blue corrupted to near black, except for the occasional page in a faded red that smelled of distant summer roses.

Each entry began with a list of names, yet it was what followed the names that chilled me to the bone.

I scanned the room, paranoia kicking in. I cleared the coffee table with one hand, clutching the book to my chest with the other. I set it down on the glass to read.

Oisin, pearl

Foley, phoenix feather

Wesley, gold coin

The last entry was from the day before he died.

Malik, a song

I traced my finger through the rest of his writing.

More are on the way, it is confirmed. Sent word to Vester. Sharon knows, or so Ansel claims.

Below this was a drawing I recognized. A ring, several stars around its orbit.

His writing continued underneath the drawing. "There is an amulet, in addition to the Circle. Can't leave, but to stay is a certain death."

Another roar sounded from the walls next door. The sound echoed in my heart.

~

"Where is your boss?"

I'd wrapped myself in a sweater, shoved my feet into shoes, and stormed over to the pub.

The woman behind the bar wasn't Iris, nor was she the man I sought.

Tiny and elfish, she appraised me with eyes of sea foam green. "Detained," she told me in an accented voice.

"For how long?"

"Couldn't say. Can I get you a drink?"

"No, thank you. I'll wait."

I leaned against the end of the bar, tapping my foot in a staccato rhythm against the brass railing. Another roar drew my attention to the far side of the room where a rousing dart tournament occupied the attention of half the pub. There was a silent pause, a solid thwack, and more cheers.

"Does this happen every week?"

"It's become that way, I'm told."

Cheers again. Several people clapped each other on the backs, and I ground my teeth together. "Any chance you could ask your boss to come down to see me?"

She appraised me. "I'll ask. No promises." She ducked into the back.

A rowdy group pushed their way to the bar. They tapped their glasses against the wood, calling for service. The woman returned. Back in command, she eyed me with suspicion and turned her attention to the other guests.

The first two ordered another round but the third man, bearded and brazen, rested his arms on the bar and winked at the bartender. "I'll take an Irish car bomb...and your number."

Her back was to him, but from my angle, I watched her tilt her head up and run her tongue underneath her lower lip, nostrils flaring. She pulled a pint, poured a shot, then rolled her shoulders back before turning to serve the man.

"Come on, now. I even like to cuddle—after." The man reached out his hand to wrap it around hers.

She leaned in close, and lower than most could hear, whispered to him. "What's your name, sailor?"

The man's eyes glazed over and he said, "Jim."

"Well—Jim—do they not tell American children never to give their names to one of the fae?"

"The fae?" Confusion clouded Jim's otherwise vacant face.

"We're none to be trifled with," she said, and with a quick twist, snapped his pinky finger backward.

Howls rang out from Jim. He clutched the finger in the opposite hand. It stuck out at an odd angle. "You crazy bitch!"

The dart tournament paused, players and spectators turned toward the commotion, murmuring among the crowd.

The woman stepped back from Jim's reach as he lunged for her just as Ansel appeared at the landing. Jim's buddies spotted the pub owner's approach and dragged him back.

Boots clomped down the stairs and the pub held its breath —all except for Jim. The man applied every swear word he knew to the bartender and hollered for his buddies to call the police.

Ansel addressed his employee. "Where's Joaquin?"

"Left." She glanced around, then added, "Got a call."

"What about me?" Jim butted into the conversation. He was ignored.

"What did I say about injuring patrons?"

"But he—"

Ansel cocked an eyebrow. Even silent, he was intimidating. A towering figure, he loomed over the tiny woman.

The woman crossed her arms. "No violence in the pub."

"Hurry up and fire her. I need a goddamn doctor!"

Ansel faced Jim. The pub owner took two steps forward, forcing Jim to retreat. "You are in *my* establishment. I am the only one permitted to order anyone around within these walls. If you ever insult one of my employees again—"

"But I didn't—"

"Or lie to me again," he added, with emphasis, "you'll never darken my door, or any other in this town, again. Do you understand me?"

Jim remained silent, tears of pain streaking his cheeks.

"Brigid will take you to my personal nurse to see *if* she's willing to treat you. Keep your mouth shut, mind, and you may keep that finger yet." With a nudge of his chin, he signaled Brigid, the bartender, and Jim to exit. Ansel then turned his attention to me.

Confronted with the man himself, my earlier resolve wavered.

Ansel growled. "What do you want? Don't you have a shop to run into the ground?"

Consider that resolve returned.

"Tell me what you know of my uncle's death. And don't you dare pretend it's nothing."

Ansel's eyes turned a slate gray and a muscle in his neck bulged. "Did you not just hear me speak to that bar trash? No one comes into *my* bar and makes demands." His voice held depth and something dark within.

"So, it's fine for you to come into my place?"

"I sent Joaquin to help you."

I poked his chest with my finger. "You let people into my home!"

"It was an emergency," he said. "They were firefighters."

"Give me my key!"

My pulse raced. Ansel's chest heaved as did mine. He squeezed his hands into fists, and I paled. Falinis got up from his corner and lumbered toward the back and up the stairs, away from the building drama. Smart dog.

"You have no idea what you're up against, woman."

"So, tell me! That is literally why I came into this oversized locker room."

Without another word, Ansel stormed out the back door. I looked from him to the stairs to the customers and ran out behind him.

He waited at the base of the stoop. I let the door slam behind me and clattered down the steps. I paused on the last so as to stand nose to nose with him.

"Stay out of my bar." His voice thundered against the walls of the courtyard. One of the crows flapped its wings, then resettled. The sky above us darkened as the air chilled.

I stood my ground. "Stay out of my shop."

"Sell it to me."

I blinked a few times before I could respond. "What?"

"You and I both know you're in over your head. I'll pay a good price."

My mouth open, I shook my head, willing a sensible response. "No."

Ansel mounted the steps, forcing me back. Heat radiated from his chest to mine as he brought his face inches from my own. I tilted my chin up, matching his glare. A ghost of stubble shaded his jaw. The cold of the door pressed at my back as he drew closer, his thigh brushing mine as he bent toward me.

His voice softened, and he placed one hand next to me on the brick. "Sell me the Apothecary and all of this goes away. You can return to whatever life you led before, but a much richer woman. We never have to see each other again."

One of the crows flapped its wings and cawed as though in warning. My brain swam with the proximity to this man. Thick eyelashes framed irises that shifted from silver to blue. His skin smelled of soap and pine. I gave an involuntary shudder I masked—or attempted to mask—as a reaction to the cold.

Hormones be damned, I would not be bullied. "You can't have it. I found things in the shop. Hollis's things. I need to figure out what they mean." His eyes darkened to cobalt. I squinted, curious if I needed glasses, more sleep, or coffee. Likely all three. "Your name is mentioned. Others, too. What aren't you telling me?"

The second crow joined the first. Their caws grated against my nerves.

Ansel stood one step below me, his lips inches from my own. "Sell me the shop and I'll tell you."

The warmth of his breath tickled my ear, and I melted, gripping the handrail. My lips parted, watching his. *Get a grip, EJ.* I looked away. "Tell me what I want to know, and I won't report you to the police."

"Boss?" Joaquin hung out the door to the pub. Ansel and I parted like teenagers caught sitting too close when the lights came up. "Nurse would like a word."

Ansel slammed a fist into the brick next to my head. I flinched. "This isn't over," he said. He stomped the rest of the way up the steps.

"I want my key!" I yelled to his retreating form.

Alone in the atrium, I faced the tree, willing my pulse to slow. I pressed my hands to my temples, closed my eyes, and exhaled. When I opened my eyes, both crows sat on the lowest branch, watching me with black, beady eyes. My conversation —a generous term—was so heated I'd been left to vent with birds.

"Now you're quiet?" I said, crossing to the tree. In response, one of the birds made a clacking sound from deep within its throat.

The bird flitted to a higher branch as I reached out to

touch the satiny trunk. I ran my finger along a branch to the end.

The crash of glass broke my trance. The crows squawked in unison, wings flapping. A second crash had me running.

EIGHT

I yanked open the door to Apothecary with both hands. My foot crunched glass as I stepped inside. Papers were scattered across the flooring. Many had landed in the remaining pools of water, their ink spreading in splotches. When I looked up, my heart sank into my stomach.

Anyone who's dropped a glass knows all too well how it shatters. Explosions of crystals scatter like the four winds. You do your best to sweep, vacuum, and mop up each piece. The clear and the sharp still find the bottom of your foot months down the road when you've long forgotten the break.

In this case, a single window, the pane closest to the front door lock, was nothing more than a jagged hole. The door, unlocked, swung open on its hinge, winter air blowing in.

The second crash had been ceramic. My coffee mugs—what was left of them—were scattered in mosaic pieces across the cement. One mug remained, teetering on the countertop. World's Best Plant Parent, indeed.

My stool, too, lay toppled, the canister of pens dumped across the sales counter. Vines, whether snagged or grabbed by the entrant, were strewn across the floor like streamers. Hollis's ledger lay abandoned next to a pot.

I pressed my fist to my mouth to stifle a scream.

The key. In two strides, I crossed the floor. My hand rose as though to check the ledger when I froze. What if the person who'd done this was still inside? Or if they'd left, watched me from outside in the dark?

I flicked my eyes to the windows and up toward the stairs. I waited. Nothing moved.

I extracted my phone from my pocket and dialed. When my call was answered, I made my request. "You said to call. Please come...yes, now. Please."

My hands shook, knees quavering. *Fall apart later, survive now.* I climbed half the stairs to peek over the landing. Whomever it was hadn't made it to the second floor. Not an object was out of place, including the board beneath the window. For assurance, I removed the piece to verify the heavy book still nestled within its hiding space.

I ran for the windows and dropped the shades. I shut the front door, locking it, however pointless the gesture, then backed my way into the corner of the shop. I wouldn't reach for the key, not yet. But I did try the door to the little room. It was locked. I slid my back against the wall and waited, shivering.

Minutes later, a face appeared in the broken pane.

"Knock knock," Joaquin called. "EJ?" He reached in through the hole in the glass, unlatched the door, and entered. "EJ, it's me."

"Here," I called from the shadows.

I winced at each crunch of his boots as he approached. When he reached my feet, he crouched to my level.

Later, he would tell me I had the look of a lost puppy, scared and vulnerable. I remember the kindness in his voice, the way headlights flashed against the plants and the walls.

"I'll call the police. They'll come and do their thing. Take notes. Dust and UV some surfaces. Put some plywood over the hole—maybe. What they don't do, I'll take care of myself. Including sleeping here tonight." I opened my mouth to protest, and he shook his head. "No way am I leaving you alone until that window is fixed and we install some cameras."

"But I don't—"

"The cameras are on Morgan's. Call it a housewarming gift."

I struggled to speak, residual adrenaline stealing my thoughts. "Thank you," was all I could say.

I let Joaquin handle the police. He answered their questions, took their cards. I crawled my way back upstairs and collapsed onto the makeshift couch. My teeth chattered as I listened to them talk below me.

"No, she didn't see anyone." I hadn't, only heard them. "No, they didn't take any money." There was no need to highlight that the shop was without cash of any kind. "No, she doesn't know who would do this." He didn't say this was because I was new and knew next to no one. "Yes, she will call if she thinks of anything that would be helpful. Thank you, officers."

There was the sound of a broom across the floor. The whir of my vacuum.

Then Joaquin called up from below. "I'll be at the bottom of the stairs if you need anything. Tomorrow all will be fixed."

I didn't ask how he would sleep on the cement floor. Instead, I stayed up far too late, staring at a crack in the ceiling, praying he was right.

A rogue sunbeam and the aroma of coffee woke me from a deep slumber. Downstairs, I found a note from Joaquin propped against a to-go cup from Second Shot. He'd scribbled on an old receipt from the ledger, spotted with ink. "Gone to the hardware store. Back with supplies."

I palmed the still-hot cup, grateful for its warmth. I stood in the sunlight, regarding the mess.

"Gods—what's happened?"

I fumbled my cup, and a splash of scalding coffee scorched my thumb. "Sweet Lady Necnevin! Gaven—I almost pissed myself."

Gaven made a face. "Sorry missus, eh—EJ. I was surprised, that's all."

"*You* were surprised?"

The teen swam in his oversized jeans, checkerboard sneakers, and a host of friendship bracelets looped around one wrist. His jacket was bulky on one side, his arm pressed against his side at an awkward angle. He meandered to one of the tables, facing the window. He shifted his awkward stance. I frowned, considering him.

"Gaven, how did you know that person?"

"Who?"

"The one who came in the other day. The one you chased off."

"I didn't."

I watched him inch away from me. "But you knew about them. What would scare them. *Fallen.* What does that mean?"

Gaven shuffled a foot. "They aren't right, that's all. Dangerous"

"But how do you know this? *Why* do you know this?"

"There are things you don't understand. History that–"

"Everyone says that. I *understand* that a person out of their mind attempted to assault me in my shop. Someone else broke into my shop last night and trashed it. Something serious is going on yet no one–even those who pretend to be my friends–will tell me what is going on."

Gaven looked at me and I saw something older in his gaze. Not the vacant, shiny pupils of youth, but something ancient, worldly. "It isn't easy, not belonging to anyone anywhere. I thought you of all people might understand that. Might understand *me*."

Another non-answer. Christopher says we reap what we sow. He's referring to which bars you choose for pickups, but this applies in many situations. I wanted friends that added sanity and support to my life. *Order, not chaos.* "I think you should go," I said, crossing my arms.

Gaven lifted his eyebrows, nodded a few times, then left.

I wanted to call him back the moment he was out the door. When he stepped from the shop, it was my son leaving home all over again. The crushing black hole of absence.

I busied myself with straightening the mess. I found shards of glass in every corner, sparkling in the crevices of the shop. I paused at the orchid table, Gaven's favorite. In his visits, he'd fussed over the remnants in the pots, convinced they would return to life. Little more than a collection of sticks, the pathetic husks of petals filled the containers fashioned with air holes. He'd told me they were the most beautiful of the flowers, his personal favorites.

In one pot, set apart from the rest, a single, crooked stem stretched upward. Gangly roots stuck out from all corners, some still bent and broken, others newly green-tipped and healthy. This was miracle enough, yet what set a lump in my throat was a single bloom, large and snow white, where none had been minutes before. How could such a bloom sprout from a plant left for dead?

Next to the orchid was a small, thin volume. Cobalt canvas stamped in gold. *Tales of the Gentry.* There on the cover was a circle of stars, the same constellation drawn in Hollis's journal.

I picked up the book and flipped open the front cover to the first page. There in classic ballpoint ink was a message. *To*

EJ, for your studies and entertainment. —Gaven. I looked from the bloom to the book and back. He'd brought me presents and I'd kicked him out. A lump caught in my throat as tears welled.

Outside the shop, I willed his familiar figure to be among those in the square. His classic cords, shaggy hair and birch tree frame a beacon. But he was gone.

Overhead, the neon of Morgan's sign blazed in the growing dusk. I could call the pub, ask if he was in. But the possibility that Ansel would pick up made me shudder. And what would I say? *I was just a complete ass to your employee, can you send him over?*

～

From across the street, a black dog watched me. Bigger than the German shepherd I'd had as a kid, it was shaggy, collarless. The animal sat on its haunches, regarding me as if waiting for direction.

"Hi, boy," I said, fully aware the dog may be a girl. "Don't suppose you know where Gaven went?" The dog tipped its head to the side, watching me. "Guess it's just me then."

"But not for long." A honeyed voice all but sang in my ear. Rowdy approached, a jar in the crook of his elbow. His hair was damp, jaw freshly-shaved. He'd stepped out of the shower and into an ad for cologne, or one of those European vacations in which everyone is gorgeous and you never have to stand in line.

"Oh. Hi." Why do we revert to our awkward teenage selves when confronted by anyone who makes us hot and sweaty? Maybe that's just me. Over Rowdy's shoulder, the dog got to its feet, ears up and teeth bared. *Uh oh.*

"Nice night."

If you consider snarling dogs across the street a good thing, sure. "Didn't see you at the market this last week. But I suppose the farmer's life is sunup to sundown and all that."

A full wattage grin lit his face. "You're not wrong about the endless tasks. We had some new staff show up. Needed training and all that," he said. "But visiting you was on my list. I wanted to bring you this," he said, holding out a jar. Inside was a honeycomb. Its hexagonal pockets oozed viscous golden liquid that puddled in the bottom of the jar.

"Thank you," I said. "This looks incredible. You didn't have to bring it all this way."

"I wanted to," he said. "To sweeten you up for a favor."

"How's that?" The idea of helping this man with anything gave me a tickle up my rib cage.

"I thought we could work out a trade. I would love the recipe for that French beverage—and any others you know. I want to post them at the booth. Give them away. You know, get more people interested in our honey for more than the basics." He winked at me. *Oh boy.*

"I've got a few ideas," I said. "I'll dig through my notes. Should I bring them by your booth?"

"I should be back at the booth starting this weekend," he said, and put his hands in his pockets. "See you...soon?"

"Count on it." Inside my head, I could hear Christopher plead with me to invite him in, supply him with beverages, and roll that golden god right into the sack.

I stood on the sidewalk for several minutes, staring in his wake as my knees solidified. When my ex and I split, it wasn't as though my sex drive dried up and dropped off the face of the planet. In contrast, it was the opposite. I wanted more than ever to experience what I'd missed. I thought that when I was finally free, I'd get a string of lovers. Maybe one of those walks of shame glorified on television. But a toddler and a tiny apartment saved me from the fate of shallow interactions and a host of STDs. Instead, I threw myself into my job and tried to ignore my cravings. The absence of a lover became a habit—a lonely one.

I remembered the dog, then, only to find it gone. Resigned to another night of solitude, I trudged back into the shop.

I cleared the rest of the debris from around the bloom. What kind of orchid, I wasn't certain, but if this one show-piece of success was a beacon, I would do my damnedest not to kill it. Instead, I took an old toothbrush from near the sink and whisked the glass shrapnel from the drip tray.

The plant rested in a unique pot. Ceramic like most, but full of holes. Through the openings, I could see clay pellets the size of my aunt's rum balls interspersed between chunks of bark. I considered how I would water this resurrected plant.

A quick flip through my new-old book informed me that orchids are often epiphytic, growing in the nooks and crannies of trees and other unusual spots. Their roots soak up water in the rain, storing it in the plant until the next downpour.

Under the sink was a plastic tub. I filled this with tap water then settled the orchid pot to soak. There was a big debate in a website forum as to whether to treat the water, but I didn't have the potions or patience necessary.

"You get water," I said, setting the plant in the tub. "That will have to do."

When I jostled the tub to shift it and its contents to the side of the sink, a green moth flitted out from underneath the petals of the single flower. It settled on the screen of my phone, drawn to the light. The insect spread its wings, stretching against the glass screen. Two spots like eyes adorned its lower wings, their tips extending into long tendrils.

"Gorgeous," I whispered, my voice soft so as not to disturb my guest. "You're welcome to join the others."

Should I be welcoming those who would chew up my sweaters, nibble holes in my pillows, and attack the rugs? I peered at my new friend. "You wouldn't, would you?" The moth raised its wings and lifted off, landing on one of the clearstory window ledges.

I picked up my phone and the book and dialed a familiar number.

"Tell me you shagged a hot cowboy."

Christopher's voice was the warm hug I needed. "No one says shagged anymore," I said, laughing.

"I do. So?"

"Sorry, no," I said, then heard his snort of frustration from the other end of the line. "But I did meet a man who walked off a stage at Paris Fashion Week."

Christopher obsessed over that event every year, showing me picture after picture of models in outrageous outfits and the celebrities who came to watch the shows. His lifelong goal was to make it to one of the events, like a basketball fan after court-side seats to their favorite team.

"And?"

"He gave me honey."

I could hear the sounds of the city in the background. Voices growing louder, the honk of a horn. I could visualize myself at his side, on our way to the Billy Goat for drinks and a gripe session about our boss and our stalled love lives. I missed my friend.

"Is that a euphemism? Please say it is."

"Sadly, no. But he wants me to work up some recipes for him. In exchange for some of his products."

"I'm going to pretend my bestie said in exchange for some—"

"Christopher!"

"Wait. Does he like boys?"

"I guess I don't know. Should I ask?"

I could picture him then. Navy slacks, a dark sweater, brown shoes. A peacoat and perfect hair. "Maybe don't bother with talking."

"Naughty," I said. "How's work?"

"It's...going. Without you, it's half the fun and twice the work."

"Still hasn't hired anyone?"

"Magda is drowning in weak applicants. The last one she interviewed couldn't create an invoice let alone single-handedly get an entire wedding party to do the cha-cha."

I grimaced, memories squeezing into our conversation. That was the wedding that came before Magda gave me little choice but to quit. Or rather, before I gave her little choice but to fire me.

"Can't pretend I'm not easy to replace," I said.

"That's enough about this frigid place and your former boss. How is it being in charge of your own sweet self?"

I wanted to tell him it was awesome. I was thriving, the shop bustling with customers from open to close.

But you don't lie to your best friends. You serve them the truth in the hopes they'll return the favor when you need it most.

"I'm...it's..." I faltered, fighting back tears. I pressed one hand to my forehead to stop the rush of emotion, but it flooded forward, overwhelming me. "I've been broken into. Twice, maybe. I'm not even sure at this point. People seem to come and go from here at all hours somehow. I have two friends, or I thought I did, but neither are honest with me. And it's full of plants—the Apothecary. Christopher—plants! —so I'm going to kill all of them and have nothing to sell. And Hollis didn't leave any kind of savings, or business plan, or directions of any kind, so I have no money to buy more plants, or products, or anything. And the bills, so many bills. The bar owner next door hates me but to be fair I kind of hate him too. He has this employee who seems to be everywhere somehow, but I can't trust him either. There was this one kid—well almost a man, but still a kid—who reminded me of Patrick but now he's gone too. I think we had a misunderstanding and I chased him out but I—"

"Whoa there. EJ. Take a breath."

My chest heaved from the effort of spilling the disaster that was my life. I closed my eyes and forced air into and out of my lungs. *Breathe-one-two-three...*

After a moment of quiet in which Christopher, no doubt crossing street after street, one gloved hand pressing his phone to his ear, the other one flagging cars to stop so he could cross, gave me the space to settle. I tried again. "I don't know what to do. About any of it."

"Oh, hun. For a rockstar like yourself, that has to be crushing you."

I nodded, though he couldn't see me, and fought back a sob.

"Remember the Kavennaugh wedding?"

I sniffed. "The one where they draped everything with lilies from the grandmother's garden, so you snuck around snipping off all the stamens?"

"The very same," he said. "That poor bartender couldn't stop sneezing and had to leave. You stepped right in and sold out our entire stock."

"So, the attendees wanted to drink. That's nothing new."

"What was new was your signature drink."

"A sazerac is nothing fancy," I said. "I worked with what I had."

"That was just the first drink. You somehow knew what everyone wanted before they did."

"It was fun," I said. "A game."

"You have a sixth sense about those things, and you need some cash," he said. "Play to your strengths. Make the short term count. You might surprise yourself."

Ideas sprouted in my head like seedlings. What if I made a pop-up night at the Apothecary?

"Look, you have every right to complain about the mess you've inherited. But hun, then it's time to embrace that reality. Own this story, EJ, if you want to decide how it ends."

Outside, I watched a person slip down from the tree. Their nimble movement suggested someone who could slip easily from sight. They skirted the cars across the street and peered into the shop. I waved. Their eyes went wide and they moved off. Christopher was right. So I had a mess on my hands. I could whine about it, or I could get my ass moving and do what I knew how to do. "Thanks for the pep talk. I miss you."

"Anytime. Call me when you want to talk about decorations."

NINE

Another week went by. I got antsy and made the call. "I need your help."

"Shoot."

Desperate times call for desperate measures.

"I've fucked everything up," I said.

"Can't be that dark. You've seen those movies about the small-town guy who's widowed, and the long-lost sweetheart comes back to scatter her mother's ashes. He risks falling in love again only to find out she's a succubus—"

"Joaquin. I mean it. I...can't be trusted with people."

"Uh...are you sure I'm the right audience? I'm not the best at regrets."

I hesitated. He may be right. There was something cavalier about him. But maybe that's what made him the best listener. "I need to talk to Gaven."

His tone was incredulous. "The bus boy?"

"I know he's not just a bus boy."

Joaquin was quiet on the other end of the line. I pictured him, muscles tense, torn between wanting to know what I meant and not planning to offer any affirmation.

"I owe him an apology," I said.

"Oh. Okay. I'll let the kid know. He...uh...isn't always around," he said.

"I know." Silence again. "One more favor?"

"Yeah?"

"Who do you know at City Hall?"

I stood in line with a dozen other people in a dingy, gray room. Stanchions linked with fraying velvet ropes herded us like cows. In front of us was a host of cubicles, each populated with an aging computer, cheap ballpoint pens, and a stalwart government employee.

Inside this office, at least, the world took on every flavor of normalcy. The woman in front of me fanned herself with in-home daycare paperwork while the man behind me yelled into his phone about getting "all these damn tickets dismissed!" Another day in city government.

As I stared at the peeling walls, I second guessed my plans, looking every which way for an alternative.

No chickening out, EJ.

Christopher had told me to use my strengths. Leverage what I know. So, twenty minutes and a stack of paperwork later, I'd filed for a temporary permit for pop up liquor sales.

I was going to throw a party.

On the street outside, winter sun glinted through the tree trunks. A giant horse statue reared from a place of prominence, its danglers out for all to see.

The crows darted overhead, aiming for their roost near the Apothecary. Had they waited outside for me? I considered them my outdoor pets at that point.

Sure enough, they were waiting outside the shop. "Hello, fellas."

One cawed at me, tipping forward in earnest protest. I bowed low. "My apologies—*madam*."

A woman on the street clutched her bag, eyeing me.

"It's been a week," I said. She shook her head and kept walking. The crows cawed after her.

Inside the empty shop, I paused. I'd half expected to find a new visitor, enemy, or flying animal, but I was alone. For now.

I used an *It's Always Sunny in Boca!* magnet to hold my receipt to the fridge and set to work exploring Hollis's kitchen cabinets. The first cabinet was full of junk–ancient dishware, a jewelry box, wooden chopsticks stuck in a fancy vase, a pile of soy sauce packets in a bowl—but I found my jackpot in the next cabinet over. Tea. Mom would brew a big pot every morning, adding all manner of ingredients, and I'd hoped my uncle had the same habits.

In a drawer, I found sugar and prickly pear jelly, a bright pink spread. I'd need to pick up a lemon but was otherwise set.

An hour later, I set several jars of makeshift tinctures to cool along the counter when my new job bell jangled above the door.

"Hello," Lotte called as she entered.

"In the kitchen," I called.

"Are you open? I can come back—"

"Because people keep sneaking in here and trashing the place, so I might be busy cleaning up, yet again?"

"Yeah, that," she said, appearing around the door frame. "I brought the lavender you asked for. Last summer's crop was amazing. Wow, you've been busy."

"I have," I said.

Lotte handed me the packet of dried flowers. "Brought this for you. Can't wait to see what you do with them."

I unfolded the brown paper sack and inhaled. Sweet summer with a spicy endnote. "Tea?"

"Sure," Lotte said, and took in the changes to the shop. "You've made plans?"

After vacuuming up the glass, I'd rearranged the plants, yet again. I placed the largest near the back of the displays, bringing others forward. I put plants that needed the same care near each other and began labeling those without tags. The last step took the longest as I combined the powers of Hollis's books and a good old internet search. Still, I was getting somewhere, and that work was paying off.

"More like a gamble." I leaned against a counter and took a sip of the tea. A cool calm slid down my throat. "I had to do something. A friend reminded me that I'm not the type to sit back and let chaos take over."

"Own your life and all that?" There was a twinkle in Lotte's eye as she regarded me.

I nodded. "Something like that. If—when—the permit goes through, I'm throwing a grand opening. Lure people into the store with food and drink. That, I'm good at. With any luck, they'll buy some plants and tell their friends."

"And then?"

"I pray it's enough to jump start this business."

The bell on the door jangled for the second time. A man in a suit breezed in. He slid his sunglasses on top of his head and scanned the shop.

"Can I help you?"

He spotted the two of us. "Hi. I'm wondering if you have something for my wife."

I stepped forward. "I'm sure I have something she'd like. Is it a special occasion?" I thought through my offerings, willing one of them to be in good enough shape to sell.

"I'm a...it's her...well. I need to make up for a few things."

"I see," I said, wary. "I have plants of all sizes, shapes, and even a few colors other than green." He would need to decide his own level of commitment for this situation. "Feel free to look around and let me know if you have questions."

Please don't have any questions.

"How about this one?" He'd spotted Gaven's orchid, its mammoth flower on full display, and walked toward it, hand outstretched. "She loves purple."

"Not for sale," I said. "My apologies."

The man frowned, considering me. I grabbed one of the smaller versions of pothos. Lotte claimed they are indestructible. "How about this one? It would look great in any space, home, office, you name it. This kind alternates yellow and green leaves. I can tie a bow around it?"

The man checked his watch. "That should work."

When he'd gone, Lotte joined me in the front room.

"Feeling antisocial?"

"He's a dog," she said, shaking her head. "It won't work. She'll see right through him."

I looked from the door to Lotte's fixed gaze on the exit and back to the door. "How do you know that?"

She shrugged. "Sixth sense. I know his type."

"Then I'm grateful he bought something before she tosses him out...and before any more of them die off."

Lotte considered my offerings. She held out her hand to cup a leaf. It snuggled into her palm as though reacting to her touch. "They aren't so bad, yet. And that one's blooming," she said, pointing to the orchid.

"Gaven's doing." I wondered if all orchids were temperamental creatures.

I'd considered that if the plants died, I'd have an empty shop to fill with upscale serums, hand knitted scarves, and boutique chocolates. Patrick had suggested as much on the phone. Then again, I wouldn't have the money to stock the shop with such things. I had to make the plants work.

"Spiky Bush? Rippled Fern? What are these labels?" Lotte peered at the bamboo tags I'd stuck in some of the plants.

I shrugged. "They looked...naked. So I put in temporary tags. When I figure out what they actually are, I write it on the back."

Lotte chuckled. "Dripping Hearts? You aren't too far off on this one." She fingered a delicate strand of leaves on a hanging plant.

"See, I've got some kind of innate ability."

"Hey now—cool find." Lotte crossed the room to the cabinet I'd cleaned. Her candle remained the focal point, but I'd added other objects to the shelves. A silver thimble from my grandmother's sewing kit. A small sickle I'd found in Hollis's tools. A shell. Several pearls I'd rescued from the floor and threaded on a string. A bottle of olive green ink. "Or was this always here?"

"I cleaned it up a bit."

"Looks like an apothecary cabinet." She pointed to the uppermost nook, the one with the stone and the plant from Patrick. "Was this one ever alive?"

I sighed. "It *was*. My son gave it to me when he left, so I can't bear to toss it."

Lotte reached up as if to touch the pile of crunchy leaves but retracted her hand. "Ah, well. I think that's alright. Most people save bouquets of flowers. Yours is just...different. Besides, from most angles, you can't see it. Kind of blends in with the wood."

"Ha. Ha."

"I'd better get back. Let me know if you need any taste testing for your plans. When's the party?"

"First of February," I said.

A look of concern crossed her face. "Oh. I have an appointment that day."

"At night?"

She crossed her arms, tucking her hands behind her elbows. "I...uh...will see what I can do."

When she left, I plugged in my portable speaker and connected it to my phone. While waiting in line at the hall, I'd read that plants grow better with music. I turned to Mariette. "How do you feel about Nick Cage?"

The inside of the shop was cozy. Warm and tidied, the music, when added to the party lights I'd strung from the rafters and the smell of fresh coffee, was the final touch in creating a space I began to love. At the front window, I peered into the outside world. Shoppers scuttled to their cars, hands full of packages. Others stopped for selfies in front of the famous fountain. A mother pushed a stroller as she jogged down the sidewalk, her breath coming out in quick puffs.

Movement drew me to one of the elms. In the branches, a shape formed, human-like, then flattened, then formed again. The figure slipped down the trunk, then slunk toward the shop. They wore a gauzy dress in shades of pale green and were barefoot in the cold. When their eyes found mine, I flinched and ducked back.

Two heart beats later and the bell jingled. *A customer.*

"Hello," I said, and shifted to greeter mode.

It was the figure from the trees. She was incredibly tall, and her brown hair was braided in a thick rope she flipped over her shoulder. She had bare feet and not a stitch of makeup.

What added a layer of peculiarity, what had me blinking several times, was the soft blurred edges to her person.

She smiled at me, then looked over my shoulder.

"How can I help you?" I put some distance between us. Either she came from a tree or I was losing what sanity I had left. Possibly both. I went into customer service mode and waved at the wall of vines. "I have...plants."

"They are beautiful," she began, her voice the music of a babbling brook, "however sad."

Ouch. "Perhaps a succulent?" I gestured to the table.

She appraised that selection. "Cheerful, like marching soldiers. But I cannot take them where I am going."

Okay. "Well, this is what I've got, so..." I held up both my hands.

She looked at my hands, then chuckled. "Of course," she said. "My apologies for not observing the custom." She reached into a pouch at her waist that hadn't been there moments before and withdrew an item from within. With great ceremony, she set it on my open palm.

A tiny, gold dragon lay in my hand. The beast was detailed, from its scales to the flames spewing out of its mouth. It was gorgeous and heavy. Real gold.

"Uh...um. This is very nice." I tried to hand the figurine back to her.

She waved both of her hands at me and backed away, smiling. "No, no, it's yours. For the tithe."

I regarded the woman. She clasped her hands together and waited, an eager smile on her face.

"O...kay. Thanks," I said, having no clue what she meant. I knew tithes from church, and a religious house, this was not. "Truly too generous."

She nodded at me, then held out her hand, expectant.

"Do you...want it back now?"

The woman shook her head. Her face was covered in freckles, her golden hair contrasting her dark skin. "The stone," she said, as though this would clear things up.

It didn't. I shrugged. She frowned. I frowned. The clock ticked one, two, three seconds while the air in the shop pressed close, moisture filling my lungs. The pointer finger on the woman's hand twitched. Pressure built at my temples while she watched me, a slight tilt to her head.

"Stones," I said, and the pressure lifted, an immediate release. "Hollis did have some stones."

During the cleanup, I'd found a giant fish bowl filled with polished rocks. They were a jumble of colors, shapes, and patterns. I reached for the bowl under the counter. "These?"

She nodded, a rapid movement. Before I could set the selection on the table, she reached out and snatched one.

"Sure, go ahead. Doesn't seem like a fair trade to me, but if this is what you wanted..."

She wasn't listening. Instead, she patted herself down, as though checking her pockets. Satisfied, she nodded, then turned back to me. "May the rain fall softly on your doorstep," she said, and gave me a small bow. "May your hearth burn bright with the power of a thousand great lizards."

"Uh...thanks." I looked down at the tiny dragon, so shiny it glowed in my hand. Tiny red jewels studded its eyes, like rubies from a watch mechanism. I wrapped my fingers around the figure, surprised at its warmth. It was as though this creature were moments away from coming to life. When I looked up, she'd moved toward the back of the shop.

"Hello?" I called. I moved to follow her between the towering plants, but my own jungle tugged me back, the leaves pulling at my clothing. I called toward the back of the store. "I keep that door locked."

When I reached the rear of the shop, she was gone.

That night I dreamed a bear watched me from the edge of a forest. I couldn't move from my place in the meadow, just stood, frozen and terrified. But the bear didn't charge. An ethereal being appeared from between the trees, then strode to the beast's side. The pair watched me together, my feet anchored as though encased in mud, before they turned to fade back in among the trunks.

TEN

Turns out, Beastie Boys does more to rouse me than coffee. At least it did when I entered Plush to a thumping bass and fast lyrics. Bryce was up on a ladder, painting the walls an electric blue. He wore a pair of torn jeans, a paint-splattered T-shirt missing its sleeves, and a trucker's hat. His bare feet balanced on the ladder rungs. A stack of posters and framed art lay on a table, his half-eaten breakfast spread on top, a can of some obnoxious energy drink serving as a paperweight.

"Nothing subtle about your Sundays," I said, raising my voice above the music.

He smiled around a pencil between his teeth, pressing paint into a corner with a sponge brush. "I'm not one for subtlety."

The fading sheen on the walls suggested he'd been at the job for hours. And I thought I was an early riser.

Paint tray in one hand, he descended the ladder, toes wrapping the edge of each rung. At the foot of the steps, he fished a remote from his pocket and pressed it. Mike D ceased his rap, mid-sentence. Silence filled the small venue.

"What did he want me to do to his nuts?"

Bryce chuckled. "A true poet, that one."

"Changing things up?"

Bryce shrugged. He had a swipe of blue along his jaw. "Going for a different energy. Capture some new clientele."

A shift away from punk bands and cigarettes littering the sidewalk would be an upgrade. "Looks great," I said. "Like a mermaid's lair."

"A decent band name." He set the paint tray on a cloth-covered table, then wiped his hands on his jeans. "To what do I owe the pleasure of this visit?" Bryce stepped closer to me, the heat from his body palpable. At his throat, beneath a hemp necklace ringed with puka shells, his pulse fluttered, a faint movement under the skin. He took another step, squinting slightly, and brushed something off my cheek in a slow and deliberate move. The skin of my arms lit up from his touch, my cheeks no doubt pink as hell.

He smiled and sucked in his lower lip before holding out the finger. A tiny drop of blue paint dotted his skin. This man knew the effect he had over women. Or at least me. Musicians, always the musicians.

"It's...a pretty color." *Eloquent, EJ.* My heart raced.

"Bit bright in this light, but hang on a sec." Bryce wiped his finger on his jeans, adding to the stain count, and moved to the windows to lower the shades, one by one. He flipped off the overhead lights. The room pitched into black.

In the darkness, he was behind me. The sudden pressure of him, *all* of him, lit every nerve in my body. He radiated warmth from every curve. *Every* curve. I smelled the vestiges of liquor seeping through his pores, cheap cologne, and some-thing flowery. Every ounce of my being shouted for me to turn around. To press my nose to his collarbone and inhale his scent. Slide my palm down the front of his jeans to cup what was now pressed into my low back.

In my ear, his voice was soft. "Check this out."

Oh, how I wanted to do just that.

Stage lights winked on, a hazy level that distracted me from my lust. I fought the urge to tip my head back and turn my face toward his.

"And now for the best part." He held up the small remote in front of me and aimed it toward the stage. One click and a spotlight lit a circle on the platform. "Picture a blues singer, sequins on her dress. Cherry red lipstick. Eyes closed."

Another click and a disco ball descended. It wasn't the typical, mirror-plated surface. The facets were softer somehow, like scales. The effect shimmered and glowed, like light through water. Another click, and the speakers kicked on a Rae Morris song.

"Care to dance?" Bryce faced me, the flickering lights reflecting in his eyes, tracing the shape of his cheekbones, the edge of his jaw. This thirty-something owner of a music venue held out his hand to me, Rae's voice in the background. *They may not know it, they may be trying to tell you...*

There are moments in a life you never forget. The birth of a child. Your wedding day. The death of a loved one. Big events that pockmark a timeline. But ask any romantic, however closeted, for their list of the small. Those minutes, seconds even, of selfish abandonment to the magic life brings when you least expect it. I guarantee, being asked to dance will herald many such lists.

When someone like Bryce asks, you say yes.

I took his hand, and he led me to the stage. I stepped onto the rickety platform, blackened by paint and a thousand footsteps. For a few moments, I forgot who I was, where we were, and why I'd come and let him draw me in.

When the world's got you down...

He clutched my right hand in his left and wrapped an arm

around my waist. We swayed to the lyrics. I rested my forehead against his cheek, our hips pressed together.

Bryce turned his chin to whisper in my ear. "So, you like the color."

"I do," I said, eyes closed.

"It occurred to me," he continued, "that if I want to attract the right kind of customers, I need to draw them in."

Who were the right kind—forty-year-old single empty nesters with a vibrator collection? *Count me in.* The soft play of lights and sound lulled me. "I think you're onto something here," I whispered.

Sunlight burst into the room, seeping through the open doorway. A figure stood, backlit.

"Bryce, you in here? We got the wine like you asked. Only they didn't have everything so they said you could put in an order for the rest."

Bryce and I stepped away from each other like teenagers under a parental flashlight, the moment shot.

"Load them in the back. And be careful. I don't want any more breakage." He rubbed the back of his neck and turned to me. "Sorry about that," he said.

I wasn't sure if he meant for the interruption, the dance, or all of the above. "No worries," I said. "I should get going."

"Was there...a reason you stopped by?" A sheepish grin stole over his boyish features. At that moment, I knew a decade younger was too much of a gap for me.

"Yeah, actually," I said, blood moving from my lady parts back up to my brain. "I was hoping you could recommend a musician. A guitarist, maybe. Acoustic? I'm doing a little thing at the shop, and I'd love live music."

He raised an eyebrow. "At your shop? I have just the guy. Usually free most nights." He pulled a pen from his back pocket and scribbled on a flier before handing it my way. "Tell him I sent you. In fact, if you call him, let him know he should stop by here, too."

"Thanks," I said, then smiled. For the referral, for the dance, for relighting a spark I'd let fizzle out. "I'll do that."

"'Course," he said, and retreated to the back to help unload the wine.

There better be champagne in those boxes because I'll be back, if only to remember.

~

I floated my way down the street to the Apothecary. I savored the remnants of Bryce's touch, the music, and the underwater lighting that set me adrift.

Christopher was right. I couldn't languish, a decaying houseplant abandoned on a shelf. I was alive. I had wants—needs, even. It was time to honor them.

Rowdy was inside my shop when I opened the door. He'd perched on my stool, one ankle over his knee. A small box sat on the counter.

"Oh," I said. "I didn't know you were coming over." *Or that you'd be inside without me.* Vulnerability tugged at my nerves.

"Door was unlocked," he said, and shrugged. "Brought you the honey." He nudged his chin to the box.

I'd emailed him to let him know I'd penned a few recipes and asked if he'd have more lavender honey. I'd planned to hit up the market, but he'd clearly wanted early access. With a smile, I reached for the ledger where I'd stuffed my notes. I handed him my notecards before peering into the box he'd brought.

"There's lavender, a sage which is really tasty for savory use, and a little house special," he said. "Something new we've been working on."

I lifted the slimmer of the jars from the box. "Hot honey?"

He nodded, flipping through my cards. "It's our acacia with dried chilies from the farm."

"Wow. I bet I can do something with that. Thanks!"

"Thank you. They sound delicious." I'd pored through my personal collection of recipes from past events and added in a few classics. Honey had been a popular cocktail ingredient and deserved a resurgence. He hopped off the stool and made his way to the door, tapping into his phone. "Good luck with your event."

"You won't be able to make it?" My dance with Bryce restored some of the bravery I'd lost in my recent defeats. "I'm hiring a guitar player from Plush and catering—"

"You know Bryce?" There was a sharpness in his tone and his eyes narrowed.

I faltered. "Yeah...uh. He gave me the guy's contact info."

Rowdy stalked back to me. His jaw shifted. "If you want my advice, stay away from Bryce. He isn't what he seems." Without another word, he was gone, my recipes in hand.

"That went well," I told Mariette in his wake. I'd dry-humped one hot man only to piss off the next. "The universe has returned to balance."

The afternoon ahead of me, I dedicated myself to figuring out the event menu. Three hours later, I'd crafted several signature cocktails, two custom blended teas, and a selection of appetizers. Tasty bites on tasting plates fought for counter space in the cramped kitchen.

I'd also sold two plants. One to a couple that wandered in, the woman checking each and every label before choosing a broad-leafed beauty with a plastic trellis shoved into the container. "Would a moss pole work for this?"

I nodded, having no clue. "Should be fine." *Note to self: research moss poles.*

I'd meant to return to my plant studies, and had even

downloaded an identification app. Yet when it came time to sit down and assess what I had, I allowed every distraction under the sun to call me elsewhere.

I was relieved when my next customer came with her own knowledge.

"*Begonia coccinea*," she exclaimed before I could get in a greeting. "I've been looking for one of these!"

"Great," I said as I rang up her purchase. The plant in question had long stalks on which wing-shaped leaves with silver detailing mirrored each other on opposite stems. "I'm sure you'll be very happy together."

Another customer asked if I took special orders. "Not at the moment," I explained. "Still sorting out distribution." He left his number for when I had more information. This inspired me to rustle in one of my *Office Supplies* boxes, still unpacked, for a wide-lined journal. I flipped to the first page, added the person's name and contact information, then left the pen atop the book. With each new detail, the Apothecary became a living, breathing shop.

One man came in for a gift and left thinking I was a few branches short of a tree. "Does that plant have...googly eyes?" he asked, spotting Mariette.

I'd made the impulse purchase at the craft store in town. I'd needed a few items for the event to decorate and grabbed the bag of stick-on eyes on my way to the checkout stand. Mariette and several others were now gifted with a pair of peepers. Made me laugh, anyway. This guy was not amused but bought a few succulents and a shallow dish, nonetheless.

I'd invited each customer back for my opening, promising a fun night. I hummed to myself, again in my element. Planning events was my bread and butter, the way I made sense of the world. I gathered people for a purpose. *I can do this.*

The next morning, fresh stack of fliers in hand, I made my way around the square. I introduced myself to each of the business owners, asked if I could hang my signs, and invited all to take part.

Lotte had donated a couple candles for a raffle basket, and Grace from Second Shot added a bag of her roast and a cute mug. "It's a great idea. We used to do special nights like this a few years ago. Knitting, open mics, book clubs. I should do it again."

At the year-round Christmas shop, the owner asked if I'd display a small tree of ornaments with her card underneath. She brought me to the wall covered in plant-themed ornaments of all sizes, shapes, and materials, each with a grosgrain ribbon loop. In exchange, she'd display a few plants in her store with the Apothecary tag. I loved her immediately.

When we shook hands, I saw her, decades later, asleep under a pile of blankets. As she drifted away, family surrounded her bedside, softly sobbing. *May we all go so peacefully,* I thought, then frowned. This wasn't as violent as my typical vision but made just as little sense. I hadn't thought of anything when Bryce and I touched. Why did this happen every other time? *Hormones*, I thought, but wasn't convinced. I shook off the eerie feeling and continued on my errands.

The door to Plush was locked, so I rolled a flier and wedged it under the door handle. I was a little relieved, in truth. I wasn't sure what I'd say to Bryce the next time we met. *Hey, would it be cool if we slow danced again? I don't want anything from you, except maybe a little use of that rock hard body...*

Yep, glad he was out.

At my last stop, I hesitated. A familiar neon glow lit the doorway. Instead of pressing in, I faced the square. As daylight gave way to streetlights, downtown shifted. Shades were drawn while others opened. Families bundled children home to bed while adults lingered over a second glass of merlot. The square itself, surrounded by life, took on an evening identity. Enrobed in shadows, buildings elongated, looming over the park.

I scanned the trees but not a leaf stirred. All but the wildest of creatures had retreated until the morning.

Behind me, a crowd pushed out of the pub. There was shouting, and I was bumped to the wall. At this man's touch, I saw his member in my hand, moving in rhythm to the thrusting taking place on the screen in front of me. A release, a stoppage of my heartbeat, then blackness.

I clutched the paper in my grip, disgusted. These visions threw me, like those videos that started playing before a webpage loaded. Only these were personal, invasive. Whether because I was losing my mind or plain freaked out, I needed to figure this out.

"Don't come back," Joaquin said from the door at my side, his voice cold and level. "Unless you plan to order an ass beating."

"You're chicken," one of the ejected said, eyeing Joaquin from head to toe. The man wore his football days like a sagging skin, yet his broad shoulders were twice the width of Joaquin's. He leered at Joaquin as the air filled with the electricity of testosterone and alcohol. "All bark and no bite."

Joaquin smiled, flashing his canines. "Buddy, you have no idea," he said, disgust twisting his handsome features. "Now go, before I set my sights on proving you wrong–and I won't be gentle."

The group shuffled off, revealing me, cowering against the wall.

"Great," Joaquin muttered. Both hands on his hips, a black leather belt with a silver buckle circling his waist and a silver chain poking out of his shirt collar, he sighed and looked at the ground. He nodded once, opened the door, and said,

"Welcome to Morgan's. Feel free to check your chaos at the door."

Making a face at him, I pushed past him, noting that he was careful not to touch me.

Inside, Morgan's was calm, quiet. *Too* quiet.

Patrons leaned over their drinks, shifting their gaze toward the front of the pub and back to each other. Ansel brooded behind the bar, arms crossed, brows knitted. He stared at an unseen spot on the opposite wall, his gaze focused and menacing. Some of the lights flickered and the air was stiff with electricity. The bar top was covered in a thin sheet of ice, its edges dripping.

Joaquin followed behind me. I whirled to face him, and he jumped back. "What did I miss?"

"Those idiots salivating over Iris which caused her to get pissed which made Ansel get huffy. I was called to take out the trash."

At the mention of the owner's protective side, something akin to jealousy tugged at the back of my mind. "Where's Iris?"

"Upstairs, warming up." He faced me, then his eyes dropped to the papers in my hands. "So, whatever this is–he gestured between me and Ansel–I'll be over there with a bucket of popcorn, watching how well it goes." With a wink, he left me in the entryway.

I pressed my lips together, determined. I took a deep breath, then made my way to the bar.

Up close, Ansel was more than intimidating. His hair, graying at his temples, was wild—did he own a brush? People with long hair needed to take better care of it. His eyes narrowed on my approach. His arms were folded over his massive chest, muscles shaping the tight bar shirt. My toes curled within my boots as I willed my spine to straighten, my resolve to solidify.

"Hi," I opened.

Ansel's gaze remained fixed in front of him.

"I'm, uh...going around to all the businesses. Talking with everybody, and I wanted to invite—"

I stopped. Ansel hadn't moved. Hadn't bothered to look my way, let alone acknowledge my presence. I'd done nothing to this man save have the poor luck to inherit a tiny business next to his behemoth. The least he could do was look at me.

Own your story, Christopher had said. How could I reclaim my strengths, let alone leverage them to turn a shit pile of a business situation into something livable, something sustainable, if I couldn't even speak to this brute of a man?

"Hey," I said, a sharp rebuke. He turned his head, the lion's mane of hair framing darkened features. "I was talking to you."

He turned back to his watch. "I know. I hoped I was dreaming and you'd stop."

I sucked in my lower lip, then continued. "Look. I'm having a thing at the Apothecary. An event. Like an open house. There'll be music, food, and drinks. I'm inviting everyone and I wanted to—"

"Drinks?"

"Yeah. I applied for a license for the night. Anyway, I—"

He cut me off again, his voice a low growl. "You came over here to tell me you're throwing your doors wide open to *anyone* who wants to come in and serving them *drinks?*"

"Yeah." I breezed on. I'd encountered his type before. Fathers of the bride, snotty venue owners, the occasional groom. If I pushed forward through the initial meetings, I'd get far enough into the spiel where it would become too late for their protests, their daughters/sons/second fiancés were off and running with the plans with nothing left for these men to do but foot the bill. "I thought it would be a great way to get people together to check out the shop."

"On Imbolc!?" His eyes flashed. Outside, the wind had picked up. It whipped a newspaper against the glass. Inside, a few beer signs shifted against their mountings. Customers eyed them and a few moved tables. Falinis lifted his great head to assess the situation.

I frowned. *Im-bolk?*

"You should go," Joaquin said, appearing at my side. He didn't look at me, instead watching Ansel turn a deepening shade of crimson.

Dismissed, I stormed out of the bar and into my shop. I flipped the sign to *Closed* and willed myself not to cry, not to waste energy and emotion on a man so cold, so volatile, his own employees cowered to his moods. Alone in my own shop, the world locked out, I vowed to never let a man talk to me that away again.

~

That night, I opened the door to Hollis's room.

I'm not sure what I expected. A secret lair, perhaps. His spirit, busy at the small desk, filling the pages of his journal.

Whatever I'd thought, it wasn't this. The room could have been a suite in any bed and breakfast. Clean, crisp linen. Spotless dresser, empty nightstand save a small clock, its brass hands in want of a battery. On one wall was a painting of a countryside spilling down a hill and into the sea. A ship bobbed on the waves, a lone figure on the beach holding a spyglass.

A pair of windows opened into the atrium. I opened them to the night air and leaned out. Stars winked into place above me. I searched them for a circlet, a match to Hollis's sketch and the old book, but found none. Orion looked back at me, but nothing more.

Today had been far more triumph than tragedy, yet I couldn't shake the energy from my encounter with Ansel.

I considered the room I'd expected to be haunted but found it homey. My neck and back eyed the bed, firm under a soft gray duvet.

I started for the door, building a mental list of the items to gather should I move in when from the courtyard below came the sounds of a heated debate.

"Not inside. Iris doesn't know—" This was Ansel. I didn't need to look out the window to picture him. Black Morgan's shirt, sleeves rolled up at the elbow, collar buttoned to his chin. He wore a frown like most wear a favorite pair of jeans.

"—and I haven't told her," Joaquin snapped. A jokester in most interactions, he was anything but in this moment. "You'll make it. It'll be fine."

"You don't know that. You can't know that. This is all but a guarantee I will be anything but *fine*."

Was it the play of the sound against the brick walls, or did I detect a hint of fear in Ansel's voice?

"Come on," Joaquin said, his voice now playful. "Good news or bad news?"

"Bad," Ansel said, and meant it.

"So she throws this party. Someone shows up. I'll be there the whole time, watching. Take them out before they even find the weir."

The weir? Take them out? I stiffened. I'd seen what Joaquin was capable of. I shivered in the dark.

Ansel grunted, unconvinced. I inched over to the window and peered out, sticking to the shadows.

Joaquin continued, "Okay, now for the good news. EJ pulls it off and nothing happens. We make an arrangement like we did with Hollis...before."

Before?

Ansel stood in front of the tree, glowering. Joaquin sat on

the back of the bench, feet on its seat, forearms resting on his thighs.

"Too risky. She can't be allowed to have it."

Is he talking about the party?

"I'll be there to make sure it stays shut." Joaquin put a hand on Ansel's shoulder. "After that, you'll be free."

I stared, open-mouthed, at their plan for my own undoing. They plotted for the demise of my event, the shop. My livelihood. *What did I do to deserve this?*

A rapping at my front door drew my attention from below in the shop. I stepped back from the window. On a whim, I grabbed the letter opener from Hollis's desk and ran for the stairs.

I tiptoed to the front door, sticking close to the plants. Wilted, they did little to hide my movement from the large front window.

Gaven waited outside.

"Gaven," I said, surprised.

He stood there looking everywhere but at me. "Joaquin said you wanted to speak to me. So...here I am."

"Are you...on your way to work?"

"Yeah," he said, and shifted the weight from one foot to the other.

Every nerve in my body fought the discomfort. I wrestled between wishing him a good night and following him over to Morgan's for my usual order, pretending nothing was wrong. Why is admitting we're wrong so damn hard, no matter how old we get?

Confronted by the boy, my rehearsed apology sounded fake in my head. I needed to tell him how I sucked as an adult role model. That I'd jumped to conclusions, freaked out, and didn't listen. I was no better than the adults I'd butted heads with as a teen. I thought of my son. Considered how I'd want him to be treated.

"Gaven, I'm sorry. I was...stupid, the other day. I was a wreck from the break-in and I took it out on you."

He kept his eyes downcast.

"I was an ass," I said, continuing. "Then when I found what you'd left for me...I saw the circle of stars."

I struggled to get out the last of my thoughts. I'd read the book he'd given me. It was full of magical tales of the fae. There were epic battles and endless love, tricksters, and those who did good deeds for the ungrateful. "Hollis knew about those stories, didn't he? He knew who you were."

For I knew, now, too. Or at least, had a solid guess. He'd given me more than a book of the mysterious and mystical. The tales of the Gentry, inhabitants of this world long before humans began their reign, were his stories. Without saying a word, he'd tried to let me know why life for him was different. Complicated.

Guilt washed over me, a cascade of emotion. How often do we do this to the people we care about—put our own bull-shit on them and play the victim?

"I've been having these weird visions," I began. My confession tumbled out. Something about Gaven's silent witness, his personal reveal, required a trade. My vulnerability for a return to his good graces. "When I touch people. Most people. I see them, their lives. Sort of. Not who they are now, but who they will be, and...how their lives will end. I think. And I'm kind of freaked out about it. The shop is about to die, I'm putting everything on the line for some half-baked party, and I'm—" A tear snaked across my cheek. I took a deep breath and released it, the stress of decades seeping out from my lungs. "Anyway. I hope you'll forgive me. I miss your visits."

Gaven watched me, quiet, uncertain. He held a backpack over one shoulder, his hair tucked behind one ear. To anyone else, he was a teenager on the way to a friend's house. But I knew he was so much more.

"I'm rambling. Would you like to come in? That is, if you have time. You don't have to. I'd understand if you don't want to deal with a stupid mortal woman who can't keep her shit together—" I didn't have time to finish my sentence before he brushed past me to enter the shop.

Inside, he pushed back his hood before turning a slow circle. I wondered what it looked like to him now. While he looked around, I took mental note of his appearance. It's a mom thing. With the ever-present hoodie, he'd donned a pair of dark green pants, as baggy as they were long. His fingers, with skin so pale it was almost translucent, stuck out from a ratty pair of knitted, fingerless gloves. His hair, black as pitch, stuck out in all directions, tousled by the hood.

Gaven reached out his hand to a yellowing leaf, its tip brown and dry. He looked at me, an expression of judgment. "Did you water like I told you?"

"I tried," I said. "I did. But...it didn't help."

Gaven shook his head, appraising the others. At the orchid, he said, "That one looks fine."

I shrugged. "That was all you."

He turned back to me. "You need to—how did you put it? —get your shit together."

"I will," I started. "If you teach me how you do it."

Gaven's eyes locked onto mine.

"Please," I said, and waited.

He shook his head. "You don't know what you're asking."

I pulled the blinds in the front windows. "I don't have a choice. It's not just the visions. It's the break-in. My so-called customers dragged out in chains or at the point of an arrow. People crawl down from the trees and offer me dragons—"

Gaven's eyebrow rose at my last example, but I pressed on.

"Your book," I said. "*Tales of the Gentry*. I found it mentioned in online forums. There are people who believe in the ancient ways. They think that the folk still walk the earth, shrouded from humans. Abandoned in this world to make their way through time. The stories they told matched those in the book, descriptions matching the people in my shop. And I think some of those stories...are about you."

His eyes widened, like a trapped squirrel. I stepped closer in case he tried to bolt. I doubted I could have held him back with my measly human ability, but I wasn't finished.

For in that internet dive, I'd learned the Gentry were creatures bound to nature. In the times of old, when suspicion and reverence flavored the everyday, they triumphed, their command over humans an established fact. But as the world changed and the strange became mundane, forgotten, reception for the old ones shifted. Now, faeries were a myth, relegated to television stories with swooning heartthrobs and glorified paranormal love triangles. The word and work of the ancient ones was brushed away, the masses too enraptured with screens and donating their lifeblood to technology.

"Gaven," I said, and held out my hand to him. I had to know.

He hesitated. I watched a wave of debate stripe his expression, fear and interest swapping places. At last, he placed his hand in mine.

Where our skin touched, it vibrated with energy. But it wasn't death I saw. Instead, it was life. A reel of events that stretched so far back, I lost the end as they played, one after the other in my mind. In most, Gaven stood at the edge of a field, a town, a school. A child would be found wandering, lost, hurt, or running from danger. As though I were he, we would take the young one's hand and guide them to safety assuring them with kind words and tales of woodland creatures we'd spot on their journey home. In some scenes we strode over great moors, heather scenting our path. A child was reunited with loving parents, then scolded for running off. In other visions from the current day, we carried a limp body full of needle holes to the nearest hospital, depositing the frail being in a wheelchair and alerting the staff before slipping back into the night. Across continents and across time, the stories marched. In many, we fled from angry farmers, bullies, and police, all after someone they believed to be a troubled teen. I saw Gaven's life for what it was now. Not a life at all, really, but an enslavement to a storyline that would play out for eternity.

I released his hand. "So you're—how old?" I stared at this boy-man-youth in front of me, mouth agape.

He shrugged, then ran a finger down a vine. At his touch, it grew, the stems creaking as it popped out a new leaf. I tried not to gape. "Can't remember my last birthday, actually."

"But...you...work with Ansel. And Joaquin. They have to know...Do they...do you...but..." I sounded like a parrot, stuck on a new word.

"We...understand each other," Gaven said with a little shrug.

"Oh god, are they...?" Panic zinged through my bloodstream. Had I been the lone human, failing miserably in front of a pack of superhuman beings? Joaquin's superhuman strength. The way the very air shifted around Ansel. No wonder they wanted me gone. I was pitiful compared to them. Humiliation locked me in place.

"Like me?" Gaven stroked one of the winged plants. Its leaves deepened to a purple-red at his touch. He shook his head and gave a little smile. "No."

I exhaled in relief.

"But," he began again, and I froze. "They have their own stories, so I wouldn't underestimate them. Or anyone around here, really."

Lead dropped to the floor of my stomach. The past few weeks crashed back into my conscience like a tsunami of regret. Every interaction, every glance, every footstep held new meaning. Lotte? Iris? The adorable woman at the Christmas shop?

"Is everyone—?"

Gaven shook his head. "No. There are many of your kind here. Everywhere, really. There are just more of my kind here because of the...amenities in the area."

"Amenities?" My brows rose.

Nonchalant, Gaven peered under leaves, propped up stems, and rotated pots under the lighting. Each plant he touched revived with attention. It was as though now fully exposed, he didn't bother hiding his abilities.

"This part of your world has a lot of...*special* energy."

"You mean Sedona?" The red rocks were a famous draw for those in search of the mystic, the alien, and the misunderstood.

"Decoy," he said, a dismissal. "The energy flows here," he said, and pointed to the floor.

"One more question," I ventured. "In case this is another weird dream and I'm about to wake up."

"Sure."

"How did you get into my shop? The first time."

Weirs.

Not fish dams, but something similar. Or at least that is what I gleaned.

The foundation made sense, in a way. The Gentry traveled between this world and their own, using the supernatural subway, of sorts. Weirs were the stops, the portals between realms.

"So the woman with the dragon..." I said, putting the pieces together in my mind like a jigsaw. Gaven waited for me to assemble the rationale. "Wait. I have a weir. *Here?*" Gaven nodded. I turned my head back and forth. "Where?"

Gaven pointed to the glassed-in porch. The tiny room crammed to the gills with books.

"Impossible. I've been in there. It's nothing but books and shelves with more books crammed in between."

"I'll show you, but you've got to be careful. Hollis wouldn't go near it, and I think that was smart." Before I could point to the key on the ledge, the little door popped open at Gaven's touch. He stooped to shift a few books out of the way.

A hat tumbled down from a shelf. It was well worn and homemade, a thick, knitted wool. I picked it up.

"That's mine," he said. I frowned, turning the brim in my hands. There was a sprig of heather jabbed between the stitches. "I...uh...keep a change of clothes here. For when I...go back," he said. "Hollis didn't mind. I can move them—"

"It's not a problem," I said. If I was honest with myself, I'd missed tripping over Patrick's shoes on the doormat and finding random articles of clothing strewn about. The things that drive you nuts about a roommate, the same ones you miss when they're gone. "Wait, were you and my uncle in a...you know...dating?"

Gaven laughed. "No," he said, matter-of-fact, then smiled. "I like girls. Not sure about Hollis, though. He never said. Now if you're done poking into my love life, I've something to show you. Mind you keep your distance."

Breathless, I leaned in to peer around his angular shoulders.

Under the window, Gaven had cleared away the books. Where a brick wall should be was instead a hole of blackness. A tunnel. There was a tugging sensation, as though an unseen force acted on my body, pulling forward. My mouth rounded as shock kept me silent.

"Not something you'll want to advertise, I'm afraid," Gaven said.

"What would happen if I was to...if a human person was to...go through?"

Gaven looked from me to the weir. A faint sound of suction came from within. I shivered. "I've never tried it," he said. "Though a milkmaid or two tempted me. There are many stories of those who have. Nobility, mostly, who refused to leave a human lover behind. From what I heard, humans never came out the same as they went in."

"Cover it up, please. This is one milkmaid who doesn't want to take any risks." Gaven returned the room to its inconspicuous, miniature library form, while I brewed a new pot of coffee. I pretended I could handle this new information, but my leap-frogging guts said anything but. I knew sleep was a long way off for me—might as well enjoy the caffeine.

"So, the dragon-gifting woman—left. Through there." That explained why the back door had remained locked.

"Tithe," he said. "In payment for her travels. Not a gift."

"Like a ticket?"

"Something like that."

I thought of the box of trinkets I'd found. Could this be a collection of tithes? And what of all the other trinkets around the shop? "Did you pay Hollis?"

"No, I watched the shop when he traveled." Gaven poured each of us a steaming mug.

"Through the weirs?" I looked back to where the gaping hole waited, a silent maw in my shop.

"Pretty sure he flew commercial," Gaven joked. "Hollis was a weirman for the Gentry, but his job was only to watch. In exchange, there are certain...benefits."

"Like bottles of Dom Perignon and blowies every night of the week?"

Gaven spit out his coffee. "Do not ever say *blowies* to me again."

"You can't play the part of a teenager if you don't cringe like one."

Gaven huffed. "*Anyway.* Hollis, this place, and to an extent, everywhere around was under protection. He vows to let the right folk in and keeps the wrong folks out and he gets a cush shop."

"And to keep the tithes." I thought of the dragon, the price it would fetch in a jewelry store, or heck, a pawn shop. Was this how he kept the Apothecary up and running?

"But there was that other one," I said, remembering the first day I met Gaven. "You called him *fallen*."

Gaven pressed his lips together. "Weirs are for the Gentry and their occasional companions. The Fallen are forbidden from using them."

"So," I began, attempting a lighter question, "will you always look like this?"

He looked down as though I'd spotted a stain on his shirt, then back up at me. "What's wrong with how I look?"

"Don't people eventually notice you don't age?

Gaven flipped the hood back over his face and fished an eyeliner pencil from one of his pockets. With deft hands and no mirror, he applied the makeup. "If you didn't know me," he said, looking down with kohl-rimmed eyes and shuffling his feet. "What would you see?"

Instead of Gaven, then, I thought of my son. I thought of all the extra jobs I took to send him to the fancy preschool, the cello lessons, and lacrosse. The wardrobe I purchased to match. The day I'd flipped out when I ran into him at the mall in a grungy flannel and torn up jeans, his own eyes lined in defiance.

"A rebel," I said.

"Exactly," Gaven said. "You'd walk the other way and put me out of your mind.

It isn't hard to fade into the streets. You make friends for a while and then it gets...complicated. Then it's time to leave for a while. Let the seasons shift. Staying in one place for long is an impossibility, but as long as I move about, it's fine."

"This explains why Ansel was cool with hiring a some-times-dishwasher."

"And dog walker. Falinis won't leash up for just anyone, after all," Gaven said. "I'm grateful for him–both of them, actually. Ansel and Joaquin. Morgan's is a safe harbor when-ever I need one. Hollis was, too."

Guilt gnawed at the back of my mind and I reminded myself how fortunate I was that Gaven forgave my earlier suspicions. He'd been there for Hollis, for the Apothecary, long before I showed up. I bit my lip, debating whether to risk my next question, then going for broke. "What do you know about Hollis's death?"

Gaven regarded me, an inner debate evident in his expres-sion. He glanced around, as though Mariette and her kind were listening. "Just that he was attacked. Here."

My mouth rounded into an O and a chill zinged down my spine. "There was nothing in the coroner's report about being attacked!"

Gaven edged for the exit. "I should get to the pub."

"Oh no, you don't. You're going to tell me what you know, now."

"Hello!" Gaven's and my heads whipped around to face the front door. Ingalls had let himself in. "Glad I caught you. I've got some news."

I wanted to pepper Gaven with more questions, but this was impossible in front of an audience.

"Oh—hello," the lawyer said when he saw Gaven. "I can wait while you finish up."

"It's fine, he works next door."

"And he's going to be late for his shift," Gaven said, and scooted for the door.

"Wait, what are you doing February first? I'm throwing a grand opening, and I could use some help. I'll pay cash." I figured every teenager, real or disguised, would appreciate a little green.

"Count me in," he said. "As long as I don't have to do dishes." With a nod to Ingalls, he was out the door.

I smiled. He'd used the front door twice in one evening.

Unaware of the nuances of the exchange he'd witnessed, Ingalls dug through his bag. "I don't know how to say any of this, so I'll just give it to you straight. There've been some unanticipated challenges to your event."

"Challenges?"

"Questions about the size of what you're planning. Given the fire code, and your recent inspection failure—"

"That bastard!"

"What? Look, if you get the inspection done, I'll fight them on the size. It's not like you are throwing a raging house party."

I sighed.

"There's more. When I was down there, I looked into this property. I had to file the paperwork to move the rest of his assets into your name."

"And?"

"Hollis owed—owes—taxes. A fair amount, I'm afraid."

"How can the dead owe taxes?"

"The law," he said, and shrugged. He set a stack of papers on the counter. "Seven thousand dollars, or thereabouts."

The air was punched out of my lungs. I choked for breath. "How is that possible?"

"He was up-to-date until this last year," Ingalls said.

I dropped my head in my hands, the throb of a headache at the base of my neck.

"Totally fixable," he said. "If you've got cash."

"Which I don't."

"I was afraid of that. At present, the bank can foreclose and auction off the property."

Unseen hands squeezed at my chest as I doubled over, gasping. *Come on, EJ.* The sound of my breathing echoed in my ears. Every time I thought things were under my control, a new barrier threatened my grip on anything close to success.

"Do you have anyone you could call? Maybe a family member who could give you a small loan," he said, his voice calm and helpful.

I could call my father. That's it. See if he could front me the money. But what if he couldn't, then what? A hundred golden dragons wouldn't get me out of this mess.

"Call me if something works out," Ingalls said. "There isn't much time, but there's some."

My heart dropped to my gut and stayed there, though I didn't have long to wallow in defeat. There was a tapping at the back door and I vowed to call my father. I'd ask for a little loan, something small. Promise him interest. Mr. Marketing would front his only daughter some cash.

"Coming!" I called, convincing myself not all hope was lost.

I turned on the stoop light and peered through the windowpanes. Gaven was back with a large object, shrouded in a dark cloth.

"Now that I know how little locks matter with you, perhaps I'll rid myself of doors entirely. Why bother?"

Gaven grinned. The boy—man—whatever he was wielded a hand truck with the large, draped mass balanced on its fulcrum. "Brought you a present."

I raised my eyebrows. "Guessing it's not a canary."

"Better. Hold the door?"

Several curses—standard on my end, more colorful on his —and a few bumps and bruises later, we hoisted the bulky item up the short flight of stairs and into the shop. Gaven maneuvered the load into the front space and whipped off the covering.

"Found it in the pub's basement. It's a quiet night, so Ansel has me cleaning out the storage. It was crammed in there with a mess of broken chairs and an ancient player piano. When I saw it, I recognized the carving work. It's a solid match for your shelves."

I walked a slow circle around the piece as he talked. With a tentative hand, I caressed the dark wood, tracing the carvings identical to those on my piece. "It's beautiful. Are you sure I can have it?"

"Ansel was just going to throw it out," he said.

I rotated the furniture and nestled it in place.

"Fits like a glove," I said. "An apothecary's cabinet and desk. See the notches there?" I pointed. "And there. It would have been set up in a shop like this. A shelf for every pill and powder, drawers for bags, herbs, and anything else they needed."

"Then it's right you have it."

"I love it. In fact..." I bustled into the kitchen and collected a few of my creations. Back in the shop, I nestled them along the shelves. Canisters here, bottles and vials there. I fetched the ledger and cash box from the rickety table and tucked them both into a wide top drawer. "It's absolutely perfect."

"Looks a bit like a bar. A mini one."

In the morning, I'd apply a layer of wax and buff the new piece until it shone like its other half. I considered it, the wheels in my brain turning at this idea. "It does..."

"I wonder what stories it would tell, could the tree it came from still speak," he said.

I lay awake half that night, replaying his words.

Eleven

"Out of honey already?" Rowdy's cheek dimpled when he smiled.

I laughed. "No, my supplier keeps me well stocked. Just saying hi."

The market hummed with energy. Despite the cold, the sunshine brought droves of shoppers out to the stalls. I'd avoided the bicycle booth, opting to visit a few vegetable stands and saving Beckett Honey for last. I'd waited in line to say hello, then stepped aside to make way for customers.

"What'd you find?" Rowdy asked while his customer, a woman who glared at me for commanding his attention, pulled cash from her wallet. "Winter kale, dried beans, chicken stock. Soup?"

I nodded. "And some more herbs if I can find them. Busy day?"

"Slammed. Sold out of the bulk of our jars. Might need to close up early." Behind Rowdy, his staff darted from the customers to the few remaining boxes of products. One of his crew stopped to look at me, his eyes red-rimmed in a vacant stare.

Rowdy followed my gaze. "Lee will be okay, won't you mate?" He clapped the other man on the shoulder. "A night out leaked into his morning and he's hurting. I remember those days."

"Oh, speaking of nights, I stopped by because I want to showcase other businesses at my opening. Collective marketing. As I'm featuring your honey, I thought you might want me to display some of it."

Rowdy rang up two beeswax candle sticks before handing them to a customer. "I love it," he said. "That's class. Titanic or not, you're playing music until the bitter end."

"Bitter end?"

"Busting tail to make a last-ditch effort at Hollis's debts takes guts. And I, for one, wish you luck." He flashed me a big grin. "I'll have one of my guys drop off some products. Great seeing you."

My mouth hung open as he turned to the next in line. How did he know about Hollis's debt? And if he knew...

I shut myself in the shop and huddled behind my new-to-me-furniture, using its care as my excuse to avoid the tentative knocks on the locked front door. I'd yet to hang operating hours, so it wasn't as though I broke any promises. I'd shot the lawyer a text, asking the earliest date the shop would go to auction, then stared at my phone, willing an answer to arrive while hating that very need.

Raucous laughter erupted through the brick. I glared at the wall, then closed my eyes, resigned. Who was I kidding? I couldn't take on Ansel. It was ridiculous to try. He was waiting for the opportunity to kick me out and take over. I would be jobless, houseless, and cast adrift.

What had Joaquin said? *You'll be free.* He knew. They

knew. Once again, others knew my business before I did. I worked my fingers to the bone only to have someone else snatch success out from under me.

I could beg Christopher for an in at the department store. Get one of those walkups in the suburbs, take the train to work. I would be back in Chicago—sort of—and that would be alright. I missed the city, longed for the life I knew, the one I understood. Patrick was safe, launched into his adult life. If I saved, was careful, and planned, I could retire one day. But I wouldn't make enough to keep the shop.

I'd called Dad. He'd listened, feigning sorrow, but I heard the glee in his voice. "Sure, honey. I'll wire the money for the taxes and a plane ticket. You can put the place up for sale from here. Realtors are used to distance at this point..." I told him I'd think about his offer. I'd known his help would come with strings attached, and I wasn't ready to give in. *Yet.* Ingalls made it sound like I had time, the yellow notice before the pink. There was no other option—I had to pull off the open house.

Under the cover of darkness, I stood at the window. Ensconced in my cocoon of a shop, I did my best not to panic while the world continued around me. Without me.

Hot tears spilled down my cheeks. Each was a hope, a dream lost to the pinch of reality. I lived in a world where everyone was ahead of me, and it was time I resigned myself to second place.

I wiped the moisture from my eyes. Downcast, I almost missed the flash of movement outside. When a glint of silver followed, I was out the front door.

Sticking close to the shadows, I watched from the doorway. Joaquin slunk through the square, darting behind trunks as he advanced. His target was a group of youths passing something lit between their hands. A whiff on the air told me all I needed to know. I kept my eyes on Joaquin. He crouched near a pillar, watching the group.

Minutes later, one of the teens peeled off. He waved to his friends and angled toward the darker side of the square. He hummed a tune as he walked, a pair of earbuds drowning out the city around him. As I watched, Joaquin closed in. Like a predator, he stole around the building, inching closer to unsuspecting prey.

A branch snapped, and Joaquin leapt forward. His form, a human in all-black clothing, gave way to a darker creature—a giant, black dog. I struggled for words, for air, for an explanation of any kind, but none came.

In his new form, Joaquin stalked the figure. His target ambled across the grass, oblivious to the hunter. I started to scream—at Joaquin, at the teen, at anybody in earshot—when a hand clamped over my mouth.

"Quiet," came the command and I struggled against the gag. I tried to scream, to kick and fight at my own captor, but Ansel—for it was he, the giant of a man—who held me tight to his chest. "You wanted to know what you're dealing with here. So watch."

In horror, I could only stare, transfixed at the scene in front of me.

Joaquin launched himself at the person, a surprise that worked to his benefit. His victim, if they could be called that, was quick to respond. Face down in the grass, they rotated their neck at an inhuman angle to screech at Joaquin—or the dog, however that worked. From nowhere, a pair of wings exploded from their back. Expansive, but damaged. The feathers hung from their frame at odd angles. Dark stains splattered across white. The two creatures—for they could no longer be confused for humans—wrestled across the grass, each trading hold over the other. When Joaquin twisted out from the grip of the winged beast, he lunged for its throat. With a snarl, he ripped flesh from the body which fell in a heap.

Ansel, from behind me, said, "Wait for it."

Where the body fell, there was a shimmer of light. A flame burst forth from the ground. The dog backed away from the fire to circle it, watching. In seconds, what was left of the figure burned to nothing.

I stared, my eyes unblinking. What had I seen? What did this mean? My breath must have slowed as Ansel loosened his grip on my body.

"I'm going to let you go," he said. "But don't be stupid. No one would believe you if you tried to tell them."

He released me from his grasp, and I collapsed forward, drawing in great gulps of fresh air. When my pulse settled, I stood up and punched him.

TWELVE

For good measure, I also kicked him in the danglers. It was his turn to double over.

Then, I ran.

In my head, the scene I'd witnessed played on a loop. Fur and feathers, black and white. Flames. I passed one block and then the next, willing the oxygen flaming through my lungs to propel me away from what I'd seen, away from Ansel. Far from my shop and every burden it represented.

My feet pounded the sidewalk, the rhythm slowing as my burst of energy faded and the reality of my midlife stamina caught up to me. At a grassy field, I gave into my aching body and stopped, heaving. My chest shuddered as I worked to control my breath.

An owl hooted nearby. Something scuttled through the bushes near my feet, and I recoiled. A rabbit or a mouse, maybe, but I wasn't taking chances. Behind me, the street was devoid of people. Anyone walking by would question the grown woman by herself at a playground. But where to go?

When in doubt, stay put, my scout leader taught us all those years ago. Our group of ragtag fifth grade girls had sold enough cookies to attend our first sleep away camp. We were on the trip of a lifetime—to eleven-year-olds. No parents, sleeping under the stars, and all the s'mores we could eat. But when I stepped away from the fire to find a spot in the bushes, my cheerful trip became a nightmare. I squatted, only to have the sensation of someone's hands on me, pressing along my sleeves and down my pant legs, crawling along my spine. I screamed and ran, yanking up my pants as I stumbled into the dark. The scout leader heard my shouts and found me huddled in a patch of open meadow. She said that I must have tripped and scared myself. That night was the first but far from the last of my bizarre dreams. I dreamed I was sleeping on a bed over which tendrils grew until I was covered, suffocating under the leaves. In the morning, I went back to the spot where I'd fallen, doubtful. I found what looked like boots made of vines with even more sticking out at all angles toward the direction of my escape. My mother tried to tell me the forest was only looking out for me. World-wary me insisted otherwise.

Here in this greenspace in Prescott, I was hundreds of miles from that campground, yet the panic welled in my chest just the same.

Moonlight reflected on the many surfaces, casting shadows across the playground. I'd stopped near a ramada, a shaded structure for picnics and family gatherings. A mylar birthday balloon made me jump as it bounced against the edge of the nearby trash can, its string snagged inside.

Bars of red, yellow, and blue framed the playground structure. Several slides, a zip line, and a crows' nest perch cast a mishmash of shadows on the bark chips below. I made a beeline for the tallest spot, the top of the winding slide. From there, I watched the world around as I regretted every one of my life decisions that brought me here.

From a distant tree came the hoot of an owl. A dark, silent

shape swooped out from one of the trees. It dove to snatch a small creature from the grasses before flying off for its meal. The bob and weave of a flashlight along the sidewalk revealed a leashed golden retriever and a pair of sneakers. I watched the light cross the park and disappear out the other end.

In the distance, the low whine of a motorcycle—no, two —pierced the silence. As I waited, a pair of bikes cruised into the parking lot, one a classic Harley, the other a sleek, black speed bike. Parked side by side, they promised open roads and adventure. I crouched behind the slide, one eye on the parking lot.

The rider of the second bike dismounted. Shoulder-length, shaggy black hair tumbled out of the helmet. *Lotte.* She tucked the helmet under her arm as the other rider dug into a saddlebag. The Harley driver shoved something into another helmet and passed it to Lotte.

When the Harley rumbled off, Lotte turned to face me.

I panicked. *Did she see me? What did she want?*

I was stuck on this glorified playground pedestal. If I ran, she would see me. In the game of fight or flight, I chose freeze.

Lotte meandered over to the swings. Each rubber seat dangled from a pair of chains that squeaked in the breeze. She set the helmets in the bark chips, claimed a swing, and kicked off. Feet pumping, she swung higher and higher, her toes extended skyward. She tipped her head back to smile at the moon.

As the swing slowed to a natural stop, she dragged her boots in the bark chips, leaving two troughs. "Some of us serve in atonement," she said, her voice a little louder than conversational. "Others are bound."

I stayed silent. For all I knew, she waxed prophetic often. By herself. On a kids' playground.

"EJ, I just want to talk."

I said nothing. If anyone would be talking, it would be

her, explaining the horrors of what I'd just witnessed. Preferably to my empty shop because I was on a flight back home, pretending none of this had happened.

"There are things you don't know," she said.

"Understatement of the year," I replied, before clapping my hand across my mouth.

"Care to chat down here?"

With a sigh, I swung my legs onto the slide. I rode it down, two twists. The static between my clothes and the plastic sent sparks into the night. Without meeting her gaze, I crossed to the other swing and collapsed into the seat.

"It isn't fair," I said. We both heard the defeat in my words.

"Anyone who tells you life is fair is selling something," Lotte said, her gaze softening out into the darkness.

"Life is crap for everyone," I said. "I get that. But why me? I never asked for—" I swept my hands outward toward the night. "This."

"You prefer ignorance."

It wasn't a question, but a test. I shook my head, denying the images that flashed even now. "I prefer peace. Or at least the absence of violence. Boring problems. People's problems. Joaquin, and the others—it's too much. And those wings!"

"Feathers like these?" She held one out. The shaft was black, its fletching more dirty gray than white.

I nodded, recoiling.

"The Fallen," she said, twisting the shaft between her fingers.

"Gaven called them that." Gears whirred to life in my brain. "The people with the bloodshot eyes, they're—" I couldn't finish the sentence. This truth was unbelievable. Impossible.

"The rejects," she said, and tucked the feather behind her ear. "Like the others."

"Who?"

"The ones who killed your uncle. And the ones who came before, a long time ago."

My mouth hung open. "But...I was told..."

"You were told what you needed to hear," she said.

In the dark, I gripped the edge of the bench, everything I knew again thrown overboard, replaced by this frightening truth.

"Did he...fight back?" I thought of Joaquin, the shift to canine, the jaws of steel. The explosion of feathers and brute strength.

"No," she said. "He was a witch," she said, and I blanched. "He did what he could with other weapons. To save the rest of us."

"He—what!?"

I stared at this woman through the dim light. The breeze ruffled her hair. She gripped the chains. "A green witch, to be precise. His magic flowed through plants. He was no match for the Fallen physically, but he kept them at bay as long as he could. He died with honor."

I stood up, overwhelmed with the idea to run. The ground swam before me. I turned to Lotte. "Whatever this is," I said, rocking my pointer finger back and forth between us, "isn't normal talk. People—creatures—coming in and out of my shop at all hours, wanting to travel through a hole to who knows where, others changing shape in front of my face, and then listening to someone tell me anyone, let alone my own flesh and blood, is a witch, isn't normal. I'm from the Midwest. Normal is what we do. This ain't that." I stomped off in search of space. I was two steps away when her words yanked me back.

"Ever consider that you might be one, too?"

I chilled, the reality of her words sinking in for a beat before righteous indignation shoved possibility aside. I scoffed and held up both thumbs. "See this? Black as they come. Even if witches were a thing, alongside having wings and dog-people, I'm not one of them. Plants *hate* me."

"Have you tried trusting in your magic?" As if in unison with her thoughts, my crow friends landed on the branch of a nearby oak, jostling for space.

"Trusting in my—? I can't believe I'm listening to this madness." *She could be right.* "Even the voice in my head won't shut up!"

"Voice?"

I steamed. My neck was warm, heat rising to my cheeks despite the chilly night air. "You know, that inner dialogue where you tell yourself you do look hot in that dress or that he does like you, he's just not ready to commit, or to remember to pick up the milk. Except instead of that, mine tells me other people's business."

Lotte lifted an eyebrow, as though I'd mentioned a new restaurant or the divorce of a mutual acquaintance. "Like what?"

I swallowed. "Mostly their deaths. It's not awesome."

"Tells you, or shows you?"

"A little of both."

In the faint moonlight, Lotte blinked at me, a slow batting of her thick lashes. "Does this happen all the time?"

I shook my head. "Only when I touch...some people. It's just my stupid brain, making up stories. I'm under incredible stress."

"Can you see...my death?" She held out her hand to me, her face eager with anticipation.

I'd told Lotte I had stories of people's imminent demise running through my head and she wanted to treat me like a sideshow freak.

"Please?" she asked, as though reading my mind.

With a frown, I held out my palm. She locked eyes with

me, then set her hand on mine. There was the rush of sound in my ears, as though I traveled through a tunnel, but then... nothing. A stretch of blank canvas. I shook my head.

"We need to pay someone a visit," Lotte said, her voice taking on a sense of urgency. She stood up from the swing. "They owe me."

I pulled back, but she didn't release my hand. I planted my feet in the bark chips. "I'm not going anywhere with you."

But Lotte wasn't listening. She half-dragged me toward a copse of trees by the parking lot. "June will know what to do. But first, I've got a certain canine who'd like to meet you."

THIRTEEN

Half-naked Joaquin bounced on one foot. I did my best to look everywhere but anywhere specific. This is tough when one is faced with a gorgeous man on *full* display, so I won't be filing an application for sainthood anytime soon.

Lotte, for her part, looked away, but I wasn't buying it. Joaquin kept checking to see if she was looking at him, but she didn't, and that was all the proof I needed that there was a story here.

Lotte had dragged me along the periphery of the park until we heard a "Psst" from a short hedgerow. She'd tossed the bundle, which turned out to be a wad of clothes, from inside the helmet. A hand reached up for the catch.

Now there's an unwritten rule that it's a little okay to ogle your friend's lover-date-it's-complicated-person so long as it's a public situation and everyone's cool. Brief mental drooling—fine, and some would say, healthy. Physical drooling—never okay. Joaquin was hot, and if she wasn't going to enjoy the show, I would take mental notes in her place.

Not going to lie, I wasn't exactly suffering.

Joaquin hopped the rest of the way into his jeans with the grace of someone used to a quick change. He zipped the fly after a discrete tuck and stood upright. He did that sexy thing men do where they climb into their T-shirt. The fabric slides down their ribs, then comes a tug on the bottom hem as they shrug into the skin-tight cotton.

Fully-dressed, Joaquin stepped out from behind the bush. He ran a hand through his hair and let the dark locks fall back into place. He lifted a silver chain over his neck. The massive pendant dropped beneath the fabric to rest against his skin.

"Silver?" I asked. "And...a cross?"

Joaquin shrugged. "For my mother," he said, and wedged his foot into a boot.

I inhaled, squeezed my eyes shut, and exhaled.

"Okay." I crossed my arms over my chest. "I'm not drunk, high, or otherwise inebriated. I see you as a human. I saw you as a dog—"

Joaquin tilted his head to the side. "Eh, I'd consider myself more of a wolf-coyote hybrid."

I blinked, filing that fact away. I turned to Lotte. "You knew this whole time." My eyebrows shot up. "Are you also—"

Joaquin quipped, "She wishes." Lotte shot him a look and he winked at her. He continued, "My buddy Yanric, yes. General contractor by day. Hangs with me at night. Very strategic guy. Your kind of people."

"People," I said. I pressed my lips together, unsure which of my emotions to let loose. Confusion and irritation fought for dominance over resistance and overwhelm. At the core of each, however, was cold, clear fear.

I shook my head. No amount of breath work would wipe the visuals of the last hour from my mind. If I was going to reckon with this reality, I wanted its bulk. All at once.

"Alright," I said, more for my own centering. "I have questions, starting with who is June?"

We wound our way out of town, taking Highway 69 east out of the valley. I clung to Joaquin's shoulders, using his form as a windshield. My fingertips froze in the night air.

At the park, Lotte promised to catch up. Within five minutes, I heard a second motorcycle draw close. The shop owner rode with her arms looped around the other driver. They flanked us as we turned off the main road.

Overhead, stars scattered across the sky, a handful of jacks strewn over an inky backdrop. We skirted a neighborhood nestled in the hills along a dry creek bed. The farther we went, the greater the distance between houses. Yard lights served as buoys in the night.

At the base of a dirt driveway, Joaquin slowed the bike to a stop. The second motorcycle parked behind us. Its driver flipped up their face shield. *Iris.* Everyone was suspect at this point.

"I'll watch the bikes," she said, as the only one left to dismount. "In case that old bat uses you all for target practice."

I followed Joaquin and Lotte, unease mounting with every step. Old bicycle wheels lined the gravel driveway. Metal sculptures, conglomerations of old bike parts, hung from trees. Light reflected off a bike mirror, sending a beam across the driveway. More wheels, handlebars, and horns welded together became fence posts. Bike baskets of every shape and size served as planters. Reflectors staked into the soft-packed earth guided us straight for the garage.

Lotte marched up to the open side door, knocked twice, and stepped in.

"We'll hang back," Joaquin said, his hand extended to hold me back. "If nothing comes flying out of that door in the next minute or so, we'll consider it safe."

There was a clanking of metal hitting cement. A heated conversation. Then Lotte popped her head out to wave us in.

As we approached, I heard a guttural voice. "Then we're square, right?"

Lotte replied. "We're square."

As I brushed past Lotte, she whispered so only I could hear, "Until the next time you need me, you old goat."

Joaquin stepped in behind me, his voice booming, hands spread wide. "Hello, June. It's been far too long."

In the cavernous room, I spotted a figure addressing a bicycle with a wrench and plenty of gusto. The frame was up on a stand. From a workbench, she traded tools and went back to work.

Oh, great. Her.

The woman had a long, thick silver braid. She made gray look healthy, luxurious. On my own head, white hair popped up in patches, the marks of a badger. On her, it was classy.

She spun one of the wheels and watched it on the bias. Satisfied with the spin, she tossed a tool onto her work bench and faced us. June pursed her lips. "Not long enough by my book."

"Always a pleasure," Joaquin replied, and gave her a low bow.

"Heard those godsdamned bikes a mile away. You think I wouldn't know you're coming? Like a stampede of elephants."

"While I love our little chats," Lotte said, "we're here for a consultation."

June put her hands on her hips. "Promise you'll listen?"

"If we like the answer, yes," Joaquin said.

"We will," Lotte said, shooting him a look.

June glanced at me, then back to them, one eyebrow lifted.

"Fine. But I'm not going easy on her. I don't care if she's a Kohl." Joaquin made a guttural sound, a warning, and June glared at him. "Don't tell me she doesn't know?"

Before Joaquin could counter the accusation, Lotte stepped in. "She knows—some. What she needed to move forward. Tell her whatever she needs to know. We won't get in the way."

Assured by Lotte's words, June rolled up her sleeves, cracked her neck, and approached me. "What were her signs?"

"Crows. Moths. Visions of death. Reanimation." Lotte didn't look at me, and June never looked away.

The older woman drew closer. She peered at me as one would peer at a butterfly pinned to a piece of foam. Checking for parts, considering identification.

She walked a slow circle around me, one hand outstretched, palm facing outward. "For how long?"

Lotte looked at me. "A few weeks. Hints from childhood."

"Nothing else?"

I balked. "Like what?" As if those things hadn't been odd enough.

June stared, as though disbelieving her lot was to talk with someone so ignorant as myself. She shook her head. "I've got bikes to build."

Lotte pleaded, "Remember our deal."

June sighed. "Fine. Start with the dreams," she told me. "All of them."

"I had dreams as a kid. Dark dreams. Not scary, really. But psychological. Like people were tugging on me for attention, to hold their stories. Now though, when people brush by me, I see a scene from their lives...and their deaths. Like a daydream."

"What kind of people—everyone?"

I shook my head. "Not all of them. I get nothing from Lotte."

"Interesting, but not impressive," June said, appraising me like a side of beef. She looked back at Lotte. "Why should I care?"

Lotte lifted an eyebrow and gave June a sardonic smile. "Diana's keeper is asking me for a purpose? Think of Hollis."

"I'm not in that business anymore," June said.

"What business is that?" The words slipped out before I could limit the harsh rebuke.

June whirled to glare at me. "Charity," she spat.

Her words reached me like a slap, a stinging rejection. What had I done to this woman? That she didn't want to help was clear. Her animosity, however, was undeserved. I didn't know her–didn't want to know her. Hands on hips, I ran my tongue over my teeth, nodded once, and turned to leave.

"June," Joaquin called from a workbench. "What happened here?"

Her attention distracted, the woman shuffled to where he stood. I saw a slight hitch in her right hip.

"A new ghost bike," she said. "Toddler."

Curiosity piqued, I looked over at the bench. Bike parts lay out atop a sheet of plastic. They'd been spray painted white, the paint drying. I stared down at the bent handlebars that matched a mangled wheel. The metal twists sickened my stomach. "What's a ghost bike?" Inside, I knew.

"What remains when the rider is gone," June said, her eyes on mine.

I looked back at the bike. Pictured Patrick on his tricycle, careening around the driveway, delighted with his own power of propulsion. He'd been an astronaut, the bike his rocket ship. A lump formed in my throat, and I looked away.

"June runs the bike shop in town," Lotte said. "The whole cycling community, really. They make memorials when a rider is...killed."

"Too little, too late," June said, her voice bitter and

measured. "But haunting the memories of the guilty is the least I can do."

I looked away. I hadn't known this child, their mother, but empathy gripped my heart. June watched me, a twitch in the corner of one eye. A tattoo spider crawled up the side of her neck, its web peeking out of her collar. She reconsidered me. Her dark eyes sparkled, a decision made. "Touch it," she said.

I frowned. "Excuse me?"

"Touch the bike," she said, like a kid on the playground, issuing a dare.

Lotte intervened. "I don't think she—"

"Do it."

I looked at Joaquin. He'd leaned back against the workbench, the ankle of one boot crossed over the other. He nodded at me, stating his opinion.

Unsettled, I faced the bike—or what was left of it. My lip puckered, an unbidden response. I lifted one hand, then took a steadying breath. This woman, this night, was a ridiculous exercise. The sooner I ended this foolish errand, the earlier I could put it all behind me. I needed sleep, a fresh start. *Home.*

I swallowed, exhaled, then rested my hand on the tiny bicycle seat.

A jolt shot up my arm. Cloudless sky, then a peel of laughter. My laughter. A shriek, then a screech of tires. Sobbing. Sirens, the broadside of an ambulance. The face of a firefighter, a sheen of sweat across his brow. Blackness.

"EJ! EJ?" Joaquin's face swam in front of me. "Ember James. Can you hear me?"

I groaned. I couldn't shake the images. I clutched at my stomach and rolled to my side, willing the sick to abate.

"Hedgerider," June pronounced, a note of satisfaction in her statement.

"She's breathing," Lotte said, from somewhere far away. "She'll recover."

I wasn't sure I would. The pain of the visions laced my blood with electric pulses that slowed but wouldn't abate. These were memories I didn't want, but I couldn't unsee them. Not now, not ever.

June's shoes stepped close to my forehead. From above, she said, "I'll help. For Hollis, for a price." Her voice was measured, calculating.

"June, come on now." Joaquin softened his tone, angling for a bargain. "You can see she's got something. Why not nurture it?"

I was back to my status as a butcher's offering. I opened my mouth to protest, but my mouth was too dry for protests.

"Name it," Lotte said.

June's reply was quick, decided. "Find the bastard who did this. End him."

The ride back to the square was silent. My teeth chattered in the cold while my mind whirled. I'd been auctioned off to a woman. My services, what they were, were still a mystery—at least to me.

The desire to know fought a bitter battle with the need to forget.

I made no protest when the bikes took the alleyway into the atrium. I swung my leg up and over the bike. Weary, I trudged to my back stoop, calling over my shoulder. "I'm getting my notebook. There'd better be a plate of dirty fries and a glass of champagne with my name on it when I get there."

"Dirty?" This was from Joaquin.

"Ask Iris."

Ten minutes later, my requirements were met.

"Not bad," I said, tipping the bubbly down my throat. I offered Iris my first smile of the evening. "I like it."

Iris beamed. "Boss let me order a few samples from the distributor. That's my favorite. Some musician imports it from France, sells it out of his winery."

I appraised the glass, the soft yellow liquid sparkling within. Behind the bar, I spotted three other champagne flutes, a new addition to the glassware.

"Thank you," I said. "You didn't have to start carrying it." I flicked my eyes up toward the office spaces. There'd been no sign of Lotte, Joaquin, or Ansel since I'd arrived. The fries were hot, though, and perfect. I groaned with pleasure at the pile of tastiness.

"Carnitas, white cheddar, and some smoked green chiles," Iris said. "Might have to make those a special. They smell like heaven."

"Want some?"

Iris shook her head. "Vegan. Doesn't mean I couldn't come up with my own version, though."

"They taste amazing."

Iris breezed through conversation as though the last few hours hadn't happened. As though we hadn't ridden back from that awful woman's lair, me with a burden of altogether too much new information.

"You aren't the only customer with—elevated—tastes," she said. "Nothing wrong with adding some classy aspects to the place. Ansel even serves brunch now. He's a killer cook."

Still no movement from above. "He sounds like a workaholic."

"Never leaves," Iris said, a flat response. "This place is his everything. S'alright though, he's a big draw for customers."

"How so?"

She smiled at me. "You've seen him. More muscles than

sense. Fresh-from-bed hair. Moody as hell, and growing more so over the last few weeks. It's like something's eating away at his sanity. Women in this place—and some of the men—love that."

I raised an eyebrow. "You being one of them?"

Iris laughed. "Not my cup of tea. You can know a painting is fine art without wanting to hang it in your house."

"Truth," I said. I shoved a forkful of fries in my mouth and chewed.

Lotte descended the stairs, her black-clad figure approaching the bar. I raised my eyebrows at Iris in the universal expression for—*How about that painting?* Iris gave a slight nod but mouthed, "Taken."

Lotte took the stool next to mine. "How are the fries?"

"Incredible. Have some."

She wrinkled her nose. "More of an onion ring kinda gal," she said.

Iris refilled my glass and slid a second one in front of Lotte.

"So, are we going to talk about what happened?" I reached for my notebook.

"Better," she said. "When you finish eating, we're going dancing."

Half an hour later, we were inside Plush. Bryce was nowhere to be seen, but the club was crawling with people. Bass thumped through the giant speakers and bodies moved to the beat. A strobe light caught freeze frames of the crowd. Most seemed young, college-aged or newer to adult freedom. Sprinkled throughout were a few people my own age. Still, the target group was obvious.

I leaned over to shout in Lotte's ear. "What are we doing here again?"

"Looking for someone," was all she said.

I'd followed her suggestion to wear all black. All manner of spandex gave me curves I'd forgotten, and a swipe of lipstick painted me on the soft side of saucy. A wink from a nearby dancer grinding air had me reconsidering my discomfort.

Lotte ordered us a pair of drinks, handing me some kind of pink swill in a clear plastic cup. I lifted an eyebrow, as trying to talk over the music was pointless. She held up her own cup and winked before taking a sip.

From the stage, the DJ slowed the record to a softer beat. With deft hands, he shifted some controls while spinning others, and a rattling sound layered into the mix. Massive headphones sided his face. When he looked my way, I saw the telltale red-rimmed eyes and looked away. He was fuzzy at the edges, ephemeral like the haunting techno tune that blared through the speakers. I scanned the crowd. Every other dancer had the same, telltale signs. What kind of business did Bryce run?

Lotte was at my shoulder. She leaned close to yell in my ear. "Keep an eye out."

"For what?"

"Anyone worth touching," she said and gave me a knowing look. I swallowed.

She held her cup high in the air and maneuvered her way through the crowd. Toward the bathroom, to a hook up, I didn't know. While I waited for her return, I faced the room and gulped.

I took a harder look at those gathered. There were women of all levels of decoration. Some in slick bodysuits like Lotte, others in slouchy jeans, crop tops baring the bottom of bare breasts. Dancers ran hands over each other and themselves, bumping and sliding against each other. Coupling and recoupling seemed to shift with the music.

I took a sip of the drink and with no one to talk to, I took another. One dancer held his hands out to me like welcoming ocean waves, drawing me in. He had short, spiky blue hair and a nose ring. Cute, but half my age. I shook my head no but smiled. My type or not, it didn't suck to be asked.

Whether from the liquid encouragement or the shock of cheap sugar hitting my bloodstream, I began to move my feet, joining those on the edge of the dance floor. Bodies moved around me as we took in the music.

I spotted Lotte across the room, talking with the long-haired woman I recognized from the coffee shop, their faces inches apart. I didn't like being left out but couldn't find a way to force myself in from this distance.

I took another sip of the putrid concoction in my hand and stepped farther into the madness. In the middle of the dance floor was sweat and raw energy. Out of their mind with the rhythm, fueled by another substance, or both, I wasn't sure. One thing I did know, however, was that I was surrounded by the Fallen.

A dancer brushed me, static electricity zapping the air between us. He looked at me, confusion in his bloodshot eyes. I offered a smile, a distraction. He pressed on. I did my best to maintain a buffer as I wove through the dancers toward Lotte, aware that to touch another would expose me further.

At the edge of the group, I spotted a couple pushed up against the wall. They made out with the fury of the starved, their faces locked together. He held her ass in his hands, buttressing her with his weight. The man ended the kiss only to trail a line of others down her neck. He ground against her, and in that moment, I realized her underwear dangled from one heel, his fly unbuckled.

I turned from the scene, an awkward voyeur, only to run smack into another person. He caught me and clutched my forearms. "Easy there," he shouted into the din. I froze in place, as a flood of images played in my mind. A jungle. A blade slicing through the air. There was a hollow cry, then flames and blackness.

I stared at him, and he blinked, his lighthearted smile shifting to suspicion.

I backed away, or tried to, but he tightened his grip. He looked into my eyes. "Do I know you?"

I looked away. "Bathroom," I squeaked, and hooked my thumb toward the back of the venue.

He released me but watched me go. I turned, certain his eyes followed my back.

The pink liquid sloshing in my bladder propelled me toward the actual restroom. A line hung out the door. Lotte intercepted me, dragging me down a short hallway.

"We have to go," she said, angling for the back door. She dragged me past the two restrooms.

"But I have to tell you. I think I—"

"Not now," she hissed. Her panic sobered me as I passed a bulletin board covered in business cards, a prominent flier for Beckett Farms in the center. *New in town? In search of a brotherhood? Jobs available just outside of town.* There was a number and a picture of an idyllic field of wildflowers.

"Where are we going?"

"Out the back," she shouted.

We were almost to the door when Bryce came in, a cigarette behind one ear, a woman dangling off one arm.

Bryce said, "Bar's that way, ladies," and pointed over our shoulders.

Lotte laughed, a fake chuckle, and said, "My bad. If the bartender keeps nailing those shots, I won't be able to find my way home."

"I'll point you in the right direction," Bryce said. He released his hold on the woman who glared at the two of us.

Bryce put a hand at the small of Lotte's back and ushered her forward. I tagged along behind.

"Ever the gentleman," Lotte said, playing the part of a grateful drunk. She reached back for my hand. When I took it, she pressed a piece of paper against my palm. I closed my fingers around it, then stuffed it into my bra. I was fairly certain that whatever it was, no one would go looking for it there.

The music, exciting and young before, became a sickening rhythm, grating at my skull. We followed Bryce through the club as he nudged customers out of the way. He offered a high-five to some, an ass slap to others. *Gross.* Where was the man who wanted an elevated clientele?

A woman bent over in our pathway and heaved, the contents of her stomach splattering over the floor. Bryce pulled back on Lotte's arm. He waved a bartender over with a mop. When the man got close, Bryce yelled, "Clean this—and her—up. Then get her another drink." He winked at the woman, then ushered us forward.

"I thought you were shifting your style," I shouted into Bryce's ear.

He steered us toward the door. "This is my bread and butter, for now. My plans have—expanded."

Gone was the Bryce of the previous night, the one I'd danced with, the one who appreciated the cultured, the calm. In his place was a sleazy bar owner who exploited his clients' weaknesses.

"There you are, ladies." He ushered us through the front door and leaned out. "Turn left at the light," he said to Lotte. Then he pointed down the sidewalk. "And you, EJ, should go that way."

"Thank you," Lotte gushed to Bryce. She gave me an exaggerated hug, slinging her arm around my neck. When her lips were near my ear, she whispered, "Half an hour. Me to you." She smacked a kiss on my cheek and stumbled off, affecting the walk of someone who'd had far more than she could handle.

I blew her a kiss and headed down the sidewalk. At the stoplight, I turned to look back. Bryce and the man with the mop stood in the doorway, watching me. I gave a little wave and sauntered on, affecting my own sway. At the shop's door, I fumbled with my keys, still playing the part in case.

Inside, I pressed my back to the door and exhaled, closing my eyes. The moths took flight from a leaf nearby, and my heart fluttered to the beat of their wings.

A knock at the back door sent my pulse straight into my throat.

I hurried through the shop, the long leaves of Mariette caressing my legs as I passed.

Instead of Lotte, it was Joaquin. "Boss's office in ten." Without waiting for an answer, he dashed down the steps.

"Joaquin," I called.

He paused at the next stoop.

"What if I said no?" I hadn't planned the question. I wasn't sure what I wanted for the answer. I only knew in my gut that it needed to be asked.

He cocked his head and a nefarious grin slid across his face. "No one ever has." Then he was gone.

I discarded my purse on the kitchen counter, flipped on a few lights, pulled a sweatshirt over my skin-tight top, and resigned myself to another late night. Seven minutes to go.

I slipped my hand into my bra to dig out the paper. A sticky note. Bright pink and crumpled. I unfolded it, then smoothed its surface against the counter's edge, the way I used to flatten dollar bills to fit into my high school's vending machines.

In blue ink, the only note was an oval, studded with hand drawn stars. In reflex, I crushed the paper and shoved it in my back pocket.

Whatever meeting would take place in five minutes would include me and all my questions.

Finally.

~

Ansel avoided my gaze. He paced the short lane between his desk and another door that led off to some unknown destination. Four strides, turn, four back.

Joaquin splayed out over one of the captain's chairs facing Ansel's desk, a toothpick between his teeth. Silver detailing at the heel of his boots shone in the low lighting. Lotte had yet to arrive and the shifter—for that's as close as I got to calling him something other than human—assumed a casual pose yet had all his senses trained on the door.

After Iris handed me another flute of bubbles, she was gone. I was alone in a wolf den, with little more than champagne to keep me company as Ansel and Joaquin talked circles around the problem.

"I knew it was Bryce," Ansel said, gnashing his teeth. "That prick has been harboring them for weeks. Months, maybe."

"You knew it was Bryce," Joaquin echoed. With nimble lips, he shifted the toothpick to the other side of his mouth. I fought the urge to pluck the stick and toss it.

Ansel clenched both fists. "I'm going to smash every speaker in the place."

Joaquin sat up. "How about we wait to see what Lotte snagged? Maybe it's something we can use."

"Where is she?" Ansel flopped into his desk chair, the furniture groaning under his weight.

"I know what it is," I said, tired of being ignored. "Seven stars in an oval shape. On a note."

Soundless, Joaquin shoved a pad of paper my way. "Technically," Joaquin said, "he's violated exactly zero percent of the Concordat."

"The what?"

Ansel ignored me. "Don't you think I know that?" He threw his words across the room like darts. "I helped write the damn thing. He's going to, though. I can feel it."

Joaquin shook his head. "Can't start a war over intuition, boss."

"Regardless. He is unchecked. Yanric watched him take a bump of elixir tonight."

Joaquin had mentioned a Yanric, but I was officially lost. "Your friend works at Plush?"

Joaquin nodded in cheerful agreement. "Undercover." He went still with realization. "Wait, did you see him? And I mean, *see him*, see him."

"Don't think so. I only touched one person, other than Bryce, and he was definitely one of the Fallen." Ansel emitted a low growl. I ignored him. "What does he look like?"

"Hair like mine, darker skin. Likes silver jewelry, too. DJs mostly."

I shook my head. "Nope. The guy behind the turntable was someone else. The one who bumped me was floor staff. Both had the eyes."

"Yanric uses special eye drops," Joaquin said. "To fit in. Been on the job a week and says everyone is trying to ply him with elixir."

"Elixir?" But they'd moved on.

"We could head back tomorrow," Lotte said, entering the office. "Try to get more intel."

"I know which guy it is," I insisted, swallowing my revulsion as I remembered the visions of a bicycle bent on the asphalt. "It wasn't Bryce," I said, a weak rebuke. A part of me wanted to cling to the memory of our dance, not realign with this picture of a dealer.

"He's the leader," Ansel insisted.

"But he didn't hit the kid. You're justifying clearing out his bar for the mistake of a single person."

"This runs deeper than you know," Ansel growled.

Joaquin frowned and volleyed his gaze between the two of us. "So, what's the plan—we follow him home?"

"Too risky," Ansel said.

"Then what's your brilliant idea?"

"Lotte asks him out. You jump him after the date."

"After?" Lotte protested.

Joaquin smiled. "Got it. I take out each employee as they leave. Simple, efficient.

"That I would help with," Lotte said.

Ansel swung on both of them. "Wouldn't Bryce notice if his staff disappears, one by one?"

Joaquin parried. "Would you?"

Ansel slammed his palm on the table. "Of course I would!"

"What's the name of the new waitress, the one Iris hired?"

"I don't...I..."

"See?" Joaquin smirked.

Ansel pounded the desk. "That's not fair! I gave Iris permission to use her best judgment. I've been a little busy trying to clean up her"–he jerked his chin my way–"mess."

"Hey," I said, shooting him a glare. "I resent that."

"Fine," Ansel said through his teeth. "Then what's *your* brilliant idea?"

"We could ask around, see where he goes when not at Plush."

"Might as well put a target on your back. One of those big red and white ones," Joaquin said. I huffed and crossed my arms.

"We don't have time for this!" Ansel's shout echoed off the walls.

"You don't have time for this," Lotte whispered. The air in the room stilled.

"Hold up," I said. "I can't believe that between the three of you, nothing resembles an actual plan. Do you always just throw darts to see which solution sticks?"

Joaquin grinned and winked at Lotte. She attempted to hide her own smile. Ansel glowered at me, palms pressed to the desk surface. He held the position of a predator ready to pounce. "Our plan was to own the godsdamn Apothecary!"

"Boss," Joaquin said, his voice a soft check.

"That isn't the only way," Lotte said, a warning.

"I don't give a good godsdamn—or whatever it is you all keep saying—what you thought was going to happen."

Ansel's face reddened at my words, a pulse and his neck bulging. I didn't care. I'd played along with this charade long enough.

"I also don't give a shit about your so-called timeline. I have to save my store from people like you taking it without anyone fighting over ways to help me." I swallowed a sob in my throat and turned to leave.

"June might have answers," Lotte said.

It was late. I was crabby. I might have snapped. "I don't care if I never come within five feet of that woman again. Or any of you, really. I have a business to save and an event to plan. So, if anyone needs me, I'll be busy next door with this thing called strategy."

Ansel threw his chair across the room where it smashed against the wall. "You don't know the first thing about strategy!" He was on his feet, heaving, a rumble in the floorboards below us. "I had a godsdamned strategy until your happy ass moved in!"

There was a pounding at the office door before it swung inward. Iris appeared, her face white as a ghost. She looked from Ansel to me, then back, her eyes wide.

"Boss, we have a problem."

"What is it?" Ansel asked, fury dripping from his words.

"I'll handle it," Joaquin said, getting up to follow Iris. He turned to Ansel, his voice quiet. "Try my suggestion," he said, then disappeared down the stairs.

"As much fun as playing referee could be, I think I'd better sit this round out," Lotte said, and followed after Joaquin.

I didn't look at Ansel. Couldn't look at him. I zipped my coat up, stuffed my hands in my pockets, and followed Lotte.

"EJ—wait. I have to stay."

I paused my retreat, hand on the threshold, back to the man. Half my brain screamed *Go!* while the other half hungered to hear him out. I said nothing as waves of heat rolled off him and over me.

"Have you ever been trapped?" he asked from behind me. "Stuck someplace you didn't want to be?"

I had. I was. I listened.

His voice grew closer. Floorboards creaked on his approach. "Have you ever had to pay for someone else's mistake?"

"I have," I said, and turned around.

A raw hunger lit his eyes, like a dog on a chain. The man was less than a foot away, and I felt every inch of that distance. We were at an impasse, and the impossibility tugged at my chest. My eyes fell to his lips, the mustache above, a brief beard below. I fought the desire to reach out to stroke his chin. His wavy hair was knotted at the base of his skull, a few tendrils hanging loose. He whispered now, the air between us crackling. "Have you ever wanted a different life?"

"I have."

"Then hear me now." Ansel closed the gap between us until his face was inches from mine. He smelled of cedar trees after the rain. If I tilted my head, my lips would brush his. His breath was hot on my ear as he whispered. "You have freedom,

Ember James. You could walk out of here, step onto a plane, and never see any of us again. I want that. To make my *own* choices. I've been chained to this place for decades, since long before I knew it. You have so much potential, woman. So much freedom to do whatever you want, and you can't even see it. Instead you squander an innate ability and blame those of us who seek freedom through you."

I reacted without thinking. I shoved him. Hard.

He didn't move. That is what happens when you press up on the human equivalent of a brick wall.

"Feel better when you hit me?" His voice was husky, low. "Do it again. Give it to me, I can take it."

I landed one punch to his chest that faltered, softening before the blow. I hung my head, defeated by his words. Was he right—was I whining about needing change but too cowardly to do anything about it? "I'm...worn out from fighting. I'm too damn old for this drama."

"You say old, I say mature." He bit his lip, watching me.

I ignored the rush in my belly. Pressed forward with my questions. "So, if I'm to buy any of this, and I'm not saying I do, you're saying you can't leave Morgan's."

"Correct."

"What does that have to do with me?"

Ansel reached behind me, pressing closer. The door closed with a soft click. He didn't step back. "I am a Guardian, chosen by my queen. A watcher. It is my destiny until I earn my freedom."

Ansel's blue eyes met mine, pleading for understanding. My resolve crumpled under the increased proximity. There was something so animal, so base level with the way my body responded to his. Called to him. His eyes dropped to my neck, then locked with mine again, and I wanted to jump up into his arms and wrap my legs around his waist. I pictured him nuzzling my chest and I nipped out, thankful for the jacket I still wore. Why are the most infuriating people some of the most seductive? This man had all but thrown a chair at me and I was picturing jumping his bones. This had to stop.

"Maybe choose a new destiny," I said, breaking eye contact.

Ansel grabbed both my shoulders in his massive hands. "I can't. Don't you get it?" As I watched, his eyes tumbled from steel to funnel cloud gray. "We need you to do your job. *I* need you."

I was officially confused, a little ticked, and plenty scared. This hulking man changed at the blink of an eye. I shrugged his hands off my arms. "I'm not here to serve you."

Ansel's face fell. His reply was cut off when Joaquin burst into the room. "Boss, we've got two bodies in the atrium. Both of them innocents. Request backup."

"I'm coming." Without another glance my way, he moved past me to the door.

I turned on my heel to follow. *Bodies?*

Joaquin recited the details like a weather report, the din of white noise in the pub muting his voice. "Two women. Both in club gear. One unknown, one is—was—your new server."

"Gods."

I followed them down the stairs and out the back door.

In front of us, under the cover of darkness, lay two women, half on, half off the steps. Each appeared as though sleeping, at however awkward an angle. One had bruises around her neck. Blood gathered in a puddle at the base of the second woman's skull. I shuddered.

Joaquin was the first to speak. "Yanric saw them both tonight. Came together."

"Are they..."

Ansel turned, noticing me for the first time. Gone was the husky voice, the pleading. In its place was the cold, calculating, cruel talk of business. "Dead? Would we be out here if it was just a tea party?"

I shot him a murderous look. *"Fallen,"* I said.

"The Fallen are male," Joaquin said, in professor mode. He gestured to the huddled shapes, limp and silent. "These are their conquests."

The pitch of my voice started to rise. "I recognize her." I pointed to one of the figures. "She'd been out back with Bryce when Lotte exited the office." I swallowed my impulse to call the police. I stared at the two women before me. Hair splayed across the cobblestones. A gold hoop there, a missing shoe. One purse, half open, a phone buzzing somewhere within.

"I did find this," Joaquin said. He held up a thin silver chain with a feather pendant.

"Disgusting," Ansel said. "Foolish women."

I reached out to grasp the tiny pendulum and slow its dangling arc. When my fingers touched the cool metal, the air went still. I saw the crowd, dancing. Injection in the bathroom stall. A shirtless man, pressing himself against me, his red eyes devouring me with his gaze as I held on to nubs on his back. My face against the wall in the alley as he took me from behind. His hands wrap around my throat, and my vision fades in and out. A blinding light, then blackness.

Ansel looked at me, his eyes desperate. "What did you see?"

"He killed her," I said, then stifled a sob.

"They aren't the first," Joaquin said. "But it's damn brazen dropping them off here."

"It's a message," Ansel said, getting in my face. "Can't you see that, at least?"

"He dropped them on your doorstep, not mine."

Joaquin put his hands out to separate the two of us. "Break it up. I've got a mess to clean and you two are in a pointless pissing match."

I was numb. The stress and overwhelm of the evening were so great I could barely register my own hands in front of me.

Ansel cleared his throat. "What you did just now—I thought you could only work with people?"

"Same." I flexed my fingers. "But it worked with the bike and now the necklace. I'd love to explain any of this to anyone, especially myself. Then I would pay good money I don't have to make it all stop."

Ansel cleared his throat and stared down at the cobblestones. Joaquin was on his phone a few paces away. I heard him ask for a cleaning service, a rush job.

"I know how you feel about me. Believe me, it's more than mutual," Ansel said. "But you have something we need. Something that could help me. What would it take to make it worth your while?"

FOURTEEN

ed. Blue. Red and blue. Back to red.

R I flicked the switch that changed the LED colors on the giant light I'd installed over a plant table. With a brand-new drill and only one hole I hadn't meant to make, I'd hung the light from a solid cross beam. Now, consulting the manual, I learned one color was for flowers, the other for growth. I hadn't the slightest idea which of my plants were meant to flower—but in case some did, I went for purple. Flowers are nice, but growth is important. *Perhaps I should spend a few hours below these lights.*

In between people turning into animals, dead bodies piling up, and puzzling over my bizarre visions, I'd returned to puttering over the plants. Call it a last-ditch effort, call it therapy, but I gave it a shot.

Despite my best intentions, however, leaves continued to curl. Stems wilted. It was as though the natural world fought my every attempt to assist.

I paced the shop, reading every conflicting piece of advice about houseplant care I could find on any forum that shared them. Water. Don't water. Buy these super fancy clay-like rocks and throw out all your soil. Now water them. Go dig up your own soil under a full moon on the second Tuesday of a tiger year and strain it through cheesecloth. At this rate, I didn't know how anyone won this game.

Gaven found me frowning over a speaker, trying first one and then another song from a playlist on my phone.

"Are you alright?" he asked. He took in the multiple, half-drunk cups of coffee scattered about the shop, tools strewn across the counter, and the blazing beam of colorful light in one corner, as concern wrinkled his brow.

I faced him. "Miles Davis or Taylor Swift? Bach is calming and soothing, though, and they seemed to like 80s rap. They say plants can feel vibrations, but that seems ridiculous, right?" I barreled on, not allowing him a chance to respond. "I've got music and lights going. It's practically a disco in here. I've added those little capsules, too. The ones you stick into the sand and the kind you scatter on top of the sand. I've alter-nated between fine droplet misters and soaking. I made a chart to keep track." I held up my documentation in full, color-coded glory. "They have to start growing soon, don't they? At least some of them?"

Gaven watched me like one would watch a wounded wild animal. "Maybe let's sit down for a minute. Should I make a fresh pot?"

Sudden exhaustion crashed over me as I slumped onto the stool. The soft burble of the pot lulled my senses. I dropped my head into my hands and rubbed at my face.

Gaven dumped the stale coffee, gave the mugs a rinse, and refilled them with fresh brew. He added a splash of almond milk and a squirt of agave nectar to one of the mugs. *When did he pick up on my habits?* Gaven wiped the bottom of the mug with a rag before pressing it into my hands. "Ansel said he made you an offer."

"He did," I said.

"I think you should take it."

"On his side, are we?"

Gaven shrugged. "He's got good reasons. But he needs to make it worth your while."

I sipped my coffee. "Thank you for this."

"About that opening?"

"Yeah?" I worried he'd cancel on me. I attracted one disaster after another, so this would be far from a surprise. "Do I have to wear a shirt and tie?" He hooked a finger into his collar and tugged at the fabric.

"No, but trendy streetwear might not fit the event. How about all black?"

"I can handle a sweater for a night," Gaven said. "What do you need me to do?"

"Ring people up, wrap up their purchases. Keep an eye on the food. For all I know, five people will show up, in which case then I'll need you to help me eat and drink all the leftovers."

"No torture there," he said. I smiled.

The door to the shop opened, the bell stilled as though by an invisible force. June. She locked the door behind herself and flipped the sign to *Closed*.

"We're open," I said, frowning.

June ignored me. She moved to each of the windows in turn, facing them and muttered something under her breath. The glass shimmered, a brief flash. She continued toward the back of the store, repeating the process as she went before mounting the staircase.

"What are you doing?"

She called down from the loft. "The fact that you don't know is an embarrassment to your family. Your mother and uncle will be rolling over in their graves."

I bristled. "You knew my mother?"

"Of her," June said.

This explained exactly nothing.

"I've been doing this long before you arrived," June said, "and will continue long after you turn tail and run. It was easier when there were two of us, but I get on."

Gears whirred to life in my mind, clicking into place. "You're the reason Ansel can't come in here. You set the wards," I said.

June descended the stairs, one step at a time, a smile of satisfaction across her face. "Hollis did, too. Before. Mucked it up in the end. Weirmen shouldn't take the task lightly, not even your addle-headed uncle."

"We don't speak ill of the dead in here. At least not of my family."

"The first reasonable thing to come from your mouth," she said. "There's a small chance that with training, you could become something to reckon with. Then the rest of us wouldn't have to babysit while you play shopkeeper."

I bit back the host of swear words at my lips. "I think you should leave."

Gaven rose behind me. June noticed and scoffed. "For someone so dead set against the realities of this realm, you sure keep an interesting bodyguard."

"She asked you to leave, June," Gaven said.

June laughed. "Or what?" She snapped, and a tiny flame appeared between her thumb and forefinger. She held it toward a dry, wrinkled leaf. "One parlor trick from this old witch and this place would go up like kindling." She rubbed her fingers together to stifle the fire.

My hand holding the mug shook. I set down my coffee and crossed my arms. "What do you want?"

"I don't care what Ansel offered you," she said. "His bargain with hell's princess is none of my concern. You need to either become what you were meant to be or put this place in your taillights for all our sakes. Life is too short for me to keep cleaning up after your family."

"No one asked you to," I said.

"They didn't have to. That's what makes us different. I take my gifts as a mark of pride. I don't flap about like a fish out of water," she added on her way to the door. "You know where to find me."

In June's wake, the sign flipped back to *Open*. Through the window, I watched her mount a mountain bike and ride off.

"Don't let her get to you," Gaven said. "She's protective, that's all."

"Why do you keep defending my enemies?"

"It's not about sides. They're not used to sharing leadership, that's all. What's that phrase your kind like to say—too many chefs in one kitchen? When you fight so long, everything becomes a battle."

I reached out to the fern June had threatened. A few remaining fronds stretched toward the windows, tiger-striped with shades of lighter green. The rest had crumbled. I stroked the brown tip, the desiccated frond crackling on contact. Life and death were two sides of the same coin, one as easy to land on as the other.

June wasn't wrong, not fully. When people waffled, when they blundered around, ruining the work of others, they were in the way. I wasn't usually one of those people, and that stung. I thought of a well-meaning mother-in-law who inserts herself into wedding plans. The corporate boss who sends a salami basket to his vegan employees. Surprise parties for people with heart conditions.

Maybe I should step down, step back. Perhaps the shop deserved new ownership. I'd lived through enough drama. Married and divorced. Raised a son. At what point did I get to settle into a job that could carry me toward a peaceful retirement? I didn't want to end up like June, bitter and alone at the edge of town. I wanted to enjoy my years, watch my son take hold of his life, and make it bloom.

Memories flooded my mind. Building sandcastles at the beach in my strawberry swimsuit while my mom hunted for sand dollars. Stirring pasta into hot water with my dad looking on. My uncle's cheer of joy when I handed him a macaroni necklace I'd made at school. I pictured my son at four years old, smashing half a peanut butter and jelly sandwich into his hair, giggling with glee. Standing at his first easel, holding a chubby crayon, sketching a city of rectangles. The bazillion plastic, colored bricks that paved the floor of our apartment as he constructed one skyscraper after another. Patrick, beaming with pride, in his gown on graduation day. I'd managed to create a rich life, despite, and perhaps in some ways because of, a slew of complications. My mother's death. The implosion of my marriage. Getting laid off and losing my apartment. Why would I let a little of the extraordinary scare me now? I was a woman, and I'd lived through hell. I would do the same again and rock every minute.

"EJ!" Gaven's face was pale, his eyes saucers. He pointed to my hand. "Look!"

I'd been stroking the fern, an absentminded soothing motion. Within my hand lay the frond, green from base to tip, unfurled and luxurious. At the crown of the plant, two more fiddlehead spirals began to unravel.

"Water it," Gaven said, his voice urgent. "Then do it again —whatever you just did."

I followed his direction. This time I thought of my dinner with Patrick before he left. He promised to learn to make croissants, my favorite pastry. "I'll make them every Sunday when I'm back," he'd said. My heart soared with pride for my son, a longing born from my love as his mom.

"You're doing it!"

I looked down to find the fronds unrolling like green carpets with ruffled edges.

"Let's try another one," he said.

"I'm not a side show act," I said, more than a little afraid of my newfound ability.

Gaven blinked. "I don't know what that is, but I think you're in denial about how awesome this is. How about a palm? Or—"

Gaven consulted the range of choices around the shop. I was unsure of whether to risk a plant closest to death as it was already a lost cause or one so vibrant I couldn't hurt it if I failed.

"How about this one?" In his hands, Gaven held the clump of dried plant from Patrick.

Before I could protest, Gaven plopped it in my hands and said, "Do your thing." He stepped back, eager and waiting.

My rush of hope and cheer was crushed. Here was failure incarnate. A reminder of all I had yet to do.

"Can I help?" he asked.

"I just need to get out of my head," I said.

I took a deep breath. *In-one-two-three, out-one-two-three.* In my mind, I took all the negative thoughts and shoved them in a box. I curled my fingers around the plant as I thought of sunshine and water. *Hope.*

"It's happening," he said, his tone ecstatic.

I opened one eye to peek. In my hands, the plant began to unfold.

Gaven beamed. "You did it, you absolutely did it! We have to tell Ansel."

I stared at the plant as it continued to unfurl. "No, no. It's just a fluke. Tomorrow it will be dead again, I know it."

"You did this," Gaven said. "Why can't you admit it's incredible?"

"It...is cool," I said, a smile spreading across my face. "But I don't know what I did. What I *do*." I couldn't get used to the idea that this was under my control.

"Your fingers," Gaven said. "Look."

From the tip of my pinky, a trail of green crawled along my skin toward my palm, a tattoo manifesting along the skin.

"It's a fiddlehead," I said in wonder.

I rotated my hand in front of my face, watching the ink expand. The frond curled around my finger.

"Whoa," Gaven said, as entranced as I was. "That's no normal tattoo."

I curled my fingers into a fist, then stretched them out again. There was the frond, green and lush as though a true leaf had imprinted on my hand.

That night, I snuggled up on the futon. I cradled my laptop with one hand, a flute of my favorite discount bubbly in the other. While I sipped, I scrolled the plant groups. People showcased their water-bound orchids and indoor flowering tips, gave instructions for tying up the spent blooms of spring bulbs, and posted picture after picture of prize roses.

In one forum, I learned an entire day each year is dedicated to posting nude pictures with your plants. Might be fun. Or incredibly stupid. If Christopher were there, he would volunteer.

On a whim, I posted a shot of the shop from the balcony to Prescott Plants, a local group. I captioned the snap *Getting ready to welcome you!* and invited all the plant fanatics to the opening. Couldn't hurt.

Every few moments, I'd glance at my finger. *Still there.* I marveled at the intricate design.

Before I'd locked up and killed the lights, I checked the fern. It flourished, a bushy version of its former self. Mariette, too, had unfurled a new leaf as if in camaraderie. I stared, drinking in this fleeting success. For all I knew, morning would reveal a fresh pile of decay.

But tonight, I was Cinderella. The power of the pumpkin flowed from me, somehow, some way.

I returned my attention to the screen and typed in a few more search terms, scribbled some notes, yet my mind continued to stray.

"What could it hurt?" I asked the room.

I shoved my feet into shoes and clomped down the stairs. A vine brushed my hand as I slid it down the railing.

Before I could second-guess my decisions, I pushed out the back door, sparing a glance for the glassed-in room. Dark and silent.

Outside, cold nipped down my collar. I put one foot in front of the other, willing myself forward. In front of the tree, I stopped.

Silver branches shone blue in the moonlight. My bookend buddies occupied a pair of branches. One opened its eyes. Upon my approach, it spread its wings and issued two calls into the night. The other crow fluffed, awakening to join the watch.

I stepped over the short barrier surrounding the base of the tree. I inched forward and lifted my hand. The bark was smooth and inviting. I set my palm on its surface.

Nothing happened.

I waited, patient. I was hot, whether from the champagne or the constant heat of the shop, yet the bark was cool to the touch. I looked up into its shadowy reaches, the naked branches criss-crossing. Closing my eyes, I thought of Patrick. The morning we'd first made chocolate chip pancakes. More flour landed on the floor than in the bowl and he'd needed a bath to remove syrup from his hair, but we managed a towering stack and a morning filled with laughter.

The tree warmed under my touch. I opened one eye. *No change. All in your head.* The crow cawed as though to urge me on. I shut my eyes and tried once more.

Ansel. The curve of his shoulder. His hands on either side of my face, his breath hot and unyielding on my skin. An ache flooded my nerves. Anger roiling underneath his words. His storm cloud eyes. How could one man draw me so close, until my every fiber itched for his attention, yet push me away with every other word from his mouth? That perfect mouth. The way his lips curved to reveal teeth that could nip...

A flare beneath my skin startled me from my daydream. I yanked my hand back. My tattoo glowed, a green fire beneath my skin. As I watched, the drawing rippled as though transferring energy.

I wonder... I held my finger to the edge of a branch, a dull gray cap on the stunted wood. Perhaps a snapped limb, a winter nub. There was a spark, and a silver line shot through the wood. A bud appeared at the end of the tree, tight and pink and perfect.

FIFTEEN

I was days away from the opening with fewer answers than I started with, my own personal mystery to figure out, and a shrinking budget for the upcoming night.

Gaven helped where he could, running errands between his shifts and setting up displays. He'd had the brilliant idea to nestle the succulents into a cupcake stand he found at the thrift store and to hang the air plants by fishing wire and suspend them from the beams overhead. I needed all the help I could get with a menu to practice and drinks to perfect.

No one else came by. If I had to verbally arm wrestle with Ansel, Joaquin, or anyone else, I was afraid of the consequences. I missed Lotte though, noting her absence. Adding a visit to my list, I headed out. My last few ingredients required a special stop.

A new barista was behind the massive espresso machine. Red sweater, hair in a ponytail atop of her head, her slender fingers held the carafe while she lifted it to the frothing wand. The tip of her pink tongue stuck out from between her teeth as she concentrated on the crema.

Focus had its rewards. She poured a perfect leaf design through the foam, much to the customer's delight.

"See, you've got this," Grace said.

The woman wiped her forehead with the back of her hand. "With your training. Oat milk is next."

Grace saw me and extended a smile. "Your usual?"

"Better not," I said. "I'm so wound up from preparations I'd be up for days. I'll take a brownie, though. And some loose leaf tea."

This had been a newer idea. If I could prepare mocktails to go alongside my adulterated drinks, no one would browse the shop empty-handed. Teas made a solid base, balancing out the fruit juices while providing subtle, mature flavor. This wasn't a frat party, more like an art opening.

"I've got some jasmine pearls that smell incredible. Or an oolong?"

"I'm looking for an Earl Grey. And some hibiscus."

"Eclectic tastes," Grace said. "I like it." She plucked tins down from the shelf behind the counter. "Need steeping times?"

"Probably a good idea. I've never been much of a tea drinker, but I'm learning. My mom would be proud."

Grace popped off a lid to one of the canisters and held it under her nose. She took a deep inhalation and smiled. "This is Lady Grey. Here." She dropped a pinch of the leaves onto my palm and turned to her scale.

I peered down at the twisted curls of blackened leaves in my hand. The pile was dotted with lavender buds and delicate, dried rose petals. "Almost too pretty to brew," I said.

"Lovely stuff. Though I like the classic, too. Too many don't like bergamot. My guess? They steep the brew for far too long. Delicate flavors are lost."

Movement caused me to look down at the portion of said

tea in my palm. The twist of tea leaves writhed, uncurling. With a small shriek, I dropped them.

Grace looked up, her face questioning my behavior. "You okay?"

"Sorry," I muttered. "I think an ant bit me."

"Strange. Those containers are airtight."

"Must have picked it up outside." I stuffed my hands in my pockets and strolled among the tables, looking everywhere except at the tea sliding into measured bags.

"How's the planning coming along?"

"Tough," I said, admiring a row of moth paintings lining the short hallway to the bathrooms. Each was painted on a piece of plywood, the title and price posted on a handwritten card beneath. "But it's coming together. Hey—any chance this artist might want to hang some of these at my shop? They're great."

Grace lifted a shoulder. "She might. Here's one of her cards," she said, tucking the rectangle into a bag. She pushed the bag across the counter. "And your tea. I wrote instructions on each. Time and temperature are your friends and enemies, both."

"Story of my life," I said, and shouldered the bag. Grace's new employee handed me the brownie and a coffee in a paper cup. "But I didn't order—"

"On the house," Grace said. "New roast—give it a try. Supplying you with coffee from time to time is the least I can do. What you're putting together for the businesses is pretty cool. Besides, you gave Cass a chance to practice."

I held the cup to my nostrils and took a deep breath. Black cherry, dark chocolate, and almond. I was smitten at the first sip.

"This is heaven."

"Glad you like it. Cass is getting the hang of Old Betsy." Grace patted the side of the espresso machine.

Cass dipped her chin, a nod to my compliment. "High praise. Thank you."

"Actually, Cass, would you be interested in picking up a couple of hours? I could use another body at the opening. It wouldn't be anything too complicated and it's after cafe hours."

"Sold," she said. "Works out, too, since I could use the cash for more paint. Those paintings are mine."

~

The scent of a thousand plants hit me like a cascade of water. I blinked at the bombardment.

Lotte rushed over to me, snapping her fingers in front of my face. "Earth to EJ. Are you okay?"

"Funny." I shook my head. "Anyone ever tell you how much it *reeks* in here?"

Lotte laughed. "Yes, but not typically in those words. Generally it's a compliment."

"It's like I can't focus now. Everything plant is calling to me." I pointed at one table. "Cinnamon, orange, and cloves." Then pointed at another. "Lavender and lemons. Spruce." I clutched my stomach at the onslaught of smells.

Lotte rested her chin in her hand for a moment, then handed me a candle.

"More?" I whined. But this candle had no effect. I frowned and sniffed twice to check.

"Plain soy wax," she said. "An alternative. I think your abilities are growing."

I groaned and set the candle down as another over-whelming layer of fragrance buried me. "Don't you have any coffee beans or something to clear my palate?"

"Myth," she said. She wore a taupe-colored sweater over gray pants. The fabrics were loose and flowing. Her hair, tousled as though fresh from the shower, swished across her face as she shook her head. "Best thing is to smell your own skin. That's a proper rest for the nose."

I frowned, then held my arm up to my face for a sniff. My voice compressed into a nasal version of itself. "If I go around like this, people will think I'm a cape-less Dracula."

Lotte laughed. "Vampires aren't all as ridiculous as Hollywood makes them out to be." I blanched at her statement, but she ignored my expression. "How's the party planning?"

"Just hired myself a second server. Between Cass and Gaven, I'm set. I've got food, alcohol, and some pretty great stuff to display from the other businesses. As long as all the plants don't die before then, I should also have something to sell." I leaned on her counter, unsteady in my scent blockade.

"Speaking of the plants...how is the...uh...practice going? I mean, other than this." She gestured at my arm wrapped in front of my face, pointing out the new tattoo.

I waggled my pinky finger at her. "You'll never guess how I got it."

I told her of Gaven's and my experiments and the tree.

Lotte nodded at my story, as though it all made sense. "I've got to go see it."

"Maybe I don't need June—"

Lotte shook her head. "Don't even try to squeak out of this. You heard her. Unchecked, you could do far more harm than good."

"She called me a hedgerider. I don't even know what that means, but I'm pretty sure it's an insult."

"Hollis was a green witch. He could bring a rose bush to full bloom in the dead of winter. Sprout mushrooms from any fallen log in the forest. But you, you're something different. A bit darker. Decisions for you aren't always a matter of life or death. Some existences offer both."

I thought of the resurrection plant. "Like an ebb and flow of energy."

Lotte nodded. "More...natural. If everything lived, we would destroy this world and the next." She grew quiet, then. Thoughtful. I sensed she held a memory in her mind, considering. "A hedgerider considers intentions. The fit of pieces into a bigger puzzle."

Weddings and funerals. Christenings and retirements. I'd made a life out of this balance. "You're suggesting that I'm somehow in charge of the flow?"

"More like an usher of what is to be," she said, in a slow and careful way. "You see what is and know what must unfold. This is why you need June. As a divination witch, she's no stranger to sorting out intent."

My heart sank. I was hopeful I could avoid the arrogant, dismissive, and intrusive woman. "Your candles aren't plants, so why do I feel like I'm under attack?"

"I use natural oils, nothing synthetic. Might also be something to do with candles. I don't know a single witch without a collection."

"You know more than one witch?"

Lotte moved around the room, selecting a few pillars from the shelves, a sprig of rosemary, a few slices of dried oranges, and some raffia ribbon. She tucked them into a bag. "For the opening," she said, and pressed the bag into my hands. "And yes. There's a coven here. Tight knit. I'll be curious to find out when June takes you in."

"When—not if?"

Lotte's smile fell and her expression sobered. "If there's one thing I know about Joaquin, it's that he is a relentless hunter."

On the sidewalk, my arms heavy with purchases, I rehashed my conversation with Lotte. She'd said I walked a line between the living and the dead. Was this the reason for my visions? A crow swooped overhead, casting its shadow along the ground in front of me as I crossed the square, running through scenarios in my mind. I blocked out those around me in an endless inner debate over my purpose and ability.

When Bryce greeted me outside the door to my own shop, I yelped, dropping my bags. I'm fairly certain insurance policies should come with fresh undies for all such surprises. *Full collision with comprehensive glass, and a fresh pair of drawers when your Kegel exercises won't save you.*

"Sorry," Bryce said, stooping to collect the bags. "I thought you saw me."

Just a sec while I stuff my heart back down my throat. "S'okay, I was deep in my thoughts."

Bryce handed me the packages. "I won't keep you long, but I have a proposition for you."

I thought of the dance, the brush of his lips against my cheek. Then I remembered the bodies, cold on the bricks. "Yeah?"

"I have certain...gifts. Abilities if you will."

Uh...where is this going? I swallowed. "Okay..." *Smooth, EJ.*

"Let me be direct."

Yes, please.

"Keep our secret, and I'll take you in."

"Huh?"

Bryce flashed me a sardonic smile. "Oh, come on now. You didn't think I'd find out?"

His words had the effect of a cold shower.

"Whatever Ansel is paying you, whatever June has planned for you, I'm here to tell you that you don't need them. I can teach you. Cherish you. Set you up in such a way that you'll never worry about your future again. You could be a ruler, not a servant. Or if you just want to run this adorable little shop,

protected, I could do that, too. We could come to an arrangement. You do have choices, EJ."

What exactly is he offering me? Management? Some kind
of small town corporate overlord? Confusion squeezed at my
temples, the bag on my shoulder dragging me down. I needed
time and space to think.

Ansel needed my help, or so he and Joaquin...and Lotte
said. June didn't want to help me but would do it for a greater
good. Even Gaven encouraged me to listen to them. But to do
what, exactly? I'd been kept in the dark about so much. My so-
called friends kept so much from me, considering me a pawn
in a bigger game, with rules I still didn't understand.

Bryce claimed he was there to help, but what did that look
like? There was one way I could get closer to that knowledge.

I beamed at Bryce, like a lightbulb switched on. "Can I
touch you? For just a moment."

The corner of Bryce's mouth curled up. "Uh, okay." He
held out his hand and I took it.

Nothing.

Well, not entirely nothing. It was smooth and warm,
muscled. The hand of a man who's strong enough to build his
own world and take care of himself.

No visions, no blackness. Just his skin against mine.

"I have to go," I said, and unlocked the door.

"Tell me you'll think about it," he called, before I closed
the door tight behind me.

I would think of little else.

Sixteen

Nothing tries your patience like hand-painting six dozen fondant bees.

Except, that is, maintaining a semblance of calm as you fight to keep your one and only source of income, pretend you know anything about the source of said income when you, in fact, know next to nothing, and have to interact with a pack of paranormal beings who treat you like an ignorant child all while experiencing endless sexual frustration.

I'd finished the last back stripe on my hive when Christopher called. I shoved the phone between my jaw and shoulder.

"You rang?" With a tiny brush, I highlighted a pair of black wings with edible gold glitter. The tiny creatures would top the petit fours, a swarm of insects atop the delicate squares.

"Checking in on my princess. How goes the preparations for the ball?"

I missed my best friend. He made everything glamorous, whether a train ride, a hot dog, or a messy break up. Life was a constant stream of entertainment with him.

"They're going," I said, paintbrush between my teeth. I

swiped at an errant stroke of gold with the tip of my tattooed finger. "Dessert is almost finished. I'll prep and freeze other nibbles tonight, then make the favors. I'm using the template we had for that spring wedding."

"The Blaus? They had that nasty daughter who nicked my lighter. Wait, bees? Must be the Caplans. Tipped well, that lot. The mother loved my tie."

"She loved your ass in those navy slacks." There was a snort on the other end of the line. Removing the brush from my mouth, I consulted my creations. I puffed out a breath of air. So much left to do and my will faltered. "Am I...trying too hard?"

Silence on the other end of the line.

I sighed. "I think I'm at the end of my rope, Topher." I rarely invoked the old nickname, the one from when he was a valet at a nightclub where I served too many shitty beers and Long Island Ice Teas to Cubs fans after the games. Christopher sidled up to the bar, post-shift, hunting for prospects. One night we shared the same man—Three Ball Paul, we called him—and each of us supplied the wrong name: he was Topher and I was Emma Jane. It was my one and only threesome, a drunken mistake that led to the best friend I'd ever have. "I'm worried I'll bust my ass to throw a killer party and it won't be enough." I decided to leave out the part where my new acquaintances would use said event to lure a murderer of humans to his death.

Some stories don't translate well over the phone.

I heard Christopher's deep inhale across the miles. "EJ, if there's one woman who can make this event fabulous, it's you."

"But..." I twirled the skinny brush between my fingertips. One of the best and worst things about Christopher was his candor.

"But if you fail, there is no one who will make a more stunning phoenix than you, my love."

I nodded, resolute. "Thank you."

"Before I go—"

"Yeah?"

"Wear something super hot. That sweater with the one sleeve off the shoulder. You aren't a victim of circumstances, you're a businesswoman with serious prowess. Act the part."

The afternoon of the opening, I was hot. Sweltering. In the naturally warm Apothecary and a clingy knit sweater, my pits were damp, and I kept pulling the fabric away from my body. My strapless bra threatened to give up to slide down my torso, but I needed her head in the game.

I ditched the sweater and grabbed my black linen top instead. Lightweight so I wouldn't swelter, flowy so it wouldn't cling to my sides or hitch up under my bra, and dark enough so no one would notice any wrinkles. *Perfect.*

Cass ducked into the shop, a stack of art under one arm. "It's freezing out there," she said, calling up to me.

I descended the stairs, and she handed me the stack of paintings and shrugged out of her coat. Her black top paired with a tight black skirt had the look of an opening night. She'd tied a black ribbon around her neck, the picture of an artist. She gestured to her artwork. "Go ahead, let me know what you think."

I lifted the first to find a giant monstera leaf spread over the canvas. The Swiss cheese holes caught the light, the shading a perfect match for Mariette. "Are these for the shop? They're beautiful." In my hands was a series of paintings, each featuring a different plant. She'd chosen the most striking aspect of each species and painted a closeup, as though a human portrait. Some featured moths, another a bee. Her paint strokes brought the plants to life.

She lifted one shoulder and let it fall in casual acknowledgement. "I thought it might be a good fit. This place inspired me to paint a series. You're sure they'll work for tonight?"

I couldn't tear my eyes from them. Each was a beautiful rendition of its subjects. "They're perfect."

With her paintings, Lotte's candles, Grace's teas, Rowdy's honey, the ornaments, and other offerings, the shop was filled with products. I'd even tucked tiny glass succulents, products of the glass blowers, among the living versions. For the first time, the Apothecary took on the identity I'd dreamed it would be before I'd set foot in the doors. *This could work out.*

"*Achemon sphinx.*" Cass stared at the wall near a vine. "Stunning."

"A what?"

"This moth," she said, pointing. "It's gorgeous. Moths are symbols of change, you know. Some think it's death, but that's only one part, never the entire picture."

I looked around the shop, considering my fluttering friends. The moths had multiplied. I found a new winged beast every other day or so. "They seem to like it here. As long as they stick to the plants and leave my closet alone, they can stay."

Cass and I plated the appetizers in the kitchen. I'd repurposed some ceramic drip trays with yellow handkerchiefs. I carried a few of the finished trays to the food table in the shop.

Gaven rushed in from the back of the store, his hands full. "I brought the bigger speaker, a fishbowl for the raffle, and the wine."

"Great—the alcohol can go behind the bar. Fishbowl on top." I'd made room for an ice chest full of bottles behind my makeshift bar. "The speaker can go..." I tapped a finger to my chin, considering the acoustics of a vaulted ceiling. "Upstairs?"

Living in the same structure in which I worked didn't seem odd...until I invited countless people over for a party. I'd cordoned off the upper level with some quick macrame work —thank you online tutorials—so no one would stray up to my living space. In what was nothing short of acrobatics, I angled my body up and over the ropes, speaker pinned under one arm.

I set the cylindrical speaker on the coffee table, then snaked the cord under the futon. If I flattened myself on the hardwood, I could just reach the outlet with the plug. My cheek to the floor, I stretched my hand as far as it would go.

Gaven called up to me. "Should sync right to your—oh, hello. Didn't know anyone was here."

"I'm Cass. I'm helping EJ."

"Me, too. You work at the coffee shop, right?"

I froze in place. Not an easy feat when on your knees, butt in the air.

"I do."

"I've seen you there," Gaven said.

His voice took on a tone I hadn't heard before. Lighter, softer. Flirtatious. At that moment, I wanted to be anywhere other than eavesdropping. But to move a muscle would either ruin their moment or make me look like a total creeper. Likely both.

"You have?"

"Yeah. You're hard to miss."

Go, Gaven. At least some of us might have a shot at a love life.

"How old are you?"

It was a playful jest in tone. I couldn't see it, but I'd bet that Cass had her arms crossed, one eyebrow lifted. Her suspicions were fair. Gaven was the last person to look his age. If I had to guess, Cass was in her early twenties.

"Old enough," Gaven said, a smile in his voice.

Cass, you have no idea.

From below, my phone rang. *Damn.* Moment blown.

Gaven called out to me. "EJ? It's that lawyer."

Ingalls. Today wasn't the day for whatever new complication came up. Whatever it was—city ordinance, filing fee—I'd claim ignorance and deal with it tomorrow.

I hustled down the steps and accepted the obnoxious device. I pressed the red button and stuffed the phone back in my pocket. Enough eavesdropping. We had work to do.

"Gaven, would you stack glasses? Cass, want to practice making a few cocktails? I think if we do batches, we won't get too backed up. The recipe cards go with honey purchases, but I've got a cheat sheet taped to the bar. Maybe start with the Bees' Knees? I'll take the cardboard out back and give us some room."

In the atrium, I shivered, deconstructing boxes and tossing them into the blue dumpster. In the fading light, the cobblestones shone a soft red-gray, their surfaces worn by time and traffic. Before I headed back inside, I quick-stepped to the tree. Above, the crows kept vigil as I checked on the branch.

Pink and green, the bud was still there. Its twist of petals spun tight against the world. *What will happen if I touch it again? Will it make another bud—or bloom?*

The back door to Morgan's squeaked open on its hinges. Joaquin eyed me as though disappointed I wasn't an intruder. "Y'all ready?"

"Think so. You?"

We—or rather, they—had settled on a plan of attack. When our guest arrived, I'd find a way to touch him. If he was who we needed to find, I'd text Joaquin. When the target left the Apothecary, he'd be captured.

I didn't ask, and didn't want to know, what came next. I remembered the flames and the resulting pile of ash.

"I'll die ready," he said. "It's kind of my thing."

There under the back alley light, the night cast dark hollows against his cheeks. "Is any of it true?"

"Is any of what true?"

"You know," I said, the feeling of foolishness descending upon me by the second. "Full moons. Howling…"

He smirked. "If it is, I'm missing out."

I nodded, appreciative of the candor. I liked Joaquin. But friends of enemies couldn't be friends—could they? I'd grown used to having him around, though. Akin to Lotte, the tendrils of attachment reached out to my heart. A gut punch of caring welled up inside me. "What about the other part?"

"Devilishly handsome? Born that way."

I bit my lip to keep from laughing, then sobered. "I was thinking of a shorter lifespan."

Joaquin looked down at his feet. He scuffed the sole of one boot against the concrete of the stoop. Finally, he met my eyes and nodded.

"Damn."

"You mean damn*ed*. Yeah, pretty much."

I bit my bottom lip and regarded this man. Who cared if I could prettify plants? If I had a gift, could I not find a bigger purpose?

Without asking, I crossed the distance between us and held out my hand, palm up.

He frowned. I beckoned again.

With an exaggerated sigh, he set his hand in mine.

His skin was warm to the touch. I curled my fingers around his and my tattoo began to glow.

There was the expected flash and then a backyard setting. Somewhere sunny, but hot. A birthday party, complete with grilling, potato salad, and a game of horseshoes. A giant cake.

Then came the screaming, the loud pops. Red on white. Blackness.

"EJ—EJ?" Joaquin squeezed my forearms.

My eyes fluttered open. I shook my head slowly, unable to register what I'd seen. "You...you've seen so many endings already." The children, the grandmother...bodies mowed down on a day of celebration. The face in the window, driving away. I hadn't seen his death, but I'd seen his life.

Joaquin released my arms, assured I'd remain upright. "Know why I work for that grouchy, overgrown man-bear?"

I shook my head.

"He is the only person who's seen anything close to what I have. That kind of thing changes you. He knows what it is to carry that burden. The difference between us is that I get to come and go, set my sights on any highway I like and drive until sunup gifts me with one more day in this world. But him? He could be a father. A grandfather. But none of that's possible for his life. He's a dream lost to shackles. Me? I'm just a nightmare."

"You aren't—"

Joaquin closed his eyes. "Don't. Please. Wanting doesn't make for change." I watched his features shift back into a place of calm. He gave me a short nod, then opened the door to Morgan's. Before he slipped through, he said, "While my allegiance is set in stone, I hope you kick ass tonight."

"Thanks. You, too." I matched his newfound grin with my own. Joaquin saluted me and ducked inside.

"Napkins?"

"Check."

"Cinnamon sticks?"

"Check."

"Edible glitter?"

"What's that?" Gaven made a face. He'd been rearranging the bigger pots to frame Cass's paintings. We'd hung them in a neat line along one wall where the light hit them best. The effect was pure art gallery.

I held up the bottle and shook it, the tiny sparkles shimmering from within. "Adds a little pizzazz to a drink, don't you think?"

"Piz-az?" Gaven tried the word on his tongue. The letter Z couldn't have a large command on the alphabet where he was from—wherever that was.

Cass snapped us back on track, a natural. "Edible glitter?"

"Check."

"Honeycomb toothpicks?"

"Sticky as heck, so I put them back in the freezer." I'd spent far too long cutting tiny pieces of honeycomb, stabbing them with toothpicks, and freezing them on a tray.

"Am I to wear a bee costume?" Gaven asked.

"It's Imbolc," Cass said, shooting him a look.

I nodded. "The Feast of Light—our theme."

"Oh, I'm familiar," Gaven said. "Just curious how far you want me to go." He waggled his eyebrows and Cass laughed.

She looked at my list on the tablet in her hand. I'd given her a copy of my planning template, and she'd made it her own. "The last item says *Check in with June*. Bicycle June?"

I made every effort to sound casual. "You know her?"

"Sold me my bike. Had to get rid of my car if I wanted to afford rent. She was awesome, got me a sweet ride."

Did everyone love June? The woman must save her irritation for me. "I need to call her," I said, resigned. "I'll get to it."

"I'm not crossing it off, then."

Cass tapped the pen against her chin. Her pixie cut framed a heart-shaped face, fringe dusting her dark brows. She'd brushed on a swipe of lip gloss. Gaven watched her, too, smitten. He'd consulted her on each step of mounting the paintings and every other task. If there was such a thing as puppy love, Gaven had it bad.

Would Cass notice? I remembered the first time Patrick came home from school, stars in his eyes. He'd fallen for a girl in his fifth-grade class. Come Valentine's, she'd broken his heart by giving a card to another boy, and Patrick came home in tears. My mama bear instincts kicked in. I'd bought a container of frozen lemon custard, and we'd devoured it while watching *Love Actually*.

If it didn't work out with Cass, I'd find Gaven's equivalent of lemon custard and romcoms. This was the least I could do.

I did need to call June. Our plan—to set a lure, surround the target, and leave it to Joaquin to clean up—had more holes than a cheese grater. What if the guy didn't show up? What if he did and brought friends? All this on top of the fact that we had to play the part of average human beings hosting an opening and keep all things supernatural undercover. Take out a paranormal being at a—hopefully—packed event without anyone noticing. *Yeah, a solid plan.*

Then there was Ansel, stuck in the pub, moody and certain we'd mess up. I'd suggested involving the witch in our plans, but they wouldn't hear of it. Said that as long as we did our jobs, we wouldn't need her. I wasn't so sure.

Mine was easy. Touch the guy. Prove he was guilty. Not get killed.

Simple. Hah.

Gaven stepped to my side and whispered, "Doing okay?"

I'd backed myself into a corner, tucked behind a vine. From this perspective, the shop was ready. With my amateur attempts, the plants had shed most of their decay. Many had new leaves, tendrils snaking through the air. The hit of oxygen when one entered the shop was palpable, heady. A selection of Schlumbergera—say that six times real fast—had cascades of pink at its tips, a new fern began to unfurl striped leaves, and one of the thickly-padded hoyas—a new term for me—had an odd growth, something the internet told me would soon be a set of unusual flowers.

All the plants were labeled, no small feat. Wood sorrel, oxalis. String of pearls, a senecio. Fiddleleaf fig, a *Ficus*—a sensitive thing, taller than me, a leaf dropping if I even looked at it sideways. The place looked...professional.

A sheen of perspiration lined my upper lip. I'd been working since sunrise, but the shop continued to be its own furnace. My new digital thermometer and humidity monitor, an online splurge, had the room at seventy-five for both. "I'm going to pop upstairs. Freshen up," I said to my helpers.

Gaven nodded, smiling. He and Cass scrolled through music options, testing the speakers. Cass played Charlie Parker, and Gaven added Iron and Wine. I left the two to their flirtation.

Upstairs, I paced. *Breathe-one-two-three, breathe-one-two-three...* I'd hidden my nervous energy, but now I needed release. Pressure boiled in my chest until I was lightheaded with panic.

If the opening was a failure, I'd lose my shop. If the stakeout was a failure, I'd lose my shot with June. I'd pick up a few enemies in either scenario. I was in full freak-out mode.

When Nora Jones came through the speakers, I bolted for Hollis's bedroom and closed the door. I sat on the bed and clutched my arms around my middle, willing my heartbeat to slow.

My ex and I had listened to one of her albums when we'd first made love. A rainy afternoon, symphony tickets, and a shared plate of pasta made for a romantic set up. Back at his place, we fell into each other, trusting each would be enough for the other, until death do us part.

Death had yet to part us, but his long-haired finance partner sure had.

The past doesn't own me, and neither does the future. I own the present. As my breath slowed, calm poured through me. If I didn't want pain, I had to set it down. Let it go. *Is this what Lotte meant about intention?* I'd bristled at her initial description. That I chose my reactions to life felt like an accusation—as though feelings were something I used to torture myself. Now, I found a kernel of truth in her words. It wasn't possible to plan every action. Mitigate every reaction. Control was a facade, a thing the fates afforded us sometimes and outright thwarted in others. My best was all I could ever do.

I'd be the first to admit my best was a little bit better with this newfound gift.

I'd assured Gaven and Lotte I'd been practicing, and that was true. I'd spent hours with the plants in the shop, blinds closed, highly caffeinated and taking notes. The experiments went well—until they didn't.

When I settled myself, I could drop into a state of mind where I wasn't the focus. One in which I wasn't trying to control anything, just letting nature *be*. When I didn't ask anything of my surroundings, I could sense the flow—or drain —of life. It was as though the world was flooded with white noise, all of which kept me, and many of us, from tuning in, stepping back, and giving way. *Heck, there's a bloom on the otherwise lifeless tree because of me.*

With plants, this wasn't too complex. When I stopped hovering above them, worrying whether they needed more light, more water, or the complete opposite, I left space to get a feel for what they needed. I wondered how often people did that in life; spent so much of themselves trying to force clarity in chaos that they stifled any chance at growth.

For me, this was still a shit show. I'd built a life—a career, a reputation—on the opposite. I dedicated my waking hours to either supporting my son's success or planning for the success of others. This is a tough habit to break. Sure I could coach a few plants to remember their will to live, but all I'd done for people—er, the Fallen—was to highlight death.

I needed air.

"Going for a quick walk," I said to my temporary employees.

"Enjoy!" Cass strung tiny fairy lights between the vines, Gaven holding one end of the string. The effect was a soft glow emanating from the entire wall. It was beautiful.

Outside, I relished the cool air of downtown, leaving my gloves and jacket behind. I wouldn't be gone for long.

SEVENTEEN

Two turns around the ring of trees gave me a new perspective—and several, non-critical opportunities to practice.

The first was an accident. A tiny woman wrangling two Great Danes lost hold of one of the leashes. I managed to step on the flailing leather strap and retrieve the dog. When I handed her the loop, my hand touched her arm. Her skin was cool and soft. There was a small spark, then nothing.

She was out of breath from running after one dog while dragging the other. "Thank you."

My second attempt was a young boy. A soccer ball rolled my way. With a deft foot stop, I kept the ball from rolling into the street. When I handed the ball back, there was nothing but the light of his bashful smile.

At the edge of the large performance space, I paused. Lotte told me the area would be busy in the warmer months, filled by festivals and holiday celebrations. Now it was a smooth expanse of gray, empty except for a figure near a planter barrel. They were huddled over a small screen, pausing to check their messages or reorient themselves in the cold. When I rounded the towering courthouse the second time, their face, shrouded in a hood, was turned my way. My skin crawled with an awareness of the attention. There was a glint at their throat, then they turned away.

Spending the last twenty-five years in a big city taught me to be aware of my surroundings. Chicago was one of my favorite places—but it wasn't considered the safest. I think that's true of any big city. When you put more people together, you increase the chance that they won't all get along. From Miami to Denver, Houston to New York, population equaled crime, even with the toughest of crack-downs. When I moved there for college, my dad packed me off with pepper spray, a taser, and my own car to minimize my vulnerability. I took the campus self-defense course, carried my keys spread between my fingers like a claw, and rarely went out after dark unless in a group. What I didn't consider back then was that bad guys don't agree to some code in which they stick to the shadows. They don't wait for a helpless newbie with *I'm vulnerable* tattooed on her forehead. The real deal, the enemies who should keep you up at night, know you. Study your weaknesses to exploit them.

I know this now.

Picking up my pace, I darted across the street. The person stood as though to follow. I booked it for the door.

"Thought I'd be on my own," Cass said when I scuttled into the shop. She'd swept her hair up into a clip and perched a pair of glasses over her nose. "T-minus-thirty minutes until we open."

I paused to catch my breath. In the warm and humid space, my lungs heaved. "Where's Gaven?"

"Next door. Said he had a quick meeting with his other boss."

I frowned. Again, I was left out. Pulse slowed, I took in the shop's transformation.

At Cass's guidance, Gaven had hung clusters of hexagonal shelves which Cass filled with waxy-leafed plants whose green and white leaves popped against the honey-colored wood. She'd stacked small jars of Beckett Honeycombs behind a plant display, giving the appearance of a larger honeycomb. Over my sales-counter-turned-bar, she'd draped a sheer golden fabric, using Lotte's candles to anchor the material. She'd framed cards with our drink menu and added a strange bird house with no front and two dozen tubes inside. In front of the house was a fishbowl with a single, yellow ticket inside.

"What's this?"

"A raffle," Cass said. "For the mason bee box. The bee society people dropped it off, said we could make it a prize."

"Cass, this is..." I turned a circle from my position in the middle of the shop. I pictured the shop when I first walked in. Overgrown, dark, aimless. Now, it was organized, bright, and professional. The dingy jungle had transformed.

"Too much? I'm so sorry, EJ. You had such a great theme, and I took that vision too far. I can take it down—"

"No," I said, stopping her. "It's...fantastic."

Cass smiled and blushed. "A box came for you. A woman dropped it off, official-like. Said you'd signed for it."

The creases in my forehead deepened as I spotted a squat cardboard box on the stool by a small bar.

"Did she say what was in it?"

"I didn't ask."

I stepped to the stool, unsure whether I wanted to know what was inside or not. A line of tape held the lid closed and there was a receipt taped to the top. *Attention: Ember James Rookwood. From: Waterhouse, Ingalls, and Parker.*

I slipped Hollis's letter opener from out of the drawer and slit the tape. Inside, the box was much larger than its contents. There was a thick manila envelope, a velvet, drawstring pouch, and a small stone on a thin chain.

The first sheet within the envelope was a list of documents, everything from the deed to the shop to shares in a company named Bellwether, Inc. I stuffed them back inside. I'd need an afternoon and a tall cup of coffee for those.

Next, I lifted the velvet pouch from inside the box. I tugged at the strings, then stretched it open.

"What is it?" Cass was at my shoulder.

"Standing that close, you'll see it before I will," I said, laughing.

"Sorry," she said. "Can't help it. I was one of seven kids and we only ever got one present at Christmas. Had to extend our joy by cheering on the others."

"Forgiven," I said, then looked at her. "Wait, seven?"

Cass nodded. "I'm second from the bottom."

I upended the bag onto my hand. A worn, tagboard box slid out. The size of a deck of cards, it had the heft of them as well. There was a stag on one side, a bouquet of flowers on the other.

"The Hedgerider Oracle," Cass read over my shoulder. "I've seen one of these before. An oracle deck."

"What is it?" I untucked the lid of the box and slid some cards into my hand.

"Like tarot, but—not."

I held the cards out to her. "Maybe you should do a reading."

"I couldn't. Decks take on their owner's energy."

I peered at the images on the cards. Each was numbered with a word and image. "Rider," I said, examining the topmost card. Atop a dragon was a human, clinging to the lizard's back.

Cass nodded at the card. "Good pull. Energy and movement coming your way." She saw my bemused expression and added, "If you follow that kind of thing."

I tucked the cards back in the box. "Why would my uncle leave these to me?"

Cass shrugged. "Might have meant something to him. Didn't want them in the hands of just anyone. You put a lot of yourself into your decks."

"You seem to know more than a little about these."

"I've explored a little," she said. "Oracle decks are all about divination. Pretty immediate. You ask questions and get direct answers."

I flipped the box in my hand. "Well, thanks, Uncle. Wish you'd left some directions." I plopped the cards back into the box and tucked it under my arm. "How soon until we open the doors?"

"You've got just enough time to tuck that upstairs."

For the first five minutes, there was no one.

Then we were inundated.

Gaven made several trips back and forth from the kitchen, running glasses and trays. Cass was swamped at the bar, mixing drinks and ringing up customers. I zipped around the store, like a bee after nectar from every flower in the meadow. I answered what few questions I could, wrapped purchases, and kept Cass stocked.

"What's this plant? Hank, isn't this the one your sister has? We've got to get one."

"Do these come in purple?"

"I think I'm watering my begonia too much. Do you think I'm watering my begonia too much?"

"Who painted these? They're beautiful!"

"When's the next night like this?"

This last question came from a woman wrapped in a wool peacoat, her hair in a tight bun. She shouldered a large tote into which she'd packed a succulent and one of Cass's paintings.

"I'm hoping monthly," I said. "Some of the other businesses have been talking about rotating who hosts."

"Count me in," she said, pressing a business card into my palm. "The gallery would be a perfect spot."

I clutched the card and winked at Cass across the room. The night was a rousing success. Plants were in the arms of everyone, some with both hands full. In response to the atmosphere, many of the moths had fluttered up to the higher vines. Several customers snapped photos from below. The stripes of the Phoenix moths were in stark contrast to the soft greens of the Lunas.

"You even got the insects to participate," Lotte said. She'd snagged a cocktail and stuck to the edge of the room, watching the crowd.

"Cass set some orange slices in the clearstory windowsills. We didn't want to risk them getting crushed."

"Brilliant. And she can paint."

"How's the drink?"

"Delicious," she said. "I'm trying to get Joaquin over here to try one. Have you seen him?" That was code for, *He's not here yet, what gives?*

"He promised he'd swing by." *His ass better show up or we are toast.*

Lotte lifted a shoulder and let it fall. "You know him. He'll be around." *I'm not worried—yet.*

"While you wait, check out some of the bigger plants in the back. Maybe your shop could use something—dramatic." *Back door is clear for exit.*

Lotte lifted her glass to me. With a nod, she moved through the crowd toward the back of the shop.

"Here's your boy." Joaquin was at my side.

"Sweet Lady Nicnevin—don't do that!"

"Would you prefer I announce myself from across the room?"

"No, that's not what I—"

"He's setting up. I followed him in." This explained his delayed arrival.

Across the crowded space, the guitar player set up to play. He sat in the folding chair to tune his instrument. Cass had turned a pair of pallets and an old door into a makeshift stage by the front window. Joaquin nudged his chin in that direction. "Recognize him?"

He'd cleaned up, but I remembered the face. He was Bryce's friend, the man who'd leered at Lotte and me from the door of the bar.

"Everyone!" Joaquin said without warning. A few people stopped their conversations to look his way.

I panicked and shoved at his arm. "What are you doing?"

He smiled and leaned toward me. "Go *help* him set up."

"But I—"

Joaquin plucked a small plant from a nearby table and stepped up onto the stool. He pulled the tag from the pot and tapped it against the side. "Ahem." The sound was muted, but the sight of the swarthy man calling down to them drew the crowd's attention his way.

Startled by his sudden diversion, I scurried around the edge of the crowd, smiling at anyone whose eye I couldn't avoid. This method of act now, think later, was a nightmare to my hyper-planner brain. I narrowed the gap between myself and the musician.

Joaquin commanded the room. "You may recognize me from next door at Morgan's, where the plants we serve come in the form of fermented liquid." The crowd tittered.

I inched closer, ducking behind a trio of women smelling Lotte's candles. "Love your shop," one said, setting a hand on my shoulder. A short spark popped from her hand. Her eyes snapped up to mine.

"The original owners of Morgan's Publican started a tradition of welcoming each new business owner with a toast to their success," Joaquin continued from his perch.

The woman wasn't listening. She looked from her hand to my face, then recoiled. I masked my response, acting as though I hadn't seen anything. "Thank you," I gushed. "I hope you'll come back soon." *A little too strong on the positive energy, EJ.* I moved off, afraid to look back.

In the center of the crowd, Joaquin bent to trade the small pot for the drink Gaven handed to him. "So, please, let's all lift our glasses to the Apothecary and its owner—" Joaquin's eyes found mine in the crowd. I wasn't even close to the musician. "Wait, hold up, our hostess doesn't have a drink. Can't have a proper toast without a drink. Could we please get a couple drinks over here?" Joaquin twisted on the stool to call to the bar.

I scooted closer to the stage. The words tumbled out when I reached the guitar player. "Hey there—thanks for coming. Can I get you anything?"

The musician looked up at me, his bloodshot eyes covered with a curtain of bangs. It was him, I recognized the tattoos. He shook his head. "I'm good." He tipped the microphone toward his mouth.

"There she is," Joaquin said from above. "Hand this hard-working woman a beverage."

Behind me, Gaven said, "Two Gold Rushes for the Boss Lady." He shoved both drinks at me.

"But I didn't—" Gaven widened his eyes at me. *Oh.* "Thanks." I took the glasses, then turned to the guitar player.

"Thank you, Gaven," Joaquin said. "Now where were we? Ah yes, a toast to our hostess, without whom we wouldn't be here, enjoying so many treasures from around our downtown."

I shoved the drink at the musician. "Here," I said. He had to take it from me or risk the entirety ending up in his lap. When he took the cup, our fingers touched. There was the flash of the child, atop a bike, the scream. I shook my head and released his hand before I was subjected to any more.

"Thanks," he said. He set the drink next to his chair and reached into his pocket so long I thought I was about to get a show. Finally, he withdrew his hand and held an object. "For you." Between his fingers was a guitar pick, red flecked with gold. I accepted the gift, my hand shaking. "It's lucky," he said, and gave me a smile.

"EJ," Joaquin said at my back, and I turned, reeling. "May your fortunes blossom like the springtime, may you pick the fruits of prosperity, and may you thrive through the seasons of change. Cheers!" Joaquin climbed down from the stool. He clinked glasses with a few guests, then my own.

"Cheers!" The crowd echoed his call. I held up my glass, a faint smile on my face.

I moved away from the stage. Strumming sounded at my back as the musician began to play.

"EJ," Cass called from the bar.

I made my way to her, smiling at every congratulatory remark from the customers I passed. The guitar player broke into a Django Reinhart tune and the crowd responded in volume.

"What can I do for you?"

Cass accepted a tray of glasses from Gaven and went back to mixing drinks. "How long are we open?"

"Tonight?" I checked my phone. "Another hour—why?"

A customer dropped a tip into the fishbowl. "Thank you, please come again," Cass said. Then to me, said, "We are almost out of bourbon. And gin. Gaven's too—"

"I'll get some," I said. "No one will notice I'm gone."

Eighteen

I made my way to the front door. In the swell of the crowd, I was bumped out onto the street, shivering. My coat was still inside. I spent ten seconds on the debate as to whether to dive back in but I'd be waylaid by customers with questions and requests, putting me further behind. It was like trying to sneak out after the cake has been cut when you get caught by a long-lost uncle and are now doomed to hear all about their latest church bake sale. There was no choice, I would have to be quick.

At the corner, I veered toward the convenience store. Like beacons in the night, the building was lit from within and without in neon signage. I picked up my pace as snowflakes began to fall, swirling around the cars that passed me.

Ahead, Bryce lounged against the door to his club, a cigarette between his fingers. A sickeningly sweet smell wafted upward in the smoke. Thumping from within rattled the shaded window.

"EJ," he said, and I froze. "Don't you have somewhere to be?"

"On my way to the store," I said, gesturing with one hand as though I needed proof. "Picking up more supplies."

A slow smile spread across his face. "Thought you were here for Lotte."

I stopped. "Lotte's...here?"

"She is...was...not sure anymore. Looked like she was having a great time last time I checked."

I frowned. If Lotte was inside, then she wasn't at the Apothecary any longer. This meant she wasn't flanking the exits as we'd planned. *Shit.*

"Maybe I should say hi," I said. "I thought we had plans later. Could be she's changed her mind."

Bryce shrugged. "Suit yourself." He took another drag on the cigarette and held the door open for me.

Darkness surrounded me as the heavy door swung shut. Bryce hadn't followed. Bodies gyrated in time to the music. Several were striped with paint that glowed under the black lights. The DJ from the other night was at the turn tables.

I searched the dancers for Lotte's delicate form. Overdressed, I stood out among the painted revelers. After ten minutes of hunting, I found myself in the back hallway. Could she have retraced her steps from the other night, sought more evidence from Bryce's office?

With a quick glance toward the dance floor, I ducked farther down the hallway.

The door marked *Office* was closed. There was a light from within. *Could she be inside?*

I held my hand out to the doorknob, tempted. If someone was inside, I would say I'd missed the bathroom. If no one was there, then...

Parents are right. When you hang out with reckless people, you pick up that energy. I was brazen. I turned the knob.

Inside, I flattened myself against the wall.

Bryce's office was a mess. Drawers gaped open, papers scattered across the desk. A trash can was upturned, its contents spilled on the floor. Pieces of a smashed coffee cup crunched underfoot as I ventured forward.

I tiptoed between the detritus, picking my way over to the desk. Envelopes papered the surface. There were driver's licenses and a pile of keys with address tags attached. A large case was open atop the paperwork. Rows of slots filled the container but all were empty. On a white board was a sketch of a building, an X marking a specific location within.

A loud cough came from the hall. I stiffened and my eyes snapped to the door. *Get out of here*. In a panic, I pocketed the closest item and hurried to the door.

From the other side of the door, I heard the voices move off, the music once again overpowering all other sounds. I rested my forehead against the surface, waiting. Assured the people were gone, I slipped back out in the hallway.

A blade sank itself into the drywall next to my head. I gasped and flattened myself against the wall.

Bryce stepped toward me. He pressed my shoulder back with one hand and with the other, withdrew the knife from the wall.

"Hello," I said. "Was looking for the bathroom."

He looked at the door, then back to me. "In my office?"

"Oh, haha. Is that your office?

"I think you knew this," Bryce said, his face moving closer to mine.

"How would I? I've only been here once before." My fingertips curled against the wall, seeking a hand hold.

"I think you went looking for my office," he said. "Funny, I found Lotte there too."

"Must be something about the night. Everyone's getting lost."

"I'm not so sure," he said, so close he smelled of beer and something sweet. "When I saw the two of you that day, I asked myself: Why would two people both want access to my office? My things. You wouldn't happen to have taken anything, would you?" I saw the lines at the corners of his mouth. The way his pupils dilated as he spoke. "How about," he said, "you and I both go back in there. Just to check that nothing was touched. That nothing has gone missing. That way you can let Lotte know."

I started to run. I spun for the door, only to collide with two barrel-chested *Fallen*. Beast One and Beast Two turned me around and shoved me toward Bryce. I stumbled forward. "Why don't you show me exactly where you thought the bathroom was. Was it here?" he said, lifting the stack of licenses. "Or here?" he said, tapping at the wall safe. "Or maybe you wondered why I have a diagram of the Founders Block?"

Confusion crossed my features. "Founders block?"

"Don't play dumb. Look, I'll even draw a tiny plant to indicate your precious Apothecary."

The diagram took shape in my mind. He'd captured, in detail, the entrances and exits of all the businesses on the block. *My* block.

"You could have them all," he whispered. "For yourself. If you'd just tell me what you sought within my office. I'm sure we could come to an arrangement."

Later, I would explain that, for once, I didn't think. I didn't stop to analyze every opportunity. I made a decision, somehow, in the depths of my brain, and the rest of me became reptilian-reactive.

With both hands, I dove between Bryce's bodyguards. Beast One reached for my shirt and yanked hard. I shrugged out of it in an awkward twist.

There's a time and place to find yourself standing in a crowded room in a bra. Tonight was that time, and here, among the scantily clad, was that place. I pushed my way through the bodies, some caressing me as I passed, and bolted for the door.

Outside, the crows cawed. Beast One tumbled out the door behind me, his twin not far behind. I twisted backward as I ran in order to assess my headstart, something you were never supposed to do. Had I not, I would have missed each crow plucking out the eyes of my pursuers. Adrenaline flooding my bloodstream was the only thing that kept me from collapsing at the sight. I pounded the pavement back to the Apothecary but couldn't go in the front door. Instead, I ducked into Morgan's.

The place was silent. Few gathered at tables in the corners. I threw myself against the bar, my breath coming out in heaving sobs. Falinis got up from his post and pressed against my side, leaning into me. I was stunned by his presence, yet too much a wreck to do more than stroke his wiry fur. Iris ran out from behind the bar and clutched me in her arms. "Boss," she called up the stairs. Ansel appeared a moment later.

I struggled to form words, fear stuck in my throat. "He... knows!"

～

Ansel squeezed his eyes shut, his hands rounding into fists. "I will rip every feather from their godsdamned bodies."

Iris had tossed me a bar shirt. I stuck one arm and then the other through the sleeves. "We've got to warn them," she said to Ansel. Iris stormed through the back door.

Ansel and I followed. He stopped at the foot of the stairs. "I've got the alley," he said. "Hurry." He whistled a trio of notes. In the branches of the tree behind him, first one crow settled, then the other.

Iris pounded on the glass to my back door, a signal to anyone inside. She pointed at the door handle. Through the glass, we watched a woman approach the door and unlock it. "I think you're supposed to come in the—"

"No time," Iris said, pushing past her.

"Thank you," I said, pressing in behind Iris.

Several people tried to talk to me as I followed in Iris's wake. At the bar, she grilled Gaven.

"Where's Lotte? Joaquin?"

"They were up near the front, arguing. Stepped outside for some fresh air."

Proof Bryce had lied. Lotte had been here this whole time. *Bastard.* "And Cass?"

"Haven't seen her for a few," Gaven said. "She went to make more of the brie things," he said. Alarm creased the corners of his eyes. "She left me a few minutes ago."

"It's too quiet," I said.

Iris and Gaven stared at me. We were missing Cass, our other team members were engaged in a spat outside, and I was worried about the music.

The music.

NINETEEN

I turned to the stage. The chair sat empty, the guitar in its case, lid flopped open as though the musician had every intention of returning to the sound. "Where's the guitar player?"

"He told everyone he'd take a quick break," Gaven said, his speech slowing as he listened to his own statement.

"Who?" Iris, perplexed, didn't register the name.

Gaven's eyes went wide. A woman tried to order from him, but he didn't hear her. He pushed his way through the people toward the back of the shop. Iris and I followed behind. Concerned whispers darted among the customers.

Ahead of us, Gaven came to an abrupt halt. Through the door to Hollis's library, the gateway to Gaven's world and beyond, lay Cass. Her body sprawled across the floor as though she'd tripped and fallen to the hardwood surface. She didn't move. Next to her outstretched hand was a scattering of empty vials. Her neck twisted at an awkward angle, the black ribbon untied, her mass of hair clouding her face. In the viscous puddle of blood snaking out from beneath her rested a single gray feather.

I screamed.

A pungent scent filled my nostrils. I shook my head. "What? Who? I need...Cass. Help!"

Iris's face centered itself in my line of sight. "Shh, EJ. We can't let them hear you."

"Who?" My arms flailed as I attempted to regain an understanding of my surroundings. My fingertips brushed fabric and I struggled to sit up. A wave of panic washed over me. "I have to get up. Have to help Cass."

"EJ," Iris said. She pressed me back onto the couch. "Cass is gone. The police are here. They'll figure this out."

I struggled against Iris's hold. Voices flooded up from below. She'd pinned my shoulders to the futon, searching my eyes with her own. "EJ. Listen to me. We can't go anywhere. We have to cooperate with the police while they are here." She dipped her voice to a whisper. "Get your shit together! We need them to leave."

Tears welled in the creases of my eyes.

"I'm going to let go," she said. "Promise me you won't do anything stupid."

I nodded, a slow movement as my head was sloshy.

"Now, when you discovered her body, you passed out cold. If Gaven hadn't caught you—"

"How long?"

"You were only out for a few minutes. You weren't the only one who went down, and the EMTs are with the others."

"How did I...?"

Iris was matter of fact, a steadfast relater of information.

"I dragged you up here. They will want to talk to you, though, so get this straight in your head."

"Gaven. Is he—"

"He's fine," Iris assured me. "Down there talking to them. Passing out water. They have the back door blocked off."

My brow furrowed. "Back door? But she—"

She shook her head at me, an exaggerated denial. "They found her outside."

I blinked from a combination of the jumbled details and the headache taking hold of my skull. I leaned back against the futon. I both knew too much and nothing at all, two standpoints which were hard to balance.

"I'm going to tell them you're awake. Stay here. And remember, you saw her outside."

From above, I heard the hum of many voices, anxiety rising with the volume.

An authoritative voice boomed. "Please, stay in line, everyone. Be ready with your information in case we need to call you back. You'll be dismissed as soon as possible. Thank you for your understanding."

Murmurs rose from below, fear and irritation rippling through the crowd. Gruff voices demanded contact information, asked if any of their party had left—and if so, who was missing. Again and again, officers asked who'd talked with Cass, seen anyone talking with her, or noticed anything unusual about her behavior. Frightened voices denied anything more than ordering drinks, purchasing a plant. Person after person said she seemed fine, happy to be there. No, they hadn't seen her talking to anyone, yet somehow, she'd spoken with everyone.

I wanted to be down there. I wanted to stop the pointless process, defend their innocence. Insist that Cass, incredible, talented, wonderful Cass, was the victim of murder.

"Ms. Rookwood? Your friend said you fainted. I'm an EMT, and I'd like to check in with you, if that's okay. Then if you're up to it, the officers have a few questions for you."

No need, I wanted to say to the man who appeared at my

side. *I'm feeling perfectly fine. Or as fine as one could be knowing a murder took place in my shop. I'm doomed to be its caretaker now because the horror of this night will officially haunt me forever. Could you kindly get out of my ruined shop so my associates and I can plan whatever counts as retribution in this hellscape I've inherited?*

Instead, I said. "I'm here, come up."

A shaggy salt and pepper head crested the stairs, followed by the well-built body of a firefighter holding a medical bag. He kneeled next to my feet. "Ms. Rookwood, is it alright if I check some of your vitals? We want to make sure you're recovering from earlier."

When the man reached for my hand to check my pulse, it sparked. He looked down at my wrist, limp in his warm, calloused hand. I looked away, as though I hadn't noticed. He scanned my body as though to check for the source of ignition.

Got me, buddy, I wanted to say. *It's one more item on the long list of* What the Fuck Is Happening to Me Right Now *that I've yet to sort through.*

"I'm going to recommend you drink plenty of fluids," Mr. Firefighter said, packing up his gear. "So long as nothing changes, I think you'll be back to your old self in a matter of hours. But if anything changes, you need to call for help."

Oh, the irony.

"The officers have some questions if you feel up to it."

The next hour was a blur. I alternated between mortified silence and bumbling speech. *No, I hadn't seen anything. Cass didn't seem off or worried, never mentioned a boyfriend or lover at all. Yes, it seems odd that I wasn't here for part of my own event, but I'd needed refills.*

When the officer asked if anyone could verify my errand, I blanched. "Bryce, from Plush. We talked briefly on my walk, then I came here."

"I know him," one officer said to the other. "Shouldn't take long to verify her statement."

Great.

Gaven downed one shot and then a second. The mom in me started to protest, then I remembered that I was sitting at a bar with a being many years older than me who'd seen everything I had tonight and likely so, so much more in his life. I shut my mouth and went back to nursing my champagne.

Iris had popped the cork, set two glasses on the bar top, and filled each to the brim. She slid one to me, then took a big swing out of the second. With the soda gun, she filled two pint glasses with water and pushed one my way. "This bottle has our name on it, but we can't afford to be stupid. We need to stay half sober, at least."

The cool, crisp water refreshed my parched throat. I wasn't recovered, not in the least, but I was upright and talking.

Ansel closed the pub when the news broke. He'd paid everyone's tabs and sent them packing.

Police tape still striped the Apothecary. The officer who'd handed me his card, a Detective Crawford, assured me a crew would return in the morning to collect more evidence. Their first sweep included fingerprints, backlights, and confiscating several plants along with Cass's water bottle. Iris offered to let me crash at her place.

Outside, the sky blackened, erasing the moon and stars. Thunder reverberated through the buildings. The windows of Morgan's fogged from the heat within.

Above our heads in the office, a storm raged.

Joaquin buzzed into the pub the moment the officers left.

He hadn't said a word to Iris or me and instead made a beeline for the stairs.

Muffled voices and shouts echoed through the thick walls. There was the thud of heavy furniture colliding with a wall. The stomp of boots followed by shattering glass. A grinding scrape across the floor, then a roar of inhuman proportions.

Joaquin appeared on the stairs, descending backward, his hands held up in defense. "It was no one's fault, you know this."

"Like hell I do!" Ansel clomped down the steps, advancing on Joaquin.

"We'll talk to Sharon. She'll find a way. Appeal to her pity. She *likes* you."

Ansel ripped one of the framed photo collages off its hook and threw it against the wall. Glass shattered, glitter in the air. "It's not up to *her.* "

I hopped off my stool, preparing to bolt.

My sudden movement caught Ansel's eye, and he turned toward me. "You!" He stormed my way.

Iris grabbed hold of the soda gun—was she planning to squirt him to submission? I grabbed a pepper grinder and backed up toward the door.

Ansel slammed both fists on the bar. The wood cracked, two splits marring the surface. "This is all your fault!"

I brandished the grinder in one hand. "Stay away from me!"

"Stay away from you? You're the one who came here. You and your entire godsdamned family ruined my life!" Ansel swatted the grinder out of my hand. I met his glare, defiant in my own defense, then saw something.

Tears?

The second stupid thing I did that night was reach out and take his hand.

In my dream theater, for that's what I called the place in

my mind that watched these visions, I saw a little boy riding a pony. Rosy cheeks, cowboy boots, and a hat so big it covered his ears. Behind him was the tree from the atrium, as devoid of life as it had been when I arrived. There was a birthday, complete with a cake holding sixteen candles and baked by an old woman, a checkered apron tied around her waist. A wake in Morgan's, singing and drinking. Ansel, alone in his office. Then there was me, from the night we met, damp and freezing in my towel. A blinding light, then nothing.

"Don't *do* that," Ansel said, jerking his hand back.

I stared at him. Half my brain insisted I run. Grab my purse and take the first plane out of here. The other half wanted to stay—at least long enough to unravel the chaos.

Ansel was a volatile force, a dangerous energy. Here, I was subject to its eruption. If I left, I'd carry questions with me wherever I went.

I did what any full-grown woman would do when staring down a man she wanted to both get to know and throttle at the same time. I flipped out on him.

"You don't get to throw a tantrum about whatever problems you have and blame them on me. I have enough problems. My *own* problems. And don't, for one minute, pretend you aren't one of them because blame flies in multiple directions, buddy."

Joaquin sucked in his bottom lip. Gaven stared into his empty glass. Iris watched us in open awe.

Ansel's face darkened. Before he could interject, I continued. "I'm the one with a shop wrapped in police tape. I'm the one who had someone murdered in said shop and found the body." As I ranted, my back stiffened. The fire of all I'd seen coursed through my being. "And before I leave here tonight, someone is going to explain why and how the police think Cass died outside when I know godsdamned well she was dead inside the shop." My hands were warm, my words a river through which my demands flowed. "And someone is going to tell me why I just said godsdamned because I've picked that up from you crazy lot which means I've spent far too much time with every one of you."

My anger dissipated like a balloon with a pinprick hole. As I waited for someone else to speak, to say something acknowledging my demands, I deflated. This—the night, the week, the month, all of this—had been more than I'd signed up for.

Ansel opened his mouth, but Joaquin piped up. "Well, that's easy."

Both Ansel and I shot Joaquin a look. Mine of surprise, Ansel's of murder.

"What's easy?" I was so winded, I'd forgotten my questions. They'd buried themselves in a mounding disease. I wanted the world to cease its incessant spin.

"There's more than one god, always has been. Thus the plural." His voice was chipper.

"Joaquin!"

The man-sometimes-shifter turned to Ansel. "What? If you ask me—"

"I didn't!"

Joaquin huffed. "Well, you should have. Because if you had, I would have told you to tell EJ about the weirs. About you and the queen. She would have known what to look for, could have protected you. Could have taken over for Hollis as watcher and—"

"Enough!" Another splintering blow to the wood.

I stared at Joaquin. His words, a gibberish of epic proportions, threatened to make sense in my mind.

Iris threw her bar towel on the countertop. "I quit," she said, rounding the bar.

Ansel roared again. "What?"

"I've watched you fall apart over the last few weeks, and I won't put up with a boss who's weak. Guess what? It's seven more years, and that blows. I can see what the first six seasons did to your sanity, and it ain't pretty. But you know what? I'm done taking shit from you or any man who wants to dump their own failings on a woman, not to mention one who is entirely innocent. All you do is fester in this place, a victim of your childhood and a mad queen. Well, I've had it. Come on, EJ." Iris wrapped an arm around my shoulder and steered me to the door. She unlocked the latch, then tossed her keys to Joaquin. "It's been real."

Joaquin looked at Ansel. "Don't let her go—say something!"

Iris paused our march, walked back to the bar, and grabbed the bottle of bubbly. She turned to Ansel, pointing the open end his way. "When you pull your head out of your ass, call me."

On the street, snow swirled around our feet, landing on Iris's beanie and kissing the bare skin at my wrists. My puffy jacket was in the shop, forbidden until released. I hoped she lived close.

Iris took a swig straight from the bottle and passed it to me. I looked at the green glass, liquid swirling within, and followed suit. We leaned on each other, winding our way toward the fancy homes east of the courthouse.

"How much do you want to know?"

Her question startled me. "Know?"

"About Ansel. That hot dickbag of a boss—ex-boss—of mine."

I peered at her. As she walked at my side, the streetlights lit her face, snowflakes dusting her lashes. "You...like...him?"

Iris burst out laughing. "Oh, gods no. Not like that. I order from the other menu. Doesn't mean I can't admire a dish though, even if I plan to dine on something else."

I frowned, sorting through her metaphor. Whether from

the champagne, the yelling, or the cold, my brain fogged, slowing its processing speed.

"Oh," I said, catching up. "Cool."

Iris nodded and took another swig from the bottle. "I care about folks from day one. It's my downfall," she said. "He's got a sad story, that one. Made him the hot mess he is today. I can feel sorry for him and want to kick him in the same breath."

I nodded. I knew the feeling well. Some people in life were sources of endless frustration. You loved them, so you put up with it, but everyone had their breaking points. Iris had found hers.

"We're almost there." She held the bottle out and watched me drink. "Did you make any money tonight?"

My mouth hung open. After what had happened, money was the last thing on my mind. "I have no idea."

"You know," Iris said.

I pressed my lips together, then licked them. "I...locked it up. Didn't count. But...it won't be enough."

Iris nodded, then stopped before a white house with a long driveway leading to a two-story garage. She pointed at the single light above the garage. "My place. So?"

I cemented my decision. If I was to make peace, I needed information. If I was to plan, I needed comprehension. "I want to know whatever you're willing to tell me."

"It started with the queen," she began, "and her idiot husband."

~

An hour later, we were in Iris's studio apartment, a tiny home above the garage of a bigger house. She'd handed me a clean pair of pajamas and bustled me into the bathroom to wash up.

She made each of us a cup of tea, and we sat at either end of her loveseat, sipping.

"If I'm following you—and mind you, that was the good champagne and I'm really, really tired—when the fae king was murdered during the first arrival of the Fallen, the killer escaped. The fae queen locked down their world to hunt for the murderer."

Iris took a sip from her mug and nodded. "Yep. And when he couldn't be found, her people rebelled, demanding she free them. They resented being cooped up, forbidden from venturing out. Rather than deny them and risk mutiny, she trisected the world of the fae into three distinct realms."

"And made the weirs their links," I added.

She nodded. "The fae, mollified, found a tentative peace. Those who wanted to escape the realm of the queen took one of two paths on this world. They either assimilated to the human way of life and became the Gentry, or they faded into the natural world, preferring to observe from the background."

I thought of the tree spirits, the wisps of light and leaf that peered at me from among the branches.

"This is where that blowhard comes in. After the threats to her rule, the queen couldn't trust her own people. She'd failed to find the murderer and her court was split."

"Understandable," I quipped. Like her or not, this was a woman with whom I could relate.

"She also had to punish the Fallen for disrupting their world with greed and destruction. They'd committed acts of violence, laying waste wherever they went. The queen, grieving, exacted her vengeance. She slaughtered all the Fallen but five who escaped her wrath. She sentenced their halfborn children to guard the weirs until the king's murderer was found. Finally, the broken ruler retreated to her castle in Elysium, locking herself away from those she's meant to lead."

"Halfborn children." My lips moved over the words, tasting their definition.

Iris unfolded her legs at the whistle of the tea kettle. She brought over the steaming pot to refill our mugs. "The First of the Fallen enjoyed every earthly delight they could find. Women were their favorite."

"I see. So Ansel is...how old, exactly?"

Iris shook her head, resettling herself on the couch. "Nothing like that. He's no Gaven."

I made a note to bring Gaven up later. I didn't want to interrupt Iris. I ate up the story like a starving beast.

"After she'd damned the innocent—or mostly innocent—halfborns, the queen relented. It wasn't their fault their parents had wreaked havoc on the world. So, she changed their punishment to an atonement."

I took a sip of hot tea and burned my tongue. I pressed the tip to the roof of my mouth. "Like in church?"

"You're not too far off. Halfborn children became guardians, those who would atone for the sins of their fathers through service to the queen. If they could protect a weir for seven years, never letting any of the Fallen through and back into the fae realms, they would be freed. Most failed, again and again, living out life sentences despite the queen's leniency. When they died in the line of duty, they were replaced with another—their next of kin."

I set my mug down and began to braid my hair. The triple strands weaving in and out soothed my mind as I wrapped my thoughts around the story. "So, Ansel is the son of a..."

"Well, yes. Or great-great-grandson—something like that. Ansel was dropped off one night, and a patron found him in a basket at the back door of the pub. The Morgans hadn't had children of their own, so they adopted him. As they aged, they turned the business over to their son. For he was never anything but their darling boy, whatever his origin."

"That's...awful. Succeed at an impossible task for seven years and you're free. Don't and the chains remain."

"I assume it gets lonely, being a weirman. Though I imagine more than one found a mate willing to overlook their inability to go on family vacations." Iris gave me a wry smile.

"I see."

"Over time, the halfborn evolved alongside the world in which they live. Many, like Ansel, run decent businesses and try to enjoy some kind of life. Those of us who know about them try to help out however we can. Been to Sedona?"

"Not yet. I heard I have to go. Gorgeous hiking among the red rocks—and something about vortices?"

"A farce," Iris said. "All of it. Sure it's pretty, but there's nothing metaphysical about the place."

"Really?"

"Complete PR stunt. The Gentry built the resorts and sent rumors far and wide that it is a sacred place. This serves as a first line of defense against the dumbest of the Fallen and any wayward fae. It distracts the majority of humans foolish enough to seek entrance to the fae realms. They've done the same anywhere there is a weir."

I bit my lower lip. There was so much to unpack, so much I wanted—and did not want—to believe. But how could I deny what shook out like the truth?

Halfborn. I understood what Ansel had been trying to tell me. He *couldn't* leave. Everything clicked: his and Joaquin's talk of timing, their worry over my event, the date. *Seven years.*

"So if I'd moved my party one day later, this all could have been avoided."

Iris put her hand on my shoulder, stopping me from walking further. "You can't think like that. Blame takes you to dark places, I should know."

"If I'd known, Cass would still be here–"

Iris shook her head, the bottle clutched under her arm like a rifle. "One might have broken in anyway."

"Wait," I said, sitting up. "If he guards a weir under Morgan's, then what's in my shop?"

"There's a saying in our world, my friend. As above, so below."

I was now, entirely, wide awake.

"Remember, the fae queen didn't trust her own people, and she definitely didn't trust the halfborn who failed, again and again, at the impossible task she set before them. She'd pictured them sitting next to weirs like unpaid doormen, yet they rebelled, attempting to carve out little lives in their servitude. The Fallen continued to find their way through, whether through bribery, coercion, or worse. There were now three realms and the queen was losing control."

I could relate to the feeling. "How did Hollis get involved?"

"Who better to guard an entry to an important fae realm than their natural enemy?"

"Witches are the enemies of the fae?"

Iris cocked her head, considering. "They were—then. Witches resented sharing this world with the invaders. To them, fae are vain troublemakers who take first and ask questions later. The queen made a political move that placated the covens while ensuring respect for her rule. She gave control of the Parallel to those most motivated to ensure that fae, and only fae, made it through and stayed put–the witches. They could succeed where the guardians had failed."

"Parallel?" I was a parrot, stunned by each revelation to the extent where I could only repeat words and phrases. "Is that like the other place—E-lee-see-um?"

"Yes and no. Elysium is the court of the fae, the most beautiful place that neither you nor I will ever see. It is reserved for the revered, those of the Cardinal Courts. You'll find no entrance to Elysium here, only in the Parallel."

"Elysium is where the Fallen lived, too. Before," I said, confident in my guess. "The Fallen would try to go back home, so it didn't matter if the guardians failed their weirs, only that the witches succeeded. But, there are more Fallen now."

Iris nodded. "The queen sequestered herself in safety and her loyalists continue to scour the kingdoms for traitors. Her court does their best to defend the realm, removing those who threaten her rule. Yet, even the truest to her reign squabble amongst themselves, leaving the court vulnerable."

"How do you know all this?"

"I'm a bartender. Iris lifted a shoulder in a small shrug. "I listen—even when I shouldn't."

"Right." I shot Iris a look. "So if Elysium is like heaven, Parallel is..."

"Like France."

"France?"

"Maybe more like the Italian countryside. Somewhere you'd love to live one day but it will probably never happen."

"If the fae can go to...Italy from my shop, what does Ansel guard? Texas?"

"Depends on if you like Texas."

Over Iris's protests, I bundled myself up and called a cab.

"I don't like this," Iris said. "You don't know what you're dealing with."

"I'll be back. Promise."

"If you aren't here in an hour, I'm coming after you. And you know how much I want to go back there tonight." She tucked me into the cab with a threat to the driver to return me in one piece.

In the short ride, I debated what to say over and over in my head. Nothing stuck. Unlike the snow, my thoughts couldn't land in any one place. I wanted to scream at him. I wanted to growl back, show him I was no one to trifle with. Turn myself into the victim no matter which way he looked.

At the same time, I wanted—no, needed—him to let me in. Not just for myself, but for Cass and anyone else who'd become prey to the invaders, the unwanted. The selfish beings who made a mess of their heaven and expected us to bow down and take their shit on Earth.

This fight had cost me my family, would probably take my business, too, but I'd be damned if I let another innocent person die on my account, in my shop. I'd made a career of turning empathy into action, and Ansel would start to include me, or I'd go it alone.

The cabbie let me out with a promise to return. In front of the doors, I summoned every shred of compassion I could muster and raised my fist to knock.

The door flew open. Ansel stood, steaming, as the cold air blanketed his bulk.

I froze, my hand still lifted. Confronted with his eyes, I faltered, then stiffened. "I'm not here to argue. Iris already told me everything." Ansel's jaw shifted, but he said nothing. I took another breath and continued. "I didn't *know*—how could I? It isn't fair to hate me because of something I didn't do. I could have helped. I can't guarantee it would have made a difference, but I would have tried. I'm *nice*. It's what I do, even to people who are jerks. Ask my clients. I'm not here to be your enemy, I never was."

Ansel stood, one hand on the edge of the open door, the other on the door jam. He looked past me at the snow. He pressed his lips together and his nostrils flared. "Doesn't matter anyway." He walked back into the bar, leaving me on the stoop, the door open. I followed him in, pulling the heavy door closed behind me.

Inside, a single light beamed over the bar. A bottle of bourbon sat, half-drained, on the polished surface, a glass nearby. Overhead, the horse head sculpture loomed, its wild features alive in the lighting.

I sent Iris a text—*Going in to talk. Not murdered yet*—then turned to the brooding man with his back to me. "Is there anything I can do?"

Ansel gestured to the bottle. I shook my head.

He took a stool. I remained standing. "Suit yourself," Ansel said. "Can't say that I blame you."

An hour ago, this man pounded holes into solid wood and all but kicked me out of his bar. Now he was calm, sullen. Offering me drinks. One man didn't track with the other. The layers of Ansel ground against my patience like sandpaper, yet I wanted to know more. He was a force that pushed as much as it pulled, a typhoon of mystery.

The tick of an antique clock over the mantle broke the silence. I followed. "What's in your basement?"

Ansel looked at me, then back to the bottle in his hand. "I thought Iris told you everything."

"I want to hear you say it."

He lifted an eyebrow. "There is a place forged with night-mares, run by the twisted who chase souls into eternity. Where the darkest of demonic beings play out their fantasies. A place where the damned are left to rot, their life forfeit in an endless cycle of torment. *That* is what I guard."

I bit my lip. Iris was right. *Netherworld.* She'd told me that the worst of the fae, and any other creature foolish enough to anger the queen, were sent to the world below. A one-way ticket.

"And your job is to escort them."

Ansel nodded. "And prevent their escape."

Across the bar, our reflections mirrored back at us. A couple in another time, another place. Opposites. In another realm, we may have been friends. Here, we were at odds in duty and drive.

Ansel poured himself another glass and held it up, studying the golden liquid against the light. "Ever seen a hunk of amber?"

I looked at his glass. "The rock? I have."

He frowned at me. "The sap of trees, hardened and preserved in time. To some, it's sacred, you know? A jewel from the tree of life." He swirled the liquid in his glass, then downed it. "The tree lives on in the amber, a piece of its existence preserved long after the rest has died."

Where was this going? Had I dragged myself back here for a philosophy lesson? Ansel might be too far into his liquid amber to talk. I glanced back at the door.

"There's one thing," he said.

"Hmm?"

Ansel pressed the glass between his palms. Cut crystal. As he shifted his hands, the light caught the facets, sending tiny prisms onto the bar. "There's a crown. The Crown of Immortality, to be specific. Were it returned to the queen, I would be set free."

"Crown of...Immortality? Does that mean she would use it to..." I could picture the scenario. Your incredible man dies far too early, so you do what any all-powerful ruler does. You bring him back. *Zombie king.* I shivered at the thought. "Okay," I said. "So, where is this crown?"

"Lost to time."

"Well, shit."

The Ansel and EJ in the mirror contemplated each other in the reflection. Mirror Ansel refilled his glass and passed it to his left. Mirror EJ downed the shot.

I shuddered, the alcohol burning a path down my throat. "So, you're fucked."

Ansel nodded.

"Damn."

We sat like that until the cab arrived, its lights muted through the condensation on the windows. "Got to go," I said to the mirror, wobbly on my feet.

Ansel raised his glass to mirror EJ.

On the curb, the driver held the door open. I frowned. "You aren't the guy who brought me here."

"Rick called off," he said, a smile on his lips. "I'm your chariot."

Hands shoved in my pockets against the cold, I considered the vehicle, then its driver.

"You know," I said. "I think I'll walk." I flipped my hood over my head and dialed Iris, my thumb hovering over the button to connect.

"I had strict orders to pick you up," he said, the edge of his words a sharp threat.

"I know where I'm going. Thanks, though." I set off for Iris's place, two blocks up, three to the right.

The cabbie sidled up to me, cruising along the street. He rolled down his windows. "You sure? I was told to give you a ride."

I stepped off the sidewalk and onto a lawn. Without taking my eye off the driver, I used my peripheral vision to scan the yard ahead and debate whether I could hop the fence.

"It's not safe out here, you know."

The driver pulled the cab to the curb. I bolted.

Full-on panic drove me forward, over the squat fence and through a yard. But I wasn't fast enough. Supernatural creatures are obnoxious that way.

The man tackled me to the ground. I winced when my knee wrenched sideways. "You won't get hurt, just don't move." I opened my mouth to scream, and he clamped a hand over my face. His hands were warm and dry, and the contact sent my mind into the future. Piercing pain, flames, and then nothing. Armed with this knowledge, I would fight back.

The cabbie dragged me to my feet, one hand still over my face, the other arm a vice grip around my torso. He wore a thin shirt despite the snow, his breath puffing out in thick clouds, his body warm against me.

"Look. I'm not going to hurt you. My boss wants a few words and then you can go. If you run, if you scream, I have a roll of duct tape in the car that will make this less fun for everyone. Can I trust you to stay quiet?"

"You're about to die," I said, my words muffled. He removed his hand, and I repeated myself. "Just thought you should know."

"Shut up," he said, gritting his teeth in frustration. With inhuman speed, he extracted a knife from his back pocket and held it to my neck. "Or I'll make it so that even the gods won't recognize you. Are we clear?"

I nodded, a lie. His grip was strong and the tip of the knife was sharp. A drip of blood trickled down my neck. Yet, from my self-defense classes as a teen in Chicago, I remembered one clear lesson. *Do not go with your attacker to another location.* I searched for an opening as he led me back to the car.

With one arm still wrapped around me from the back, he extracted a vial from the pocket of his shirt. He popped the top off the glass cylinder and drank.

"Disgusting," I said. "I know you cannibalize each other for that. It's self-destructing madness."

This is what I'd realized when I saw Cass's body. She'd been part fae, after all. I'd considered her uncanny ability to manipulate humans and her unwavering ability to design. The empty vials found near her body hadn't been drained, they'd been prepared. We'd found her body before it could be used to make elixir.

A muscle under his eye twitched. He squeezed the vial, cracking the glass. A rivulet of blood trickled down his hand. "You don't know anything, hedgerider."

So, everyone knows? "First, you can't insult me with something that so far has been equal parts cool and underwhelming. Second, I know you've taken the lives of others to extend your own miserable existence like a true coward."

He spat on me, a glob of disgust.

"Spineless and fragile," I said. "A useless combination. It's almost as though you weren't meant to be." I kept talking and continued to prod. If he faltered, I'd take off. The longer I delayed getting in that car, the better chance I had of escape. "Go ahead, sprout those decaying wings I know you're hiding. You're nothing but an abomination that didn't have the sense to die."

The man sneered, his face inches from mine. His breath stank of rot and seawater. "Had I not sworn to deliver you *whole*, I'd shred you like the trash you are."

"Blah, blah, blah. If you're going to threaten someone, do it with a little more mystery, a little less obvious prick. How about this? Let my friend go and I'll consider burying what's left of your body. See? Much more exciting. You get to imagine what I mean."

The cab driver and I swiveled our heads to find Joaquin sitting on a fire hydrant. He flipped a blade with one hand, catching it by the handle, but his attention was lasered in on my captor.

The knife left my throat as the cab driver dove for his car.

Joaquin didn't need to shift. With deadly accuracy, he threw the knife into my attacker's neck. The man—being?— grabbed at the blade, but it was far too late. A moment later, he was engulfed in flames which died out into a pile of ash.

I regarded the leftovers, dispassionate at the blackened dust.

"It's the elixir. It's keeping them alive–like a morphine drip–until they can make it to the Parallel." I told Joaquin what I'd figured out between finding Cass and what Iris told me.

"That tracks," Joaquin said, kicking at the ash to uncover his knife. "They're pre-zombies on that stuff."

I crossed my arms over my chest, the cold seeping into my bones. "If I keep watch at the Apothecary, they can't leave. Then, we find the source. We just have to cut off their supply."

"There's just one problem." Joaquin looked from the ashes up to me.

"Which is?"

"That supply is bottomless."

TWENTY

In borrowed clothes, I stared at the envelope.

"Glad I caught you," Ingalls said. "I would have come yesterday but I didn't...well..." Instead, he'd met me at the Apothecary. Tape still crossed the doors, so we talked out front, my tragedy on full display to all who walked by.

I tapped the envelope against my palm. "You didn't want to spoil my night? S'okay, it was awful."

"Yeah, um." He shifted in his suit and licked at his bottom lip, uncomfortable. To be fair to him, what does one say to that?

I crossed my arms. "So, what's the next step?"

Ingalls looked away, then back to me. "It's February, Ms. Rookwood. This is the notice of auction."

"Fuck."

"I'm guessing that means you haven't raised the funds."

I hadn't checked our sales from the opening. What with throwing a party, finding a body, and getting kidnapped, I'd been occupied. "I've had to cover everything else and..." I trailed off. My stomach soured as I blinked into the sunshine. I needed a shower, a gallon of coffee—and thousands of dollars.

Back to the door, I faced the park. As Ingalls talked, detailing exactly how I'd failed to save my business, I watched a being slip down from one of the trees. Lithe and sleek, they snuck around the trunk and slipped between two cars.

Oh no. Not today. The shop was locked, the sign marked Closed—not to mention the bright yellow tape proclaiming it off limits to all.

"Here's my advice," Ingalls said. "Get together as much as you can. Call a few relatives. Bid like crazy and you may get to keep the place."

"Should have sold it when you had the chance."

The voice made my skin crawl.

Ingalls turned to face the newcomer to our conversation. "I don't believe we've met. Stuart Ingalls, EJ's attorney."

"Bryce Mallory. Venue owner and...investor. I was stopping by to see if EJ wanted to talk business. A partnership. But I see she's already meeting."

"That's right," I said. "Then I'll be busy at Morgan's for the day." I hadn't cleared this with Ansel, but it would have to be the truth.

Bryce's eyes narrowed a split second, then rounded in innocence. "I'm a patient man. Besides, I have more...guests... arriving any minute." He flashed me a smile. "Better go and get them settled. I've got more coming next week, too."

"Hah," Ingalls said. "My wife will barely let my mother-in-law come for the weekend."

"In my case," Bryce said, "the more, the merrier." He winked at me.

I glared at his back as he walked off, no doubt to roll out a red carpet for a new group of Fallen. They'd be hooked on elixir within days.

∾

"It's hopeless."

"That was fast." Joaquin smirked into his drink.

I paced the floor behind the stools. "Bryce is on his way to usher in another batch of those creeps as we speak. My shop is a crime scene and y'all need some crown that may or may not exist."

"It's not a crime scene."

"What?"

"Cops cleared out," Joaquin said. "Left an hour ago. The rest is true, though."

"But they didn't take—ugh." I pressed my hands to the sides of my face until the pressure faded. "If you need me, I'll be next door trying to clean up the mess that is my life."

Back in the Apothecary, I fingered a loose strand of fairy lights. Sunbeams striped the walls, the morning light piercing the dusty interior of the shop. Exhausted, I collapsed against the wall. Tears streamed down my face, silent and hot.

I spotted the dragon on the floor. Knocked off the shelf by a partygoer or the police, I didn't know. I reached for the little figurine, turning it between my fingers. "Hollis, what do I do?"

The doorknob turned, a slow click-click of the latch opening. I grabbed the nearest potted plant, ready to launch it at the intruder.

The figure from the tree peeked in. She was older, her hair a long thick twist of white. Her clothes were a diaphanous silk, the pale green of spring shoots. She clutched a pouch in one hand.

Spotting me on the floor, she knelt down with a smile. Her face was kind, and while not withered, it was wise. She reached into her pouch for something, then held it out to me.

I cowered. Her power filled the room, pressing on every living thing. I couldn't move, let alone take what she offered. Her eyes creased with concern. She reached for my hand.

There was the familiar spark. Instead of showing distrust or confusion, she smiled at me. The woman pressed something round and firm into my palm and squeezed my hand in a gesture of reassurance.

She stood then, and with a nod, crossed to the back of the shop. I twisted to watch her open the door to the glassed-in room and disappear.

My phone buzzed in my pocket. I took an embarrassing amount of time to notice because when I answered, Christopher was testy.

"Been trying to get a hold of you for days! Your message was you ugly crying for two minutes—had me freaking out."

"Not freaking out enough to answer."

There was a pause. "I nailed one of the banker brothers."

"No—you didn't!" The banker brothers were twins who spent every Friday happy hour at the bar down the block from Christopher's place. "Which one?"

"Scott. I think. Maybe Jason. No, had to be Scott. He had this dimple on his—"

I interrupted. "Don't need to know that level of detail, thank you very much."

"Interesting since your bestie would love to hear that amount of detail from you. Found anyone yet?"

"Funny. And wait a minute, how do you know I was ugly crying?"

"You did that thing where you pause between tears, when you shudder like you're cold and the waterworks start all over again."

"Never crying in front of you again."

"Best friends are honest," he said. "So, what is it?"

I sighed. "I'm job hunting. Will you put the word out?"

There was a sharp intake of breath on the other line. "What—why?"

"Can't do it. I tried."

"But the opening. Your recipes. I thought you were even kind of getting along with that sexy brute next door."

I laughed bitterly. "A woman died."

"Oh, shit. EJ, that's horrid."

Tears streamed down my face, and I snorted, trying to hold them back. "Dammit. It was awful. I've never seen...she was full of so much potential and then she was...gone."

"I don't know what to say, EJ." He was crushed with me, and that was something I needed. I'd held it all in for so long. Stuffed down the horror at seeing Cass dead in my shop because every other person I interacted with chalked it up to some bad guy and moved on. I still mourned the woman and my lost innocence. I hadn't realized I'd been missing empathy until Christopher gave it to me.

When my tears slowed, I took a deep breath. "And to top off that shit sandwich, Hollis hadn't paid taxes since...well, the dark ages. The lawyer tells me the place is up for some kind of auction. So, you see, it's a bit of a mess here."

"You aren't kidding."

$\sim$

After my chat with Christopher, I grabbed my keys, locked the door, and ducked into Morgan's. I needed to be anywhere but the shop. Looking at all the life was so...depressing.

Iris took one look at my face and tucked me into a booth. "What was it?"

"What was what?" I frowned at her. "Wait a minute, I thought you quit–?"

She tilted her head to the side and pursed her lips. "I did. But Ansel apologized. Said not only was he an ass and I was right, but that the last thing he wants to do is start making small talk with the locals. Made me a manager. Gave me a raise, too."

"Glad to hear it," I said.

"Anyway, what was the thing she put in your hand? The old one."

By old did she mean the rock or the woman? "A moonstone," I said, pulling the small, smooth rock from my pocket.

As a kid I'd collected rocks, adding to my mom's pile of much more refined specimens. I hadn't noticed until now that she and Hollis each had collections. The pale glow of this stone mesmerized me, shades of pink and blue lighting from within its depths.

Iris touched its smooth, luminous surface "A tithe," she said. "Boss never gets those."

"People don't tip an escort to the underworld," Joaquin said from his spot at the bar. He nursed a beer, a wedge of lime floating in the bottle like a captured ship.

Iris ignored him. "So, then what happened?"

"She...went."

Iris mused. "I wonder why so many come from the trees." Standing, she lifted a trash bag from the oversized bin and knotted the top.

"It's not like we've got ocean front property on offer," Joaquin added.

"So funny," Iris said, dryly. She hefted the bag over her shoulder on her way out to the dumpster. "You should become a comedian."

"I shed too much," Joaquin quipped without missing a beat.

I thought of what Bryce had told me. Fallen arriving any day now, with more on the way. Fae elixir their means for surviving this world long enough to make it to the next. "Maybe it's an escape route. To avoid what's coming."

"You've been hanging around us too long," Joaquin said.

"Is that a hint?"

"No. Fair warning. This shit jades you."

"Only if I stay."

Joaquin's brows drew together and his mouth opened to respond.

"'Quin? I need you." Iris called from the back. Her voice wavered, a plea that attempted to maintain calm.

I followed Joaquin around the stairwell and into the sunshine. I blinked back at the light, midday arresting my senses.

On the steps to the Apothecary lay a pile of gray-black feathers, streaked with white. Rather, the half-folded wings of the Fallen covered their body. There was a sickening scent of rotted sweetness, like a peach orchard late in the season.

Without hesitation, Joaquin crossed the short distance between the steps. He grabbed the railing and leaned over the bars to peer down at the figure.

"Hey," he called. "Hello?"

The body moaned.

"Looking for a houseplant?"

There was no response. Joaquin reached down and flipped them over with the care a butcher might give a slab of meat.

I recoiled at the sight. Blackened teeth, eyes crusted over. A hand outstretched, as though willing the door to Apothecary to open and for an invisible force to pull them inside to safety. Overhead, the branches of the tree—empty save the single, tightly closed bud—creaked in a breeze.

"Did you think you would escape? That no one in the Parallel would notice a ruined heap of heavenly trash trespassing in their realm?"

Teeth cracked open in a smile. With a voice raw and broken, the ruined figure croaked, "Had to try."

Joaquin shook his head, forearms resting on the rail. "That's what they all say."

"You don't know what it's like—dog." He chuckled, a faint sound akin to a weak cough.

Joaquin landed a swift kick to his side. The figure groaned. "I've seen enough," Joaquin said.

"Stop," I said, putting a hand on Joaquin's arm. "It's not like he's going anywhere."

Another bitter laugh crested from the filthy face. "That I am not. And no, dog. We aren't related. I'm descended from the gods. You though," he turned to spit up blood, a tacky black liquid, then lay back against the concrete, "you're a mistake."

"Don't!" I grabbed Joaquin's arm before he could land another kick. "Wait."

"You're on borrowed time," Joaquin said, as he glanced around the atrium for witnesses.

I bent down over the figure, one hand on the rail. I spotted a newer brick jammed in the wall ahead, fresher mortar holding it in. I focused on this brick so I wouldn't have to look at the ruined, rotting face so close to mine. "Why here? Why my shop?"

Choked laughter. "Can't stay. Have to go."

As though this answered my question. "But...what happened to you?"

He sucked in his lips as though to wet them. "Cut me off. Bastard. If you don't work, you don't play." He coughed again.

Joaquin cleared his throat. I looked at him, then back to the figure. Iris watched from afar, hands held out in front of her body as though holding an imaginary softball.

"What do we do? We can't just leave him here."

Joaquin gawked at me. "I think you know that answer." He slid the knife from out of his boot. Cleaned from the night before, it glinted in the light.

"But what if there's something we can do? Get more information, find a way to—"

In a whirlwind of feathers, the figure leapt up from the

steps and wrapped two hands around my throat. My feet left the ground as he clutched me to his chest, wrapping his wings around me in a cocoon of rotten flesh. I gasped for air, my feet dangling.

Next I knew, I was in a heap on the cobblestones. There was a flash of flames, then nothing.

"EJ–are you okay?" Iris's hands were icy as she touched my cheeks, felt my forehead. The coolness was a balm to the skin around my neck.

"I'm..." I struggled for air, a latent panic holding my thoughts hostage.

Joaquin kicked his way through the pile of ash. He found a stone among the powder. Blue-green and shimmering. "He planned to pay you. Mermaid's tears."

I shook my head, disbelieving. "He...I wouldn't have..."

"Is there any chance Hollis might have?"

"Never," Joaquin said, before I could say the same.

"Sorry," Iris said. "Had to ask."

I ripped down the yellow tape and unlocked the door. The inside of the shop was every bit the morning after. Empty cups were strewn on the floor, a couple discarded in bigger pots. Food left out on trays, lights still on. I sighed, then shuffled over to the coffee pot to turn it on.

After the last splutter of the machine, I set the stones on the counter and reached for my favorite mug. The scent of liquid heaven filled the room, the coffee warm in my hand.

When I turned around, the mug fell to the ground and shattered.

Where I'd set the stone next to one of the spider plants Cass had potted, carefully adding fertilizer beads to the soil, the leaves had blackened.

As I watched, the blackness spread until it reached the tips. Then, one at a time as though on cue, each leaf fell, fluttering to the countertop in a heap of decay. I willed myself to focus, to concentrate, to drum up whatever crap level of magic I could manage but it failed me.

I reached for the plant and attempted to stroke the leaves that were left, trying to revive the frayed remains. The pieces crumbled in my hands. As I watched, the next plant over began to rot, leaves falling from the vines that hung over the countertop and dusted the floor. I grabbed the stone, flung open the front door, and tossed it into the street. A woman stopped to stare at me, her dog sniffing in the direction of the rock.

Back inside, I peered out at the stone as though it would find its way back of its own volition. Assured it stayed put, blackness against the asphalt, I beheld the square. There among the trees was a group of Fallen, their definitions soft in the weak light.. Eyes still bright, however, they had the look of tourists taking in the area. They were everywhere.

My phone rang, somewhere in my pocket. I answered.

"Mom?"

"Patrick, how are you? What time is it?"

"Almost eleven. We just got out of a show."

"How was it?"

"Good, really good. Listen, when you come for Spring Break, you'll bring my lucky protractor, right?"

"That and your good suit. Got it." I thought of the tickets I'd yet to purchase.

"You are coming, right?"

"Of course I am," I said, and bit my lip. I didn't have the money for property taxes, let alone a flight to Europe. "How's school? You still loving it?"

"I am, Mom, I really am. I'd better go, we're almost to the metro and I'll get cut off."

"Be safe, talk soon."

"Love you, Mom!"

Silence. I stared at the phone for another minute, then dialed.

"Any chance you can spare a few minutes? I've got a fresh pot."

❦

Lotte sipped from my second favorite mug. "What did you see?"

"See?" I'd detailed everything from before the opening to the moment my son called, all the way from Paris.

"When he touched you."

I hadn't told Joaquin or Iris. When the Fallen had turned to dust, they went back to Morgan's, quiet and satisfied the threat was gone.

"It's how I knew I'd live," I said. "I saw myself, then Joaquin. The flash of Joaquin's knife. Then the blackness."

"And when you came inside, you brought that decay with you."

I considered what she said. "I did, didn't I?"

"Have you ever tried to give instead of take? With people, that is."

"What do you mean?"

"When you reach out to the Fallen. The fae. You're looking for what you can gain from them, learn about their lives. What if instead you tried to give them something?"

"But what could I possibly..." I trailed off. "If these are beings on the edge, what could they gain from me?" *Hedgerider.* I heard June in my head.

"That's a good question." Lotte stepped to the sink to wash her mug. She set it on the drying rack, then turned back to me. "So, what do you plan to do?"

I looked around the shop. My existence alternated between saving and killing, neither of which made for a solid business plan. "It doesn't matter what I plan."

"I know a candlemaker who would be happy to meet a new apprentice."

"Thanks," I said, draining my own cup. "I think I'll return to what I know. See what's left for me back home."

"Home," Lotte said, as though I wasn't in the room. "Funny how that definition shifts."

When Lotte left, I looked around the shop. I would pack, but it wouldn't take long. I'd been so busy, there was little of myself in the shop. I'd spent so much time on the plants, they'd become my furniture, my home.

I picked up the tiny dragon again, holding it. Some things could stay up, for now. No need to denude the place until I had an end date. When I set the dragon on the shelf, it gleamed in the light. I thought of the traveler from that morning and set the tiny figurine next to the moonstone.

On impulse, I reached for the peace lily next to the register. I stroked the plant, thinking of the woman and her kind smile. Next to the stem, a leaf sprouted, then unfurled.

"Too little, too late, my friend."

TWENTY-ONE

I've read moving takes years off your life. I don't doubt this is true.

There's the putting stuff in boxes, yes, but it's so much more than that. There's sorting, debating, wrapping, and unwrapping. Rehashing memories you don't want to experience again but can't avoid because you've got to decide where to put Great Aunt Gertrude's quilt your mother guilted you into keeping. Old love letters. Copies of taxes. That shirt you swear you'll fit into again—one day. And this doesn't include coordinating movers, utilities, change of address, and the rest of the logistical madness that is icing on the Moving Sucks cake. Multiply the measurement of awfulness by the distance you are moving and you'll have an approximation of how many times you'll swear to Never. Move. Again.

Yet here I was, packing.

Half my stuff was still in Chicago-packed boxes, jammed into the corners of the shop and the upstairs apartment. The other half was either everyday stuff I couldn't pack until the last minute or the things I treasured so much I wanted them out. No easy wins. To top it off, I had to deal with Hollis's belongings, too, something I'd avoided for weeks.

Instead of bringing me closer to my uncle, my finds made me feel further away from understanding him. Pictures from a safari. A collection of throwing knives. Detailed maps of a defunct copper mine, a handheld note scrawled across the top —*Possible relocation spot?* I started Keep, Donate, and Toss piles, only vaguely certain I would know the difference when it came to Hollis's things.

Then, there were the plants. I could ask Lotte to look after them until the new owner showed up, but there was no guarantee the newbie wouldn't toss them in the trash. I'd grown accustomed to living in my jungle yet as I'd yet to figure out where I'd be living–let alone a job, car, and all the other details–I couldn't plan to take any with me. I picked up one pot and then another, miserable at the loss.

"Never thought I'd see the day when you'd be hugging a plant like a long, lost relative." Gaven stood in the archway to the shop, his arms crossed, a smile at the corners of his lips.

I smiled. "Funny how things change."

"Can I help?" Gaven didn't wait for my answer. He retrieved the long-spouted can and set to work. I watched him check the soil, fingers slipping beneath the leaves. Some plants were misted, others received a long drink. This was a moving meditation, a task to sooth the mind.

"Haven't seen you for a few days," I said. I brushed some soil off the countertop and into my hand. I dumped the bits into a nearby pot.

"Went back. For a bit. Needed the familiar."

I assumed he meant home, wherever that was. "I hear that. Right about now I could go for a Chicago hot dog and a long walk along the lake."

"I've never been to Chicago," Gaven said.

"You'd like it," I said. "Though maybe not in the winter. Or the summer."

Gaven finished watering and set the can by the sink. "Don't go during half the year, but the rest of the time is fine. Got it."

I laughed. "So the weather isn't awesome, but the city... well it's practically its own living, breathing beast. I could head out any time, night or day, and find something fun and fabulous to do. Christopher—my best friend—and I would dance until our feet begged us to stop. We'd duck into some hole-in-the-wall for pizza, then take the train to his apartment only to do it all again. Even after I became a wife and a mom, I could take the family to plays, comedy shows, and every sport you could want to watch. There's freedom in so much choice." Until the words left my mouth, I hadn't considered how much this business, my life here, had stifled me. Little by little, I'd let my obsession with raising the shop from the near-dead drain my adventurous side, like some kind of responsibility nightmare.

"Sounds...exciting," Gaven said. He reached for a sharp pair of scissors to remove some dry fronds from a fern. "Why'd you leave in the first place?"

My face, joyous in the rehash of all I'd loved about the big city, fell under the pressure of that scrutiny. "I...couldn't keep up." The loss of my job, my apartment, and proximity to my son had been a one-two-three jab to the gut of my life.

Gaven looked at me, resting his wrist on the table. "Think about this," he said. "Is something really so great if it can't be maintained? Like this heartleaf fern."

"Bess? I hate her."

"That's what I'm saying." Gaven stroked the edge of one of Bess's leaves with the tip of a finger. "Is it not better to accept a new reality rather than continue a losing battle?"

"It's not as though I can see into the future." I wasn't sure he was talking about plants anymore. "So, you're saying I should let Bess die?"

"No. I don't think even you hate her that much." Gaven shook his head, his curtain of hair obscuring his face. Bess curled a leaf around his finger. *Traitor,* I thought, but couldn't blame the plant. There was something about Gaven that made you believe in the tender and wild. "A wise person once told me that once you leave, you can never go home. I think about that a lot."

I stepped toward my hundreds-year-old, teenaged employee. "May I?" I held out my hand.

He set his hand on my palm. There was a bright pop, a white spark, then quiet. "I think I already kind of knew," I said, releasing his hand. Gaven was one of the Gentry. "So, when you leave here, you go...back?"

Gaven snagged one of the stoppered bottles from last night, flicked the cork out with his thumb, and took a drink. "To where I'm not wanted? Yeah."

"What do you do...there?"

The wine in the bottle sloshed against the glass, a Red Sea. "You know, find lost children and return them to their ungrateful parents. Avoid shepherds who think I'm a poacher. Dodge the bullets of the farmers when I dare to sneak a carrot. When I've had enough of that, I come here. Or I go to one of the many other places I know. Maybe I'll go somewhere new, one day, but I'm a glutton for chasing an impossible ideal. I keep thinking that one day they'll quit trying to hunt me down. But the fates are cruel and our time is limited—even mine. I spend my days running from one place to the next."

I held out my hand and he passed the bottle. The pinot noir was earthy and rich in fruit. The aftertaste left a bitterness on my tongue. "I understand a bit why my uncle rarely left here. He had a whole life to look after, friends to care for. He had you. I'm the one who failed to hold it all together."

Gaven smiled at me. "He would have loved to see you here." He reached behind her ear to withdraw a rose, tiny and pink. Gaven tucked it behind my ear. "You haven't failed him. Or me."

A booming knock rattled the glass in the door.

"Guessing that's my cue," Gaven said, and slunk toward the back of the shop.

The knob turned and the door opened. When wide and gaping, I noted no one outside it.

I stepped forward to swing it closed, chalking everything up to the wind, when a booted foot jammed itself in the doorframe.

"Quit feeling sorry for yourself and get up. We've got work to do."

Twenty-Two

Without ceremony or introduction, June brushed past me. She stopped in the middle of the shop and looked around. "Didn't Hollis have a library of sorts around here? Keep some notes?" She paced the shop, eyes darting over every surface.

I spluttered. "What are you doing here? We didn't—I didn't—the guy escaped."

June regarded me, then looked away, pursing her lips. "The way I see it, that's half my fault."

"I won't argue that one."

"When you get old, you forget sometimes that you don't know everything." June put her hands on her hips. She stared at the floor, then expelled a huge sigh. "I'm sorry I didn't help you. The whole disaster would never have happened if I hadn't let my godsdamned pride get the best of me."

I stared, mouth open. The same woman who'd reduced me to an outcast apologized to me.

"Don't stand there gawping like a widemouthed bass. Get me Hollis's books. The real ones. Not whatever this mess is."

She buzzed the pages to the ledger, scanning the figures Hollis left behind.

"There's more books in the back."

June left the ledger and followed me to the shelving in the glass room.

Gaven surprised us both. "June. Decided to be a team player for once?"

"All I do is consider my *team*, as you call them. Kept us together through this nightmare so far."

"Didn't keep the little one safe."

At his mention of the white tricycle, June's eyes flashed. I gulped.

June stepped toe-to-toe with Gaven. "You're one supernatural chromosome from being one of those walking nightmares. Of the two of us, one is far closer to a threat."

"We lining up bodies now, June? What's your count?"

I interjected, an attempt at distraction. "What exactly are we looking for?"

June glared at Gaven, then turned back to me. "Something —anything—that would tell us what Hollis was after. He sent us a cryptic message the day before, then poof, he was gone."

Gaven shot her a look. I swallowed. I wasn't used to the idea that Hollis was murdered.

We pawed through the books, flipping through the texts. Most were dusty, untouched. Books on botany, philosophy, astronomy. Everything about the natural world and how it worked was on those shelves.

"A guide to the night sky," Gaven read. "Might need this."

I flipped through vintage copies of Shakespeare, a Good Housekeeping cookbook, and a guide to insects of the desert southwest.

In this last book, I flipped through the pages. In the section titled *Lepidoptera*, I found it.

"Sphinx Moth." I held the image up for Gaven.

"Nice find! One down, only..." He looked at the growing collection, flitting about in my urban jungle. "A dozen more to go?"

"Better keep this one out." I tucked the book under my arm.

June pursed her lips over a book on modern witchcraft. "Moths symbolize death," she said, the factual statement of disconnect.

I thought of Cass. Hollis. The others. The Apothecary was a place for death. It was also a place for life.

"And growth," Gaven said. "Don't forget that." He set his book back on the stack. I spotted the cover. A set of seven stars, linked together on the cover.

Stars.

I grabbed for the ledger and breezed through the pages. Too far into the book, I'd made it to my notes, so I started over.

There it was. The circle, the set of stars.

I handed it to Gaven. "Any idea what this is?"

He took the book, his fingertips pinning back the pages. "A constellation?"

June looked over his shoulder. "Not one I've ever seen."

"And you've seen them all, have you?"

"Pert near," she said. "Divination, remember?"

I sat back on my heels and blew out a breath. We were getting nowhere fast.

June watched me, calculating. "You sure this is it?"

"I'll look." I stood and brushed off my jeans. While they continued the hunt downstairs, I took the steps up two at a time.

From below, I heard the shuffling of pages and stacking of books. When I was certain June and Gaven were deep in their own searches, I lifted the wood plank at the base of the window.

I'd taken to using Hollis's secret cache for my own safe storage. In addition to what Hollis had, I'd added his journal and the velvet bag. I removed the journal now and held it in my lap. I turned the pages, one by one, watching—hoping, praying—that something would jump out at me. But there was nothing but Latin, idle drawings, and scribbles I couldn't figure out.

I stuffed the items back into the compartment and fitted the panel back in place. I scanned the upstairs.

Hollis's room. There had been books at the bedside table. I stepped inside.

Most forty-something year olds wouldn't opt to sleep on a futon when a perfectly good bed exists. But I wasn't most of them. I owned a veritable supernatural train station I was about to lose to a fae drug-peddling creep all while sprouting latent witch powers I couldn't begin to understand. My sleep wasn't going to be solid anytime soon.

The last two nights, I'd dreamed of a garden in which every manner of flower burst forth with color. Like a mash-up of Alice's looking glass adventure and a Georgia O'Keefe painting, they beckoned to me, promising sensual depths. I'd run, knowing flowers had roots, but wherever I went, they sprang forth from the earth. I'd awoken in a sweat and did that dance where you don't want your feet or hands hanging over the bed in case something can get you. When my conscious mind caught up, I decided that creepy or not, I would check out Hollis's room. In case.

The room had a quiet mask of dust on every surface. Clean and tidy, it smelled of faded lemon.

On the side table was a short stack of books.

The first was a copy of *Herodotus*. I flipped through the pages but found nothing other than a few dog-eared pages, flattened out to indicate the end of their purpose. Below this was a slim copy of *Paradise Lost*. Last was a book on medicinal plants. I lifted the book and it fell open. The card serving as a placeholder fluttered to the floor to land under the bed.

I bent down to retrieve it, fishing it out from the shadows. When I picked it up and flipped it over, I gasped.

Hurrying downstairs, I held the card in front of me as I walked. I was afraid that if I looked away, I'd lose the image.

June and Gaven were where I left them. June had Hollis's notebook in one hand, her own page of notes next to her. "Did you know your uncle collected more tithes in the month before he died than the entire year before?"

Gaven's brows drew together. "I wonder why."

"I'm going next door," I said, infusing my voice with a casual calm. "I'll be right back."

"Something you need to share?" June regarded me, one eye raised.

"Only if you follow me."

~

June crossed her arms and scowled. She'd chosen the corner in which to stand. Protected from all directions. I sensed she wasn't the biggest fan of our host.

Gaven bounded up the stairs, two at a time. He picked up a few shifts and made plans with the dishwashers. Moments like this, he looked every bit the part of an average teenager.

Joaquin peered over Ansel's shoulder, studying the card.

"This is what Lotte described when she scoped out Bryce's office," I said. "This was in his notebook. Same description, same drawing Hollis had in his. It's got to mean something." The two men ignored me, their eyes searching the card.

Joaquin said, "This definitely puts a spin on things. You have to tell her."

"Sharon? Not happening. Not until we know for sure."

"Why do you have this?" Ansel's tone was accusatory. He

glared at me as though I'd hidden this from him all along. "Where did you get it?"

"What my boss means to say is, how did you come across this item?"

Ansel shot Joaquin a murderous look.

"Hollis had it. And I will want it back."

"It's now officially in my collection and under my protection," Ansel asserted.

"Like hell it is," I said, striding forward.

A chill dropped in the air. Tiny ice crystals formed on the windows. "Because you are doing something magical with it? You are nothing more than a failed weir watcher."

Ansel's words stung, calculated. The low blow hit home.

"Enough," June said. "Some of us have yet to see the thing in question. Ansel, you must uphold our agreement."

"What agreement?" I asked.

June held Ansel's gaze. "The one in which we share all matters related to the Fallen."

Joaquin leaned over his boss and snapped a picture of the card. Ansel set the card on the desk. "Only looking," he said. "No touching."

June approached. "Out of all of us, I am the best equipped to understand what we have here. I refuse to be treated as the least. You will let me ascertain divine intention."

"Give it to her," I said. This was an empty threat, since there was nothing I could do to force him. Still, it was my card, and I would decide who held it and when.

With a growl, Ansel crossed his arms and leaned back in his chair. When June picked up the card, I took my first look at the pattern on the back. Roses and filigree.

"Death," she said.

June was accurate. Beyond the calligraphy on the bottom of the card, the image was a match. In it, bodies lay about the ground, many in the robes and jewelry of royalty. Above was a bright, hot sun. In the foreground, a skeleton rode astride a horse, holding a scepter topped with a large stone. On the skeleton's head was a crown, depicted as a circle dotted with bright, pointed diamonds.

"Don't tell me this predicted what happened to my uncle."

"Not at all. Hollis didn't pick this card. He studied it," she said, setting it back on the table. I resisted the urge to snatch it up. I wouldn't let Ansel keep it, but I needed more information.

"That is the same crown Bryce and Hollis drew. Death wears it. You are looking for the Crown of Immortality, are you not? Couldn't these be one and the same?"

Gaven let out a low whistle. "That sure makes things a little more interesting."

"She's on to something, Boss." Joaquin leaned one arm on the desk. "Don't hold that against her."

"If Bryce was after it, could he have found it by now?"

"If he knew where it was," June snapped, "he wouldn't be here, running a nightclub. He'd be using it. Or selling the old relic to the highest bidder."

"Guessing it used to live on the head of that guy." I pointed to the skeleton figure. "What does it do?"

"It's said that the crown allows the wearer to travel to and from the realm of the dead."

Ansel maintained his stony silence.

"Okay. So, let's say that I buy the idea that one can go to and from hell, like a train stop. Why would anyone want to go back and forth? Escape, I understand."

Gaven stepped up to peer at the card. "Remember the realms were once combined. There are those who would not have them separated. Like the Fomori."

Ansel growled and narrowed his eyes.

"Who are they?"

"Fomorians," Gaven said. "were among the first of the Fallen. They escaped the Queen's wrath and fled, vowing to avenge their brethren's deaths."

"Great, so we have pissed off customers. Where did they go?"

"Scattered to the five corners of the Earth. Forced to keep their distance so as not to alert the queen until they can unite in their power."

"Since when does anywhere have five corners?"

June scoffed. "Leave it to an amateur to neglect the divine."

"So, if that one," I said, ignoring June and nodding toward the skeleton, "is one of the Fomorians, wouldn't he be in hell, prancing about in his fancy crown?"

"Could be," Joaquin said. "But then why would Bryce and Hollis want it? If Death had it, most wouldn't try to wrest it from the old bastard. Even I'm not that brazen."

Ansel ground his jaw. He'd said he needed the Crown of Immortality, but not why. Was he willing to confront Death, himself?

"So, this guy is...royalty?"

June lifted an eyebrow, all sass. "Be sure to address him as Your Highness when you meet."

I huffed and put my hands on my hips. "Look, I'm new to all this. I get that I'm behind in my knowledge of basically everything, but I *am* trying to help."

"Then do something useful," June said.

"I have been experimenting with poison."

"What?"

Four pairs of eyes bored into me.

"Awesome!" Gaven high-fived me. "What did you make?"

"Well, I was looking for something that grew only in Arizona. Something in which I could specialize."

"Create your own market," Gaven said. "I like it."

"Originally I'd wanted to make my own things. For the shop. You know, in case the plants...well, anyway. I've been reading Hollis's books to learn about plant use. One thing lead to another..."

"And?" Ansel sat on the edge of the chair. The ice crystals had melted from the windows, but the papers on his desk began to flutter. He slapped a hand down on a stack of invoices.

"Frankincense," I said, beaming with pride.

"Frankincense?" Joaquin quirked up one cheek, as though trying to place the term.

"You know, frankincense, myrrh, and gold. What the wisemen brought."

"That's sacred," June said, "not poisonous."

"Depends on how you use it. In quantity, it's deadly to the unholy."

"So, your plan is to have Bryce drink...frankincense?" Ansel laughed, a big, booming sound. "You plan to take down a creature of the old world, one who has survived multiple millennia, with an essential oil you can buy off the internet?" He continued to laugh, slapping a hand on his thigh.

I glared at him, furious and frustrated. The man had been eager for my information one minute, judgmental and dismissive the next. I didn't know why I bothered. I snatched the card up from the desk.

"Hey!" he yelled

"If you want it so bad, why don't you come over to my place and get it? Oh, wait. That's right, you've been deemed unworthy and warded out." With that, I bolted for my shop.

I poured beans into the grinder and cranked it on, the grating sound soothing to my jangled nerves. There was a soft knock at the back door. Gaven was working at the pub and Lotte had retreated to her own shop. Weary, I padded to the back door and peered through the glass. Joaquin stood on the back steps. He was dressed in his usual black leather jacket, a helmet under each arm.

"I don't wanna hear it," I said. "Sending an employee over to apologize for him isn't going to work."

"I'm not here to apologize for anyone, least of all my grumpy Sasquatch of a best friend."

My face fell.

"I know he's an asshole, but he's damn good at being one. Don't take it personally. He's had many years to perfect it, and good reasons, too."

Against my better judgment, my mouth turned up at the corners. "If you aren't here to grovel on his behalf, then why are you here?"

Joaquin looked behind himself down the alley, then back at me. "I wanted to get a little fresh air."

Ten minutes later, I was on the highway, bugs in my teeth and my hair whipping in all directions. I clung to Joaquin as he sped his bike around first one curve and then another. He followed the lines of the road, like someone who knew them intimately, the curves of a lover.

"Where are we going?" I yelled into the night, but he didn't hear me or didn't listen. I gave in to the journey.

I hated to admit this, but I loved being on the back of a bike. In the city, I'd been on the back of a scooter too, but nothing like this. There was something about a wide-open highway that called to you. The white noise of the tires on the asphalt blocked out my cloud of thoughts. Out here it was me and Joaquin, the bike, and the twinkling night sky.

Outside of town, we pulled over along the short strip mall. There were a handful of shops, a narrow parking lot, and a pull out.

Joaquin slowed the bike to a stop and waited as I slid down from the seat before dismounting. I lifted off the heavy helmet.

"So, that was kind of incredible," I said. "I might have to turn into one of those middle-aged women who buys a Harley."

"This is no Harley," Joaquin said. "That's more of Ansel's flavor. My bike is for when you want to go fast and take every curve like you mean it. His bike is big and rumbling. You aren't gonna miss a ride on that."

"Ansel rides?"

Joaquin shook his head. "But he would sure like to start. Inherited the bike from his dad. Adopted dad," he added, before I could ask.

"Lotte told me about your driving," I said, shaking out my hair.

Joaquin perked up, his brows lifting. "Yeah? What'd she say?"

"That when she tips her head back to look at the sky, it's as though you're making the stars race for her from the driver's seat."

Joaquin had a faraway look for a moment. I didn't know what these two had, but it was something.

"Right," he said. "There's someone you should meet. Follow me." He led me toward the building, the kind with several shops lined up, a common sidewalk in front. We walked past a real estate office and down toward the end, where a tourist trap waited. The outside was covered in horse-shoes nailed to every wooden surface. Prayer flags hung in the windows and a selection of rocks and crystals lined the windowsills. In the windows, someone had taped several flyers advertising tours of Sedona, with everything from celestial reawakening to promises of alien sightings. The shop behind was gloomy and dark.

"Guessing we missed closing time," I said, as we rounded the back of the building.

Joaquin knocked on the door, a pattern of taps, then sent a text. Moments later, the door opened.

"Hello, my friends." The man who greeted us wore a tunic of blue silk, draped with strands of wooden beads. His hair had the ragged unkempt look of someone who'd forgotten they had hair to begin with. Inside the shop behind him, a single bulb lit a workbench, a discarded plate of pizza off to the side. "How can I help you?"

"Same flavor, new cake," Joaquin said.

The man looked me up and down, biting his lower lip. He walked a circle around me, nodding slowly, then glanced at Joaquin.

"Her power is fresh, tart. Like a lemon." He reached out and brushed a finger across my cheek. His touch made me shiver from the warmth. "Ooh," he said. "She sparkles."

Fae, I thought.

Joaquin said, "She needs something for protection."

The man nodded and again turned to me. "Gorgeous in all the right places. Behind on development though. There should be a stronger pull," he said. I stuck out my tongue. "A little sour, I dig it. Come with me."

I stepped into the shop behind them both and closed the door, shutting out the desert. The back room of the shop was crowded with boxes and bins.

"Make yourself comfy." There was a bean bag of unimaginable depths, the grimy floor, and the chair at which our host had been seated. Joaquin and I remained standing.

A soldering iron sat in a stand with pieces of jewelry scattered on the workspace. When he returned, I gestured to the desk. "These are beautiful pieces." There were earrings of all sizes wrapped with colored wires, glass window hangers depicting a watchful eye, and bracelets woven with shells.

He smiled, a Cheshire grin. "Have to keep the tourists happy. Or rather, keep them thinking this is the place where all their metaphysical dreams will come true."

"You're saying there's nothing special about these lands?"

The man tutted at me. "Not at all. Only in this case, humans should learn to be satisfied with natural beauty. In some cases, it is only skin deep. The places they are after are well hidden from the casual and flagrant," he said. "As you should know."

Had Joaquin told him about me? Or had he known Hollis? I had no doubt this man knew about the weir in my shop, which meant there were others.

"Don't panic, sweetheart. I've no interest in going back. And even if I did," he said, "I could afford the tithe."

What does one say to a member of the fae who claims they can afford your services, whatever the price? Not a word. I looked to Joaquin for help.

"That's a small sheath," Joaquin said, eyeing the object in the shopkeeper's hands.

"Never judge a weapon by the size of its covering, my friend."

"I've said the same to many women," Joaquin said. I slugged him in the shoulder.

"Shame you have to convince them to take a chance," the man parried with a smirk.

"Touché," Joaquin said.

The man handed me the sheathed knife, its blade twice as long as the handle.

"Little White," he said. "Carved by the Teg armorers."

"Who were the Teg?" I turned the sheath over in my hand. A delicate vine of roses was pressed into the white leather casing.

"An old name for an old people." He watched me run my

fingers over the curious bumps in the handle. "Bone," he said, answering the question I hadn't asked.

I lifted both eyebrows and resisted dropping the weapon. "Really?"

"It's rumored to be dragon, but the truth is far darker."

"How so?" I pulled the blade from the sheath. It cast a beam whichever way I turned it.

"When in need of material, they chose to honor their dead by...uh...*repurposing* them."

I grimaced at the knife. "You mean it's made of...?"

He shrugged. "Likely. No different than the human practice of keeping ashes in some urn on the mantle. Far more useful, anyway."

I slid the blade back in place. "This is...beautiful. But a bit creepy. I'm not sure I'd know what to do with a knife, though."

"I'll teach you," Joaquin said. "It's half instinct, half physics." He turned to the shopkeeper. "Name your price."

The broad grin was back. The man tilted his head, considering. "Information."

"I'm an open book," Joaquin said.

"Not you, old friend. Her."

I brought my hand to my chest, the classic sign of knowing nothing of importance. "Me?" *I don't even know where I'm living next week. What could he want to know from me?*

"The winds whisper of a woman of incredible power who commands the flighted spirits and the sleeping heat. Would you know of this woman?"

He looked at me in a way no other person has or would for the remainder of my days. It was as if it wasn't me he sought but the depths below my being, the fiber of which I was made.

Could he mean June? Lotte? Iris, Cass, or Grace? "I do not," I said, in honesty.

"Pity," he replied. "I hope you meet her."

Joaquin put his arm around me and escorted me toward the door. "You've been generous with your time and treasures, and we thank you."

"It was my pleasure," he said with a slight nod of his head.

The night air was crisp in my lungs after the confines of the building's interior. While I waited for Joaquin to ready the bike, I pulled the knife free from its sheath, curious. Under the starlight, the blade shimmered, silvery swirls glinting in the light. They reminded me of the same threads I'd seen in the tree.

"Careful," Joaquin said. "It's a witch killer."

TWENTY-THREE

Packing tape gets expensive. I should know.

Gaven and I spent the afternoon finishing my boxes. "Blue tape is for the bathroom, right?" I'd devised a color-coded system for quick identification of my boxes.

"Yes, purple for the kitchen. Red for the bedroom." Gaven made a face.

"What?"

"Nothing," the quasi-teen said, a knowing smile on his face. "But since you brought it up...will there be anyone in particular you'll miss when you move back to the Windy City? Perhaps a grumpy bartender hotty?"

I beaned him with a throw pillow. "Miss irritating him? Absolutely. Miss dealing with his temperamental ass? Hah!"

Gaven turned to the kitchen towels. In a mock voice he said, "Miss seeing his sexy ass flex? Most definitely."

I groaned in irritation and threw a towel at him.

A bell rang, and a voice called into the shop. "Knock, knock."

Gaven and I locked eyes. *Bryce.*

"Anyone here? EJ?"

Gaven mouthed, "I'm not here," then pointed to the weir room.

I nodded, then called out, "Coming!" I left Gaven in the kitchen and entered the shop. Bryce stood in the center, appraising the place. He grinned like a kid after Easter eggs, as though every plant might hide a treasure. "Can I help you?"

From his expression, you would never know he'd threatened me the last time we spoke.

"You know, the light in here is just gorgeous. Bring in a piano, put in a proper sound system, and you'd have an incredible venue. What's upstairs? Mind if I go up?"

Bryce was almost to the bottom step before I could stop him. I stepped in front of the stairwell and smiled. "Actually, I'd rather not. I have some personal stuff out. You know. Bras drying in the shower and what not."

"Another time then," he said to me with a smirk. "I'd love to talk business."

"Business?" The Bryce in my shop was a full turnaround from the other night. Had I entered a twilight zone?

He adopted a casual tone, as though I'd invited him over for coffee and he just happened to start a conversation. "A little bird told me things might be getting tough for you, so I wanted to come over and see what I could do. To help."

I seethed. Not only had the creep come into the shop, but he came in thinking we'd work together? "Who told you I'd want your help for anything?"

He swiped his hand at me, as though a paw. "Put those claws away, kitty cat."

I rolled my eyes. "How about you say what you came to say? I've got a to-do list a mile long."

"Fine. Business it is." He reached out to stroke a vine. With his touch, the tendrils twirled out to meet him, to wind around his fingers.

Fae. I should have known.

"I want to buy the shop. Let me give you a fair price."

"What? No."

"Now EJ," he said. He held out his hand to one of the giant sphinx moths. Its proboscis tapped at his finger, checking for food. "Don't dismiss my offer too quickly. I thought we were friends."

"Right now we're not." I summoned every ounce of restraint I had not to roar at this man in full Ansel-style. It was tempting, and might be the only way to quell the unease fluttering in my chest cavity.

The smile on his face cracked and wavered before returning in full glory. "Look, I'm not here to take. Quite the opposite. I'd like to be your partner."

"What?"

He gave a little boy band shrug, a humble brag that made me want to barf. "You're in over your head and I get that. It's just the luck of the draw, sometimes." I glared, silent, so he continued. "But you are obviously talented. With our abilities combined, this place could be big. Really big."

"Why would you want it?" I was stalling. If he was fae, would he already know of the weir? "You have your own already."

He put his hands in his pocket and kicked at an imaginary spot on the ground. "True, Plush is pretty great, but you know I wanted to step it up a notch. This place would let me do that. I could put on parties, host meetings...use the weir. You know, typical stuff."

My eyes snapped to him. "What did you say?"

"You haven't figured it out, have you? Gods, EJ, for someone from such a powerful line, you are hopelessly clueless. Where do you think the guy went—for a stroll? Your own help tried to stop him—her last mistake."

"You were part of this?"

He held up his hands. "No one was supposed to get hurt. His orders were to check out the weir. But he made it, I got word."

I seethed. Cass had been caught up in a dangerous web and hadn't recognized the spider.

Bryce meandered toward me, stroking a leaf here, checking a price tag there. "Your...fundraiser was interrupted, so you couldn't possibly have recovered."

"Recovered what?"

"Hollis's debts."

I narrowed my eyes. "What would you know about Hollis's business?"

"I know in the end he accepted mere trinkets when he should have required treasures." He turned his hand this way and that, watching the moth walk along his hand. "He wouldn't even let me in the door to see this place. Not very neighborly of him. But there were consequences. Unlike many of my kind, I have no problem with the Fallen. They are my cousins, in a way. Some of us value profit over purity."

"If he refused to help you...he warded you out?" I flashed back to June, reinstating the wards on the shop when Hollis died. She wouldn't have known about Bryce.

"It was a...misunderstanding. He wasn't as welcoming as you are. Come on, EJ. This way, you retain some control. The other way, I make a stop at city hall and...well. I'm sure we can come to an agreement."

He knew. "Like hell we will!"

"Now, now. I know it may sting a bit to call me boss, but think of the benefits. You could stay here, work for me. Live here, even," he said, watching the insect.

"I'd rather die than work for you!" The statement, dripping with every bit of ire to be found in my body, rang out in the shop. An eerie silence followed.

The moth vacated, fluttering off toward the vines. "Don't

be so certain of that," Bryce said. He spotted my packing list on the counter. "Contact lawyers. Hire movers. Donate clothes. Huh. Seems like you've already given up." He scanned the countertop, then looked at me. "Have a pen? I'll add Pride and Self-respect to the bottom."

My hands balled into fists. "Get out."

"A little advice, from one business owner to another. Adapt, or be trampled." He turned a slow circle on one heel, taking in the shop. "It truly has potential," he said, then added, "if you get rid of all these plants."

Twenty-Four

"I. Want. To. Smash. Things."

"You are more than entitled, but we did just finish packing your mugs," Gaven said.

"Why are the godsdamned fae so...so..." Gaven waited, brows raised. I sighed. "Great as friends when they aren't total shitbags."

"Not a shitbag. I will put this on my resume."

I looked at him. "You have a resume?"

He nodded. "Got an address here, don't I? For a while, I debated going to uni, getting a degree in something. A job. Maybe even a wife and kids. A dog..." His voice quieted as he trailed off.

"But then you realized..." I trailed off, following his train of thought. How crushing to find pure joy knowing how short-lived it would be.

"Getting my heart broken every decade sounds miserable."

"You aren't worried about the wife and kids?"

He shook his head, the straight black locks falling over his eyes. "She'd kick me out when I didn't age. Besides, if I settled down in one spot, I'd miss my adventures. So what if the villagers burn my cottage down from time to time? Keeps a guy fit."

"You'll always have a spot to crash with me," I said, and swallowed. The reality of leaving my new friends, as few as they may be, squeezed at my heart.

"Thanks," Gaven said, and gave me a half smile. "I'm dish-washing tonight. Want me to bring over some dirty fries later? We can tuck into some trashy rom-coms."

"I'll bring the champagne." I'd toasted my beginning with Lotte and would toast my end with Gaven.

∼

Hours later, I'd little left to do but confront the mound of paperwork.

I despise paperwork. Who doesn't? In the twenty-first century, there's no reason to keep every tiny receipt. Scan that sucker and save it in the cloud.

I started with the top, snapping a picture, labeling it, and storing each file in a folder. The whole time, I grumbled to myself, knowing it was likely the only time I would ever see them.

Darkness fell as I continued the mind-numbing task. I'd locked up early, flipped the sign, and relegated myself to the sales counter. Hair in a messy bun, camouflage tank top and cut offs plenty to keep me comfy in the warm shop, I became one with the mess of papers.

Hours later, there was a dent in the stack and my butt was going numb on the stool. I figured that once I finished the last year's worth, I would take a stretch-and-coffee break. Gaven might be slammed until late, cleaning up after the rowdy basketball fans watching the games next door.

Determined to finish December, mere weeks before I arrived in Prescott, mourning my uncle, my past life, and daring to hope for a fresh start, I reached for the stack, only to knock the slips to the floor. They fluttered like ticker tape, scattering around my seat.

I crouched down behind the bar to gather them again. There were fewer in the pile. It was possible Hollis hadn't been open, but in the rush of the Christmas season, this didn't make a lot of sense. Why miss out on one of the biggest times of year? Had I been able to keep the shop going, I would have brought in poinsettias with their cheery red leaves. Maybe organized some Christmas tree sales. I would have held a special cocktail night with warming flavors and a gift exchange.

In short, I would have loved it.

I sat on the floor where I crouched, crossed my arms over my knees, and rested my head, letting defeat wash over me. I mourned the life I wouldn't have.

I'd been in this same position in Chicago when Patrick's dad had packed his bag and left me with an infant, a rental agreement, and a bitter heart. I hadn't planned to get married only to end up divorced. I'd been blindsided by the turns life took and it hurt.

Slowly, day by day, I'd gotten out of bed, put on one shoe and then the other, worked three jobs, then two, then one good one so I could keep a roof over my and Patrick's heads, feed us decently, and contribute as much as I could to his college fund. Over time, I'd gained a foothold in the finance district, then with the entertainment crowd. In my job, I'd become ruthless, believing that when people were prepared, they could take on any event in life, no matter how big. I managed weddings for five hundred, corporate holiday parties, and baby shower after baby shower for the wealthy. Poor preparation was a choice, a failure. I'd brought that determination with me to Whisky Row, determined. I was flawless—until I fucked up.

I hadn't prepared to battle supernatural forces to keep my little shop. Even me, Ember James Rookwood, event planner to the stars, couldn't make this work.

I'd failed. Again.

Hot tears fell to the floor below. *Plip plip.* The drops fell on one of the receipts, blurring the printout.

"Sweet Lady Nicnevin," I said.

I picked up the receipt. It was for a bag of cement and a single brick. "Bizarre, Hollis, even for you."

Another paper was stuck to the back of the receipt. I flipped it over and read the handwritten note. *Send EJ the coordinates.*

I stared at the paper. The coordinates to what? Puzzled, I pushed myself up to a standing position, scrutinizing the note.

A fist smashed through the front door, just above the latch.

I froze, blinking, then felt the cold blade of a knife at my throat. "Can I cut her, boss? Please? Just once." I recognized the voice of the DJ. Smooth and measured.

"No. And whatever you do, don't touch her."

Bryce's cold voice came from outside. The hand returned through the hole in the door, rotated downward, and unlocked the bolt. The knob turned, the door opened, and through it walked Bryce.

Bryce stopped to wave his hand in front of the window. The air in front of the door became wavy, like when the asphalt heats up in summer, and the broken glass appeared whole. "No need for anyone to discover that until the morning," he said, and turned to me.

Behind him, one of the Fallen followed. He held a bloody fist, the thick liquid oozing down his fingers and dripping onto the floor. This one was in bad shape. Black feathers covered his wings, with little white remaining. His eyes were crusted and raw, his cheeks gaunt and hollow.

Bryce addressed me. "Miss me?"

I kept my tone measured, even, while my brain screamed at itself to *think, think, think!* "You won't stay gone long enough. Maybe fuck off for a bit and give me a chance."

The person behind me, no doubt far from human, hissed. "You let her talk to you this way? In my day, women would burn for such talk."

"Guessing your dating profile is fun. 'Paranormal with a great voice but if you piss me off, I'll burn you.' How's that working out?"

Another hiss and a brief press of the blade to my neck. I couldn't see the person behind me, but Bryce shot them a warning look and gave a brief shake of his head. I was on the Do Not Stab list—for now.

"This is the witch they left guarding the weir?" The disgust was evident in the voice at my back.

Bryce pursed his lips as though to say, *I know, right?*

"Will someone please tell me the big deal about these stupid weirs? You can't tell me all of the fae come to Prescott when they want to travel."

Bryce tilted his chin toward me. "You don't know about the weirs?"

I debated keeping my mouth shut. Probably should have, but when you're over forty and don't know how long you have to live, you want answers, and you want them yesterday.

"I get that they take you to other realms. Whatever that even means. But why is there one here? Aren't there others? Couldn't you go ruin someone else's shop instead of mine?"

Bryce shook his head as though I was the biggest idiot on the planet and he would provide this next kernel of clarity out of the kindness of his heart. *Bless him.*

"In ancient times, weirs were as common as bus stops. If you wanted to go anywhere, you found the closest one and went."

"Convenient," I acknowledged.

"But when the king was murdered, the killers escaped through them. In a vast network, it is nearly impossible to trace all travel. The queen spent her first hundred years of mourning sealing as many weirs as she could, leaving some for her own use. The remaining few that lead to Parallel are guarded by weirmen, like your uncle. Those to Nether, the underworld, are protected by the guardians."

I thought of Ophelia's threat. It had only been a few weeks back yet it seemed ages ago. My knowledge of the world has come so far since then. "What about Elysium?"

Bryce rolled his eyes. "Overrated," he said. "The queen has let the shrine to the old gods fade in her grief. Altars to the Goddess and the Green Man are overgrown with darkness. The great kingdoms of the Cardinal Court lay in ruin while she sobs over some softy who couldn't watch his own back."

"Sounds sad," I said. "If a touch overdramatic."

"Doesn't matter, really. Fae are happy in the Parallel. Less drama and easy enough to come here for a pleasure cruise." He winked at me and I grimaced.

The threads of understanding knotted themselves into a bow in my mind. "The Fallen go there to seek asylum." I'd thought they wanted back into Elysium, but why, if they'd only be returned to Earth? A realm in which they could escape persecution and live in abundance would be a heaven for anyone.

"Smarter than you look." Bryce walked toward me, all business. Gone were the niceties of the afternoon, however short-lived. I'd kept him talking as long as possible, but he had an agenda. "I would love to wait for my grand re-opening of this place, but Rex here isn't long for this world. I'm afraid we need to speed things up."

My eyes widened and I turned to bolt but my captor was too quick. He tripped me with his foot and I sprawled flat on my stomach, palms stinging from where they smacked the concrete. My right cheek smarted and would bruise from the impact. A foot stamped down on my head, pressing my face to the ground. "Don't move," the voice said.

"Yrms zee-sjay," I mumbled.

The boot moved from my head to the small of my back.

"What?"

"You're the DJ," I said. "I recognize your voice. It's too bad you're a giant asshole, or I would totally have contracted with you for weddings and such. You're good—you'd make a killing in tips."

"Shut up," Bryce said. "We aren't here to network."

"But you said—" The boot was back on the side of my head. "Oomph."

Bryce stepped over me and headed toward the back. "Now, how do I open this...let's see..."

From my awkward position on the floor, I watched Bryce jiggle the door handle, then yank hard. It didn't budge. "Come here," he said to the Fallen. "What's one more punch? You'll heal the minute you're through."

The zombie of a being ambled forth and attempted to put his hand through the glass. I winced when he struck a solid surface that didn't crack.

Bryce whirled on me. "How does it open?"

"I don't know."

"What do you mean, you don't know?" In two strides, he was in front of me, bending low, his face above mine. "If you value your pathetic life, you will tell me how to open this door."

The boot was lifted. "I've never done it," I said.

"Lies!" Bryce's irises began to glow with a faint yellow flicker.

"I'm not lying. I don't do anything. They just show up, pay me the tithe, or whatever, and go—"

"The tithe, that's right." Bryce cut me off with a half laugh. I almost forgot. "Have either of you got something we can give her?"

Rex shook his head and the DJ said, "I'm not giving her shit."

Bryce rolled his eyes and dug in his pockets. Coming up empty, he slipped one of the rings off his hand and held it out to me. It was gold with a band of carvings in a language I didn't recognize. "Tithe paid," he said, and dropped the ring in front of my face. It bounced twice on the floor before settling.

"Seems cheap—you sure it's real? The last ring I was offered was crusted in gems. This is junk."

Bryce wasn't listening. "Tithe—check." He tried the door.

This time, it sprang open. The blast of ice-cold air burst forth in contrast to the heat of the room.

"It worked," the DJ said. "You know what this means?"

Bryce nodded, his eyes wide with possibility. "That we—I —am about to be very rich."

The pressure on my jaw lifted as the DJ leaned toward the weir room to watch Bryce. I took that opportunity to reach into my book, grab hold of a cold, white handle, and jab Little White straight into the nearest calf.

The DJ howled and clutched at his leg. I was on my feet, bloodied blade in hand, and running for the front door. I grabbed the knob, but it slipped from my hand. Each time I tried to reach for it, my hands touched nothing. The air around the door still shimmered under Bryce's control. I turned to see Bryce, hand outstretched toward me.

"Stop or I'll—"

His words were cut off when Gaven tackled him from behind, wielding my chef's knife. The two wrestled on the floor, Gaven swinging and Bryce blocking the blows. They crashed into a wall. Several of Cass's paintings slipped off their nails and slid down the wall. Bryce threw Gaven into one of the tables. Pots smashed against the painted concrete. Bryce scrambled to regain his hold, but Gaven was faster. He ran for me.

"Open the door!"

"I can't! He did something to it."

Gaven extended his fingers toward the shimmer of magic, but a cold voice stopped him.

"Don't be foolish."

Behind us, the three of them stood in a line. Bryce was flanked on his right by the fae DJ—who would forever in my mind be remembered as DJ Fae—whose murderous look was trained on me. On his left was Rex, who held a ball of fire between his fingers.

"You will get back from that door," Bryce said, his words calm and collected, "or this entire place, with you in it, goes up in flames." Rex spread his hands farther apart, allowing the ball of fire to expand.

"Neat party trick," I said. "Don't think they'd let you do kid birthdays, though."

Rex frowned, confused. Bryce glowered.

"Hey, Gaven?"

"Yeah?" Gaven's eyes flicked my way, then back to the others.

"You know how you said Scotland is the prettiest place you've been?"

"Yeah?"

"I'd like to go one day." I briefly shifted my gaze to him. "Soon."

His eyes widened as he registered my meaning. A slight dip of his chin and he was in on my plan. "I'll be your tour guide, then."

"Neither of you are going anywhere!" Bryce's face was red, his eyes the golden gleam of growing irritation.

I ignored him and reached for one of the vines. These beauties had wrapped themselves from ceiling to floor around any tubular surface they could find. *Intention,* Lotte had told me. I thought of lush fields and safety, adventure and freedom. I thought of death, often closer than we like, and life, its other side. I thought of starting over.

The plant wound itself around my finger and then my hand. I gave a short tug.

"If I have to—" But Bryce didn't finish his sentence.

Water fell from above, a cascade. The sprinklers burst open, dousing everything with a gush of liquid.

Gaven and I ran for the weir room. Inside, he shoved books aside, exposing the portal.

Like a rip in fabric, the opening was a rough-edged opening. A slip. Through it was black and cold, akin to space. I stared, transfixed. *Is this happening?*

"Duck!" Gaven yelled and chucked a book at my head.

I ducked, and the book socked DJ Fae in the stomach. He slipped on the water pooling on the floor and crashed into a stack of boxes.

"Grab my hand!" Gaven held out his hand to me. "We can't get separated."

"Like hell you will!" Bryce lunged for me. He grabbed my arm, sparks flying from the touch, and yanked me toward the door. I grabbed a book and hit him as hard as I could. He backhanded me. I became a dead weight, sinking to the floor.

Gaven went after Bryce, but DJ Fae cut him off, water splashing in their wake. He brandished Little White. Each move Gaven made, DJ Fae countered. With one wrong move and a sickening squelch, the blade slipped into Gaven's body. The DJ laughed as Gaven stumbled, clutching his side.

I kicked at Bryce. He'd dragged me to the steps and forced me to sit. The googly eyes I'd attached to Mariette gave the plant a half-crazed expression. She looked on as Bryce used an inordinate amount of packing tape to secure me to the railing.

"Godsdamned witches. Give them a little power and they think they're invincible."

I spat in his face. What can I say? I've seen a lot of movies.

"Disgusting. No wonder you're single," Bryce said.

"What is that supposed to mean?" I readied another wad of saliva.

Bryce shook his head in exaggerated revulsion. "No one wants a woman who acts like that."

"Like what?"

"Like she doesn't give a good godsdamn what they think."

"This isn't the first century. Women are sometimes allowed to think."

"And that's the problem," Bryce said. Water dripped from his brow as he talked. "They're bad at it. Especially as they age. Give a woman a couple decades and she thinks she's the expert on how the world should work. Well, guess what? The fates will twist that on you whenever they like, whether it's ten, fifty, or five hundred years from now."

"So, women should roll over and take it?"

"It's not like they know how to give it."

As if a reflex, my foot shot out and kicked him in the faery junk. He doubled over and dropped the tape.

"You sure about that?"

Bryce rested his hands on his thighs while he caught his breath. Whatever the fae had down there, it too, was vulnerable. "You *bitch*."

"Oooh, can I be next?" Iris stood near Bryce.

"It was pretty satisfying," I said, water dripping down my hair and into my mouth.

Bryce growled and turned on the petite brunette. She pressed her palms together, then twisted them in a rotating swirl as though holding a ball. In the space between, a blue sphere formed.

"Can I kick him, too?" Joaquin clambered down the stairs behind me, then hopped over the railing. "Hang on," he said, spotting Gaven, his strength waning, fighting off DJ Fae. "I need to change the music."

Joaquin drew his bow, nocked an arrow, and fired through the DJ. The Fallen took three steps, stumbled, and fell in a heap. *Iron-tipped.*

Iris held Bryce in her sights. "I'm here to give you an option, faery boy. Come quietly, and the Boss will give you passage. Resist in the slightest, and you will die."

Bryce glowered at her, then lunged.

Iris was fast. She fired several icy blasts at Bryce, slowing him to a crawl. Every fiber in his being struggled against the hold. The muscles on his face bulged with the strain. "Gods-damn...ice..."

Iris readied another round. "Where's all that big talk now?"

"And we're done here," Joaquin said. He slipped a pair of handcuffs on Bryce. The cuffs sizzled where they touched his skin.

"Where's the Fallen?" Iris asked. She held her hand out for Gaven to grasp and pulled him upright.

"I'd help you all look, but..." I waggled my hands to illustrate my predicament.

Iris and Gaven rushed to the interior of the shop. He lay in the water. Not dead, but close. The expense of generating fireballs had taken what little energy he had on reserve.

"Poor bastard," Joaquin said, shaking his head. "You did this, asshole," he said to Bryce.

"As if I was the only source," Bryce spat. Joaquin plowed his fist into Bryce's jaw, silencing further comments.

"We can't leave him this way," Iris said. "You've got to put him out of his misery.

"Wait, what?" I asked, trying to see between their bodies.

My protest went unheard. With an inhuman swiftness, Joaquin withdrew another arrow and fired at close range.

Flames shot up, only to be doused by the falling water.

Iris lifted her chin, eyes blinking shut against the drops. "Can we shut this off now?"

TWENTY-FIVE

A beautiful face hovered in front of my own. I stared at her statuesque features as she dabbed at a wound on my hairline with a cotton ball.

"You, my dear, are on the fearless list," she said.

Dressed as a nurse–if the average nurse wore stilettos, cherry red lipstick and popped cleavage like a swimsuit model–she kept her eyes on my hairline while she spoke. I didn't need a mirror to know hitting the floor left a mark, one that would stick around for a while. Still, I didn't mind the TLC from this professional. Joaquin introduced her as the nurse, and the title, while vague, fit.

"I'm not fearless, just brave. Time did that."

The woman, who didn't look a day over twenty-seven, said, "I hear that."

I frowned. What could she know? I'm sure she'd seen the gamut of injuries in her time, but she couldn't be someone's wife or mother, could she?

The nurse found a raw spot with the alcohol-soaked cotton, and I winced. I ventured a glance toward the bedroom. Joaquin had carried the fae to the bed. Whatever the nurse had done for Gaven's wound had left him dead asleep, recovering.

Each time I tried to stand up, I was pushed back into place. Joaquin kept a firm hand on my shoulder as the nurse treated my wounds.

"You don't have to be so...forceful," I said through my teeth.

"Oh, but I do. The nurse has been treating me for a long time now, and I know the drill. Behave and you'll be back to your old self in no time."

"My old self," I said to no one in particular. I wasn't sure who that old self was, let alone if she was someone I wanted to be again.

The nurse crouched near me and looked into my eyes. "I can give you something to help you heal faster, but there are consequences."

I eyed the vial she held in her hand. "Will I grow a third arm or something?"

"If only," Joaquin said. "That'd be pretty handy. Haha—get it? Hand-y."

I rolled my eyes and shook my head, trying not to laugh.

The nurse crinkled her nose. "It's hard to know what will happen," she said. "In some cases, not much. In others..." She ventured a glance at Joaquin. He looked away. "You have to decide for yourself."

"What is it?" I was used to the host of medications with long lists of horrible side effects that made you want to take nothing and deal with the fewer problems you had to begin with.

"The Angel's Share," she said.

"The what?"

"Elixir," Joaquin said. "But the purest form."

I stared at the small vial in horror. "The same stuff the Fallen are after—what they're addicted to?"

"Medicine is only that when taken properly," Meritt said. "Anything in the wrong dose can spell death."

"The Fallen are desperate," Joaquin added. "They'll take any form they can get their hands on with the promise of extending their lives. Not every drop is the same."

I thought of Cass, her brilliance ended on the floor of my shop. A life discarded in desperation. "Not all elixir is created equal."

"Something like that," Joaquin said. "The Fallen take it for survival. If they can make it to the Parallel, they heal. If they can't get enough elixir, they waste away. Quantity over quality in their case"

I thought of Rex, prone on the ground. The mercy killing. It was murder, but it was out of pity.

"I think I'll pass...this time."

The nurse gave a little shrug. "Suit yourself. If you ever need me, ask Joaquin. Gaven, too." She registered the astonishment on my face. "He'll be right as rain when he wakes, no worrying needed. Elixir has no negative effects on the fae."

I sat up a little more and stuffed another pillow behind my back. The nurse gathered her things from my coffee table. The silver stethoscope she'd yet to remove shifted into a snake and back as I watched.

I pointed, worried delirium had a hold on my fragile reality. "Was that...did it just...?

"Horace? Don't mind him," she said, apparently used to the shenanigans of a silver neck viper. She'd tucked away the last of her things when she spotted the card sticking out of Hollis' book and froze.

"Where did you get that?"

"I found it," I said. "Hollis—my uncle—had it."

"May I see it?" Her voice shook with the request.

"Of course."

With care, she opened the book and removed the card. She

stared at the back, rubbing a finger over the printed design. Then, she flipped the card face up.

With a soft gasp, she stared at Death.

I watched a thousand emotions race across her face. "You know this card?"

The nurse lifted her gaze to meet mine, a tear at the corner of one eye. "I lost it. Long ago."

"It's...yours?"

She nodded, regarding the card with reverence. "I lost it in a bet."

"Then I'm glad to return it to you.."

"Really?" She grinned, clutching the card to her chest.

"Not much fun to carry around such a small deck. Everyone guesses your hand."

The nurse stared at the card while I shifted positions. Futons are the worst. "Out of curiosity, would you know anything about this?" I tapped the image.

"A circle of stars," the nurse said. She sat back on her heels, regarding the drawing. "Death was a king once, or so I'm told. Ruled a vast kingdom until an obsession with immortality drove him mad. He searched to the ends of the realms for a means to live forever. The gods granted him his wish, but at the ultimate price—they do so love a twist of fate."

"What happened to his crown?"

"The Crown of Immortality was lost when Death was banished from Elysium. It hasn't been seen in a millennium."

"If one were to look for the crown, where would you start?" Heck, I was about to lose my job, my apartment, and my sense of direction. I could use a new adventure.

The nurse smiled at the card. "I would ask his wife."

I blinked. "Who is she?"

"She," the woman began, "is me."

I lifted an eyebrow. This woman? I had to hear this story. "How do you feel about champagne?"

"I'll check my calendar."

I did that dumb thing where you roll out of bed far too fast.

A thousand arrows bombarded my skull. I winced at the pain. There was a tender spot on my hip and both wrists ached. My body was a canvas of purplish bruises.

But I was whole, and that was something. I shuffled downstairs. Empty. Sunlight beamed through the windows, the plants turning leaves to meet the day. The moths were still, tucked under a leaf here, wedged against a pipe there. Water dripped, a constant reminder of the night before.

The plants were wet. The furniture was wet. My boxes—all wet.

I would need to repack, reassess. The weight of the work was crushing. I ambled to the coffee maker. My trusty machine would be among the last things I packed and the first to come back out of a box.

As I waited for the hot liquid to fill the glass carafe, I thought of the last conversation I'd had before I fell asleep.

Joaquin had stayed the night, ignoring my protests. He'd set up camp on the floor of the shop, rolling his jacket into a neck pillow. Part of his job, he'd said, when I brushed off his chivalry.

When everyone else was gone and I'd tucked myself in, blanket yanked up to my chin, I'd called down to him.

"Joaquin?"

"Yes, ma'am?" His voice was low, assured. With the faintest hint of an accent I couldn't place.

"What does Ansel wear in the summer?"

There was a snort down below. "Pretty much the same. Cranks up the AC, though. The heat from your place doesn't help."

"Good," I said, pleased that in some small way I irritated him, like a fly on a stallion. I let the silence sit between us for a few minutes, as headlights from the street lit the shop and were gone. I needed sleep, yet I wanted answers. "You've taken elixir." It wasn't a question.

There was a pause. "Yes, ma'am."

"How many times?"

The shop was silent. The moon peeked through the clearstory windows, casting eerie shadows. I turned over onto my other side.

"It's all about choices, isn't it? We each have a relationship with Death," he said. "Mine's complicated."

In the dark, my eyes opened. The more I learned, the less I seemed to know—about anything.

"Goodnight, Joaquin."

"'Night."

In the light of day, this conversation clung to me like a translucent fabric, weighing lightly on my thoughts. Were we all like Joaquin, balancing our choices against the inevitable outcome?

I'd dreamed of sailing an endless sea aboard a raft. Mariette was lashed to the mast, the rains nourishing our journey.

I wandered toward the back door with my cup. I avoided looking into the weir room, instead glancing out the window. I brought the mug to my lips as I peeked outside.

On the bench, under the branches, was a figure. A beanie pulled down over his head, Ansel sat, staring at the bud. Falinis lay at Ansel's feet.

I bit my lip. Like Joaquin, every moment, I had a choice.

Before I could talk myself out of it, I poured a second mug, wrapped myself in a second sweater, and headed out into the atrium.

Ansel didn't move. Not when I sat down. Not when I set the mug next to him on the bench. It steamed between us as I reached down to stroke the dog. I took a sip from my own cup and waited.

He reached out a hand and hefted the World's Best Plant Parent mug. While he took a sip, I waited.

"It's good."

I chuckled. "Don't get too used to it—my time's limited."

"You're...leaving?" He looked at me.

I frowned. Joaquin must not have told him—but why? I'd have thought Ansel would have jumped at the news. "Hollis was behind–very behind–on his taxes. Can't swing the bill myself. I'd hoped the opening would bring in a chunk I could bargain with, but...well you know what happened there." I sighed. "Going back to Chicago, tail between my legs."

"I've been here forty-five years. An occasional squirrel's nest. A twig that snaps off in a storm. In nearly half a century, that's all I've seen."

I nodded, waiting.

"But you. You're here less than a month, and there's...life." He looked back at the tiny flower.

I didn't know what to say to that. "Do you ever wonder..." I gathered my bravery before continuing. "I mean, is it possible that the Fallen could ever be welcomed here?"

"Welcomed?"

"Maybe not with open arms and campfire songs, but...I can't help feeling sorry for some of them."

"They've been banished for a reason."

"I know," I said. "But what if it's like when the whole class gets held in at recess because the one kid won't get in line. I hate that kind of punishment."

Ansel didn't respond. Was this his thinking face, or was he merely waiting for me to leave?

But I did come out there for an atonement of my own, and it was now or never. Whether it took me a day or a week to erase myself from the premises, my time was limited. I looked at his profile. Strong lines, trimmed beard, and tight lips. "I didn't understand. If I had, I wouldn't have had the party. He shouldn't have gotten through."

Ansel shook his head, then looked down at his lap. "What's seven more years? More time to look for the crown."

I clutched the mug between my hands, my forearms resting on my thighs. "The nurse said it was lost in the war. Most husbands lose their car keys, hers loses a godsdamned crown."

Ansel snorted. "You're starting to sound like us."

I gave him a wry smile, then wiped it away. "Ansel, I'm sorry."

He stared at the flower for a long moment. It wasn't that I needed a reply, but I didn't want to leave this—him—on a sour note. Joaquin's words got to me. In the end, we all dance with Death. It's what we do before that matters. He sighed, then nodded.

"What will you do with the crown—when you find it?"

"Buy my freedom. Then with the ring—"

"Ring?"

Ansel set his mug on the bench. "Yeah. Family heirloom on my father's side. Carved with our motto in the old language."

I drew my brows together and picked up his empty mug. "I'll be right back."

I ducked back into the shop, got down on all fours, and scrambled over the floor. *There it is.* I all but ran back outside.

"Here," I said, and held out my fist.

Staring at me, Ansel extended his palm. I dropped the small circle into his hand. I closed his fingers over the ring.

"We all need a little hope to keep us going." I gave his hand a squeeze and with a parting smile, headed for my shop.

∾

Wet cardboard peeled off in sections, flaking like dandruff. I needed more boxes, more tape, and loads more energy than I could muster.

I eyed the coffee maker. My bag of beans needed to last a few more days—at least. I couldn't justify another round of groceries when my days were numbered.

Ansel stayed in the atrium a long time after I gave him the ring. I watched him through the back window. He stared at the ring, turning it over in his palm, before wrapping it in his giant fist.

Exhaustion took hold of my heart. Physically, mentally, and emotionally, I was spent. Mariette looked at me, her googly eyes accusatory.

"Don't give me that. They don't let us take six-foot monsteras on airplanes." I sighed.

A knock sounded at the back door. Joaquin opened the door and peeked in. "Morning."

"Not often a man takes off before I wake up, then comes back without breakfast."

Joaquin held up both hands. "My mistake, won't happen again. Donuts or bagels?"

"Breakfast burritos."

"Respectable."

I smiled. "What can I do for you? As you can see, I'm quite busy wallowing in self-pity."

The corner of Joaquin's mouth turned up. "Official business—this time." He reached in his jacket pocket and extracted a folded piece of paper. He handed it to me and stepped back.

"What's this?" I unfolded the paper. A cashier's check. All the zeros made my vision swim.

"From Ansel," he said, as though this explained it all. "In thanks."

"But..."

Joaquin crossed his arms and lifted his shoulders in a brief shrug. "You gave him hope," he said. He shook his head. "Even I can't do that."

"This is too much. It was just a ring. I can't accept—"

Joaquin shook his head. "Take the money, EJ. He can afford it."

I folded the check and slid it into my pocket. "Thank you. Please—thank him."

Joaquin nodded, then left with a wave. "Next time, burritos," he called over his shoulder.

It was true, there would be a next time.

I spent the remainder of the afternoon unpacking the defunct boxes, checking my belongings for water damage, and convincing myself that the check was real. That my hope was real.

I mounded the cardboard in a soggy heap near the back door. It would have to go out to the dumpster along with the chunks of smashed ceramic pots and broken glass.

A jangle at the front door alerted me to a customer. I wiped my hands on a towel. "Sorry, we're closed," I called from the back of the shop. "Had an accident with the sprinklers. Should reopen by next week." Silence. I moved toward the front of the shop, grabbing Little White from its spot next to my coffee maker before rounding the stairs.

Christopher stood in the doorway. Leather duffel slung over one shoulder, sunglasses in hand, he appraised my worn out green sweats with wet knees, my arms deep in a pair of dishwashing gloves, wielding a blade the length of a carrot. He drew a line in the air from my head to my toes. "Clearly I arrived just in time to prevent any more of this."

"Christopher!" I wrapped my arms around his neck and

kissed his cheek. "I didn't know you were coming. How's the new job–you've already got vacation?"

"I lasted two months," he said, rolling his eyes. "If I hear *Run, Run, Rudolph* one more time, I'm going to choke an elf."

"It's February."

"They've moved on to *Careless Whisper*."

I cringed. "Enough said."

"Anyway," he said, stepping over a puddle. "I thought I'd take a little trip. Or move. You know, take a page out of the EJ Rookwood book and come to little old Prescott, Arizona. Get some sunshine, see my bestie." He set his bag on the stool. "Hmm. Is this one of those immersive experiences?"

I put my hand to my cheek and shook my head, looking around. "I...it's...I don't know where to start. It's a long, long story."

"Well I've got time," he said. "Do those gloves come in men's large?"

Christopher dug in, not only to help me unpack but doing what he does best. I gave him Hollis's room as a project. He'd crash with me while he rebooted his life, and in exchange, my entire place would look fabulous when he finished.

If you asked me, I got the better deal.

"So what's the game plan?" A moth had settled in Christopher's thick mop of hair, riding around as though he were its chariot.

I giggled. "Plan?"

"With this place. Are we sticking with plants or embarking on something new?"

I paused, my hand resting on the end of a mop. "I was thinking both. I can apply for a permanent license to serve food and drinks. Could squeeze in a few tables, add a couple more outside. And now that you're here I could say yes to some of these requests." Despite the drama at the opening, I'd received a few emails about catering some events in the area. "That is, if you'd be interested."

"Girl, I'm unemployed. Color me interested," Christopher said, and I beamed, excited at our prospects.

My stuff somewhat back in place and his tucked in here and there, Christopher headed to the store to purchase dinner ingredients for two. I propped the back door open with a potted fern, intent on attacking the pile of damp cardboard. Grunting, I hauled the stack toward the door, then tossed the box parts through, two at a time.

One piece became wedged between the stoop and the dumpster. I squeezed myself through the railing to reach for the slice of brown. My arm was too short. I tromped down the short flight of steps and rounded the bins. I wedged myself between the dumpsters, squatting until I could reach the cardboard. With rubber-covered fingertips, I was just able to snatch it.

I backed out of the space, retracing my steps. I was almost free when I tripped on a cobblestone. I crashed against the wall, my foot hooking on a brick. I sprawled out from the gap, landing flat on my butt. "Godsdamnit," I said, struggling to get to my feet. My ass was killing me. In the space where I'd been, a brick stuck out at an angle. Loosened from its resting spot, its corner was chipped where I'd kicked it from the wall. A glint of light caught something behind the displaced brick.

I scooted toward the wall, wedging myself back between the canisters. The smell was dank, saccharine, and rotten. A rat skittered out from under the dumpsters. One of the crows cawed from its perch in the tree behind me.

I grabbed the brick with a gloved hand, wrenching it back and forth. With a final tug, it came loose. Unlike those around it, the brick was newer, a brighter red than its neighbors. I set it on the ground, then leaned toward the gap to peer in.

Sparkles glinted from within the wall's recess. I shook a

glove off my hand and reached in the hole to withdraw the treasure.

My hand shook with the weight of my find. Seven giant diamonds. A circle of gold. Chills raced down my body as I stared at the godsdamn crown in my hands

Both crows landed on the dumpster, their caws drowning out my thoughts.

"Oh, Hollis. What did you do?"

TWENTY-SIX

Joaquin returned through the back door, taking the steps two at a time.

Ansel was behind the bar. His long hair hung in waves over his shoulders, wet from a shower. A dish towel was slung over one shoulder, the sleeves of his turtleneck pushed up to his elbows. He wiped down the polished wooden surface before setting out a napkin and a fork.

Joaquin slipped onto one of the stools, facing the man. "Good news or bad news, Boss?"

"Good." Ansel slid a plate in front of Joaquin, followed by salt, pepper, and hot sauce.

"Chilaquiles!"

"Not news," Ansel said.

Joaquin crammed a forkful in his mouth and chewed. "To you, maybe. To me, this is the best news."

Ansel rolled his eyes and picked up his own plate. They ate in silence while the food was hot.

Joaquin swallowed a bite and ran his tongue over the front of his teeth. "Outstanding, as always." Ansel grunted, busy with his own plate. "Okay, so good news: you have the ring!"

"Not the right one."

"It's not?"

Ansel shook his head. "Close, but no. Mine's broken. What she gave me is a wish ring. Much older."

Joaquin peered at Ansel. He'd let EJ think she'd helped him, then did something nice for her. He was definitely cracking.

Ansel finished chewing. "Bad news now."

"Okay, no ring," Joaquin said. "No crown, either—yet. And shitloads more Fallen on the way."

"We have to tell Sharon."

"That is bad news."

Ansel shot Joaquin a look. "You know we do. When we hand over Bryce, she's going to ask questions."

Joaquin scooped up another bite with his fork. "So, tell her. It's not like you're setting them loose."

"What if she's right?"

"Who—Sharon?"

"No," Ansel said. "EJ. What if they are meant to be here?"

Joaquin regarded his boss. He'd been miserable for so long. All hope rested on a pathetic opportunity that came once every seven years because a queen couldn't bear to be without her king. He had no patience for the spoiled and weak when it came to tragedy. Life was hard, people you loved would die. He knew this better than most. His best friend deserves the chance to learn that for himself. This time, they wouldn't fail. "So what if she is right? Someone still has to manage the influx."

Ansel shook his head, picking up his empty plate. "I want nothing of power. I want freedom."

Joaquin was quiet. It was easy to whine from his side of the bar.

"I want freedom," Ansel continued. "A plot of land, a herd of cattle..."

"A fine woman to bounce on your lap?"

Ansel reddened. "It's more than that, 'Quin." He shook his head. "I want the impossible—I want my life back. The life I never got to live."

Joaquin watched his friend, heartsick. There was far too much brevity in the world, and no amount of fast motorcycles, bottomless bank accounts, or bravado could make up for the lack of family.

"We'll get there." Joaquin knocked his fist against the bar and stood up from the stool.

Ansel nodded, then collected Joaquin's plate. "She took the check?"

"Tried not to. Did the humble dance. But I made her."

"Good."

Joaquin traced his hand along the length of the bar as he headed for the door. "You know, you could have bid on the place. Won it at auction."

"I know."

"You'd own the shop—the weir."

Ansel was halfway to the kitchen. He stopped, his back to Joaquin. His voice was gruff, impatient. "I know."

"Why?"

Ansel's shoulders tensed. "She brings life. All we do is usher death." Without looking back, he pushed his way through the swinging doors.

"Thanks for breakfast! I'll be back when I find some good news."

Out in the sunshine, he shoved his hands into his pockets and set his feet in motion. Joaquin thought best when moving, as though the action distracted his body long enough so his mind could take over.

A trio of crows squawked overhead. One held a pizza crust from which the others plucked off bready chunks. Joaquin peered up at them. "Good eats, eh?"

The crows quieted. One of them hinged from its position on the branch, cocking its head as though to examine Joaquin. It had an eerie familiarity, somehow. He saluted the birds, then crossed the street.

At Lotte's shop, he paused. Where had she gone? They'd not seen her in weeks. Joaquin gnawed at his lip. "Aw, hell."

Joaquin stepped to the big shop window. The closed sign was centered in the glass door. Joaquin tented his eyes to peer through the glass and into the shop. A fine layer of dust coated the place.

Joaquin stepped back from the window. He looked up one street and down the other, as though Lotte would be coming his way along a sidewalk.

"Where did you go?" She hadn't returned his calls or texts. While she didn't owe him anything, he'd thought they were friends—at least.

There was no answer.

Joaquin stuffed his hands back in his pockets. This was unlike him. He didn't get attached. Didn't worry about people beyond the moments they were with him.

But Ansel's admonishment of their lifestyle ate away at Joaquin's conscience. What would a goddess such as Lotte want with a glorified harbinger of death? His heart ached, and in that moment he would trade what little time he had left for another night on the bike, her arms wrapped around him, the stars their only witnesses.

"Careful there," he warned himself, shaking his heading for his bike. "Can't afford vulnerability, Joaquin—we all know what's headed this way."

THANK YOU!

Thanks for reading! If you enjoyed this book, please consider leaving me a review and I'll love you forever. Reviews help me find readers and I am grateful for all of you!

If there was something that tugged at your mind as you read, I'd love to hear from you at courtney@court neyfenix.com.

Tiara Borealis, book two in the *Four Crowns* series, releases this fall. Turn the page for access to a bonus epilogue...

Bonus Epilogue

Sign up for my monthly newsletter and you'll be sent a free, bonus epilogue to *A Circle of Stars* in your preferred digital format.

Each month I send monthly writing and reading updates, some personal stories, recipes, freebies from my author friends, cat pics, and more! I promise to never sell your email and hope you'll hit reply once in a while and let me know how you are, too. :)

READ THE SERIAL

Love the Four Crowns crew? Read the companion serial, *Weir Walker*—for free on Ream, a great platform for readers.

Hope to see you there!

Afterword

This book is an amalgamation of fantasy genre fandom. It all started with Jurassic Park.

What do dinosaurs have in common with the fae? Nothing and everything all at once.

When I read Jurassic Park, solidly in the sci-fi zone, I glommed onto the idea that humans are the most dangerous creatures, dreaming up and actualizing worlds far beyond our control. In effect, sci-fi is fantasy, as fantasy weaves pieces of our reality within its words. It's that relationship that makes them my most favorite genres to read. You can have whole new worlds, mythical beings, and it's all good. A manifestation of imagination that is wildly popular, for who wouldn't want a touch of the wild in their everyday?

People love the unknown just as much as they fear it.

For a lover of the unknown and a fanatic for characters who leap off the page, this book was a joy to write. It will also be known in my timeline as the book written across many adventures as I wrote the first draft in five states (AZ, CA, OR, WA, and AK) four foreign countries (Ireland, Spain, Portugal, and Morocco) across three continents. I wrote it on the beach, in the desert, and even at a waterpark. I wish keyboards measured mileage...

Speaking of countries, many of the characters and objects in this series are inspired by Celtic myths and legends. I spend hours diving through rabbit holes to learn all I can about my ancestors' lives as blacksmiths on the islands in the far north seas. When the winter weather set it, gloomy and gray, storytelling occupied everyone's watch for the light to return. Unearthing these treasures passed down through generations has become a passion project in which I lose myself in front of the fireplace on many a rainy night, toddy in hand, cat on my lap.

This particular story is set in Prescott, Arizona, a favorite city in my home state. While I've taken fictional liberties with much of the locations and landscape, I hope I've stayed true to the energy and draw of Courthouse Plaza and greater Yavapai County. If you ever get the chance to visit, I hope you stay long enough to explore the history of the city—and if he asks, take a ride under the stars on the back of Joaquin's bike. You'll thank me later.

— -ERIN

Acknowledgments

Three cheers to my sister Stephanie Driggs who was a brave (and timely!) alpha reader all while hiding this book from her twin, our sister Mariah. Your commentary and encouragement was what I needed most to turn good into great.

All my love to Mariah who I know will forgive our shenanigans once she sees the Dedication. Thank you also for being such a big supporter even for being kept in the dark!

Michelle Albright is to be applauded not only for her support of my work and great cheer but for her dedication to friendship. This one is coming to you signed!

Much appreciation to Terrilani Chong for your unwavering energy for supporting my writing. I love that your candid honesty never fails to teach and your voracity for reading is inspirational. Thank you my friend.

Serious props to the Livick-Laabs family for their judicial review of cover designs and to Katherine listening to me talk through the conceptual aspects of this story while sitting in a geothermal pool next to the Breitenbush River.

Thank you to Tara McCormick for your opinions and promotion of this work—so glad to have you as a reader!

Cheers to Paula Lester, my first and longtime editor who has oodles of patience.

Endless adoration for the readers who will take a gamble on a new series. Storytelling needs an audience, and I couldn't do this without you.

Thank you Bryan for shouldering the lion's share of the

dailies so I could lock myself away and write. You are an Earth-bound Adonis in more ways than one.

And never least, my love to Ava who takes great pride in her mother, even if at fourteen she wants nothing to do with my kissing books.

About the Author

Erin is a lover of fountain pens and the trail they leave behind. She is an award-winning author of the Four Crowns romantic contemporary fantasy series and the companion web serial, Weir Walker. Her work is highly praised for its heart and snark as well as her knack for breathing magic into the everyday. Erin also writes cozy mysteries for those who walk the gentler side of fiction.

A diehard gadabout and champagne fanatic, Erin is a firm believer in the tender and wild. A native Arizonan, when not behind a keyboard, you'll find her under the stars, howling at the moon.

ALSO BY ERIN LARK MAPLES

Four Crowns Series

Weir Walker (Companion Serial)

Fallen (Prequel Novella)

A Circle of Stars (Book One)

Tiara Borealis (Book Two) —Coming Fall 2024

The Declan Rosewood Mysteries

Bleeding Hearts —Coming Fall 2024

The Sheridan County Mysteries

The New Teacher

The Sled Dog

The Dead Swede

The Master Mechanic

The Banjo Player